STORM TAKEN

WILLIAM MICHAEL DAVIDSON

Happy Birthday Grandma! I love you! Thank you for always encaraging me to write and believing in me.

Bill

Clean Reads
GREAT STORIES, NO GUILT.
www.cleanreads.com

Storm Taken
by William Michael Davidson
Published by Clean Reads
www.cleanreads.com

This is a work of fiction. Names, places, characters, and events are fictitious
in every regard. Any similarities to actual events and persons, living or dead,
are purely coincidental. Any trademarks, service marks, product names, or
named features are assumed to be the property of their respective owners,
and are used only for reference. There is no implied endorsement if any of
these terms are used. Except for review purposes, the reproduction of this
book in whole or part, electronically or mechanically, constitutes a copyright
violation.

Much of this book is about the power of a good marriage.
I dedicate this book to my dad, who gave an example from which to write,
and who has shown me what it is to love a woman.

"Storms make the oak grow deeper roots"
-George Herbert

"No monsters came out of the storm; the storm *was* the monster."
-Eddie Dees, the author

Chapter One

The storm took many things, but my dog was the first.

My wife and I owned a Golden Retriever that we rescued from the pound. A decision that was, the more I look back at everything, a decision to please our younger son; he's quite an adept beggar, and we caved in way too soon.

I didn't realize, of course, that the dog had actually been taken.

And Bessie was only the beginning.

We moved to Naples Island at the age of forty-two because life had been pretty good to us. At least until that point it had. My first three novels sold very well, all bestsellers, and they even made a movie out of the last one. We'd previously lived in Seattle. When our folks passed away and we realized that money wasn't going to be a problem for us and we could have our druthers, we selected Naples Island. It's a community in Belmont Shore, California, that looks like something right out of Italy, our favorite place to vacation together. Our Cape Cod-style home sat right on one of the canals. We loved to sit outside, drink wine, admire the sunset, and watch people walk dreamily along the canals. It really was, to us at least, a piece of heaven.

The storm began on the first day of July, our first summer living there. At that point, we had no idea what we were in for. We were on the deck in the front of the house, sitting by our gas-powered fire pit and drinking Gaja Barbaresco, when we noticed the storm clouds moving in. The first flashes of lightning whitened the sky, but there was no thunder that we could hear. We laughed when we noticed the looming storm. Here we were, all giddy about living in California, and not even two months in our new home, a storm was coming our way. A storm in July? Something just seemed very un-California about it to Seattle natives like us.

I checked the weather on my phone. Apparently monsoon moisture from the deserts had drifted farther west than usual, which was causing some showers and thunderstorms. Not a very common thing to happen near the beaches in July, but we decided to make the best of it.

It was still mid-afternoon, and we thought we'd wait it out and drink more wine until the rain came our way. I have to admit, it was pretty amazing to watch. These dark, billowing clouds crawled across the sky, and it was almost like watching a fireworks show. The thunderclouds spewed out great bolts of lightning—electrical forked tongues licking the corners of the horizon. Some of our neighbors even came out to watch the spectacle.

Before long, we could hear thunder following the brilliant flashes. The wind picked up, and I thought it best to pick up our plate of cheese and crackers, gather our wine glasses, and make our way inside. But my wife, Madison, laughed at my suggestion to move things indoors to escape the impending downpour.

"Don't be so silly," she said. Reclining in her chair, she leisurely flipped through pages of *Eating Well*.

"Do you see the clouds? They're coming our way."

"Yes, I can see the clouds," she said, "and a little thunder and lightning isn't going to kill us. Where's your sense of adventure? This is kind of exciting, Eddie. It's our first storm in California. Maybe we can dance beside the canal when it gets here? It'll be a special moment."

"I think if we're going to dance, I'd prefer to dance inside."

She clicked her tongue and shook her head. "Party pooper," she whispered and tossed the magazine at me. Then she leaned back and undid the top two buttons of her blouse. "If it's any consolation, I still think you're the hottest bestselling author on Naples Island."

I thought about this statement. "Well, considering I'm the *only* bestselling author on Naples Island, I suppose that's a compliment."

"I know what we can do instead of dance," she said, and she pulled out the scrunchie that had kept her long locks of blonde hair in a bun. It fell about her shoulders. She threw the scrunchie at me, and I saw those big, electric-blue eyes looking at me. She peeled back the top of her blouse and baited me with a glimpse of tanned cleavage. It worked well, because I couldn't look away. Hey, I'm a guy. "We can do something else in the rain, if you'd prefer? Something a little naughty."

"Babe, I think that's something I'd prefer to do inside as well."

She clicked her tongue again. "It wouldn't be the first in the rain, but it'd be the first in California rain. Remember right after we got married? In the park?"

"Yes, I remember," I said, and seeing that she wasn't going to budge until the deluge was upon us, I picked up my glass of wine and made myself comfortable. "But that was a long time ago, babe. We were in our twenties."

"I still think you're hot."

"And we were complete idiots. Anyone could have walked by at any moment."

"They would have been jealous," she said very matter-of-factly. In what was clearly another attempt to bait me, she moved southward on her journey of unbuttoning her blouse and I, primitive man, watched the buttons undo themselves as if under hypnosis.

The front door opened, and Owen, our junior in high school, walked out with a can of Coca-Cola in his hand. He's a tall, gangly guy—several inches taller than me—and his headphones might as well have been surgically attached to him. Under his shaggy mop of black hair, maybe they really were screwed into his skull.

I don't know what exactly he was coming out to ask us. He opened his mouth to say something, but I assume the sight of his mom with her shirt unbuttoned and her boobs nearly hanging out was too much for his adolescent mind to cope with. Me drooling over her probably didn't help. His eyes went wide, and then he shut them. His acne-pocked forehead crinkled in what appeared to be an effort to squeeze that memory out of his mind once and for all.

"That is so gross!" he said, still looking constipated.

He turned around and closed the door behind him.

But we could hear him yell as he went back upstairs: "Disgusting!"

My wife and I looked at each other and fell apart laughing.

Chapter Two

I've always considered myself one of the lucky guys, and I really mean it. I was forty-two that summer, and more had gone right in my life than had gone wrong—a lot more. I sold my first suspense novel just a few years after graduating college, married the same woman who had encouraged me to finish writing that book, had two healthy and well-adjusted children, and I had plenty of money in the bank. What more could a guy want? I used to sit on the front porch of that house on Naples Island and wonder if I should pinch myself, because so much good fortune in so short a span of time seemed almost impossible to believe.

And most of my good fortune is because of Madison. I really do love my wife, and the older I get, the more I realize how few people can truly say that. I have three good friends from high school and college that I still keep in touch with. Two of them have been through not-very-nice divorces, custody fights, and enough drama to script daytime talk shows for the next millennium. My other buddy, Dwight, is married, but sometimes when I talk to him I get the impression he'd rather join my other friends in their return to bachelorhood.

He and his wife have three boys, and if it wasn't for them, I think he probably would have thrown in the towel a long time ago.

I think in all our years of marriage, my wife and I haven't even said that word: *divorce*. Maybe it's because we both came from divorced families and we've seen the aftermath firsthand; it's hard to drop a bomb when you've spent time standing amongst the civilians and debris. But more than that, I just think I chose the right person. Maybe all the books that have been written on marriage and relationships can be substituted for one simple rule: *Get your head out of your butt and choose the right person.* That's the advice I've always given my sons.

My wife and I are polar opposites. My friends in college used to joke with me and say that I could probably go a whole week sitting inside without talking to somebody, and there's truth in that. I'm usually the first to want to leave a social event, most certainly the first to suggest not even going to a social event, and when I can't get out of those situations, I probably look pretty pathetic following my wife around like a shadow. Being shorter than her probably doesn't help. If there's anything I like about those kinds of situations, it's the fact that I can observe, because that's what writers do—we observe things. Many a person that I've been introduced to at my wife's social gatherings has appeared on the pages of my books. But in the end, I guess I'm just a homebody. We all have what I like to think of as a daily word quota, and I take care of mine at about five o'clock in the morning with my coffee and the blank screen in front of me. That's my safe place. That's when Eddie Dees has more words than he knows what to do with.

My wife, on the other hand, can hardly go to the bathroom without giving everyone in the room a hug goodbye. She's vivacious, loud, bubbly, exciting, childlike, and my life would be boring without her. For sure, she annoys me at times and hardly lets me get a word in edgewise on most days and maybe that's why I chose a career as a writer. Blank pages don't interrupt me when I'm trying to make a point. But, in all honestly, I'd probably be some crabby author locked in my office twenty-four hours a day if it weren't for her. She gets me out into the real world and, even more importantly, she gets me out of my head.

And she definitely makes me deal with people like Marsha Walker.

I'm not sure how old Marsha is, but I've always assumed she's closing in on her fifties. During our first couple months living on Naples Island, I never saw Marsha wearing anything other than a muumuu. It looked to me like she'd bought all of these items in some thrift store on the wrong side of the tracks. She had short but very thick brown curls which sat on top of a pudgy, doughy face. Her eyes were big brown headlights that seemed to swallow up everything in her presence. Sometimes she reminded me of an oversized, over-sugared kid, with cotton candy in one hand and a soda in the other, who had been let loose in an amusement park with hundreds of dollars in her pocket. She just had this overly-enthusiastic, overly-optimistic demeanor about her and, when I discovered how so frumpy a woman had come to reside in so elegant a neighborhood, it made sense to me. She had grown up on Naples Island and from what I heard, had never married (or had a boyfriend for that matter). She never left the house she was brought home to as an infant. When her parents passed away—only a few years before my wife and I moved there—she had inherited the home along with a trust as robust as her. She really was that kid in the amusement park.

Just as my son, Owen, had retreated from what he thought was the most disturbing sight he had ever beheld—sexual flirtation between Mom and Dad—Marsha waddled over to our house. She was our neighbor to the right and, considering how close the houses are built on Naples Island, that distance could probably be measured in inches.

"Oh my dear, oh my dear, oh my dear," Marsha said. She pointed her pudgy finger toward the approaching storm clouds, and her bracelets clicked together about her wrists. She always wore brightly colored, plastic bracelets. My wife and I never quite understood it. "Do you see the storm, do you see it? A thunderstorm in July. Oh my dear, I've never seen something like this. It's so rare."

My wife, who had quickly buttoned her shirt when she saw Marsha approaching, nodded in agreement and said, "Hi, Marsha. Yes, we were just talking about it. Our first storm in California. We've seen enough of them in Washington."

"Oh, I bet you have," Marsha said. Then she looked at me. "Kind of like something a writer would have in a scary book or something, right, Mr. Dees?"

"Well, perhaps. Maybe it'll inspire me."

"Oh, I just think it's so fascinating how writers can be inspired by such things," she said. She took a deep breath and sighed. "I just think it's so absolutely wonderful how you are able to take these things that we see around us every day and make them into stories. It's almost magical, Mr. Dees, almost magical. I know I've already told you about how when I was a little girl, I dreamed of being a writer. I dug up that old story I wrote and once I'm done editing it I'll give it to you so you can tell me what you think."

My wife shot me a knowing grin.

"Yes, Marsha," I said. "I'm very much looking forward to seeing it."

Marsha had already told me about the short story she wrote in college at least a dozen times and even though she kept promising she would show me her story, I doubted she ever would. I've learned that most people talk about writing, but very few actually sit down to do it. Occasionally, I run into a person like Marsha who, because I've sold a lot of copies of my novels, thinks I'm some kind of deity. I even gave up my effort to get her to call me by my first name. It was apparent that she wasn't going to take me down from the pedestal she'd placed me on. My wife, of course, thought the whole thing was hilarious. She always thought it was hilarious when people—particularly females—went all goo-goo-eyed over me because I was a successful writer.

"He still wipes his butt, people, he's just a normal dude," she'd often whisper in my ear during certain encounters. "Oh, wait a minute," she would then tease. "I just cleaned his underwear last night. I take that back. Maybe he doesn't wipe."

"Thanks a lot, babe," was my usual response.

"How's your new novel coming along?" Marsha asked.

"Doing well. Got up at my usual five o'clock and put in a few hours. Hoping to have it done in a few months."

"And what is it about? Is it the usual suspense kind of stuff? Or is it a follow-up to one of your earlier books? Like *Redemption Awaits*? I always thought that would have been a good one to write a sequel to."

"No, this is a standalone novel, and I can't say anything about it yet. Too early. But if things go as planned, it should be out sometime next year."

"Well, you know me. I'll want an autographed copy."

"That can be arranged," I said, smiling. Why not? I'd autographed my other novels for her, and my wife and I had noticed, during one occasion when she invited us into her living room for some tea and cookies, those autographed books on display on the top of her living room bookshelf. She was mighty proud of them.

Just then, Darrel and Jenna Paisley walked by. They were followed by Samantha Wheeler. Darrel and Jenna were the typical middle-aged near-retirement family you expected to find on Naples Island, and they were our neighbors two doors to the left. Some hermit by the name of Dominic, whom I had only seen once or twice, lived between us. Darrel was a twiggy, scrawny guy with thinning hair and a hook nose, while his wife, Jenna, was a bit more on the shorter, wider side of things. Nearing retirement, Darrel was a financial planner, and his wife was an art teacher at Woodrow Wilson High School. It was pretty clear that it was his income and his income alone that afforded them the ability to live on this private nook of Naples Island.

They seemed to me, in the brief time that I'd been there, the all-American, friendly, work-hard-and-play-hard kind of family. They had one grown son, Sean, who had long ago moved out, and every time I'd chatted with them, they talked excitedly about some vacation that they were planning. They were both quiet, reserved, but the kind of people who would go the extra mile to help you out if you needed something. We'd had dinner at each other's houses on a few occasions, and we'd stayed up pretty late and gone through far too many bottles of wine, but we always walked away thinking the same thing: we hit the jackpot as far as neighbors are concerned when it came to the Paisleys.

The Paisleys said hello to us, but Samantha Wheeler was the one who caught my eye. She caught every guy's eye. Not a day over thirty-five, she was married to some young investment banker who was away on business more than he was home. We'd spoken to her briefly a couple times and once, while I was out walking Bessie, she and I chatted a bit. A tall brunette with long legs, honey-colored skin, and big hazel eyes, she was striking, to say the least. I have to admit when I bumped into her that day on my walk, I felt she desperately wanted attention. Maybe it was because her husband was away so much, or maybe it was because she was just used to having power over men, but I thought there was something quite flirtatious and inviting about Samantha Wheeler.

I think the first time I noticed Bessie missing was when our impromptu meeting with the neighbors broke up. The Paisleys, always smiling, were waving goodbye and heading toward their castle on the water, and Marsha, bracelets clinking around her wrists, was about to head back to her house to bake some cookies, when a massive, seemingly-unending fork of lightning ripped through the sky. It was followed, just a moment after, by a virtual sonic boom. I could feel it in my toes. And then the first bit of real drizzle started.

We all looked up in amazement, and then I looked around for Bessie. She was funny when it came to storms. Up in Washington, she wasn't like most dogs that wanted to hide out when the thunder and lightning were at their worst; she always wanted to be with Madison and me. I always said it was because she was a lover, but my wife thought she was just a plain sissy.

Yet I didn't see her anywhere. Strange.

Our farewells were interrupted briefly as we gawked and commented on how massive that bolt of lightning had been and how much darker the clouds had gotten in just the last few minutes, when Drake walked out of his front door. He lived across the canal in a three-story Victorian home just alongside Samantha Wheeler's. I had never spoken to him; in fact, I think it's safe to say that none of us had ever spoken a word to Drake. I didn't even know what his last name was, but, as neighbors talk, we knew enough.

He was probably in his early twenties and lived with his father, who, according to local legend, was suffering some kind of debilitating illness and hadn't left the house for months. I don't think it would be fair to describe Drake as the gothic type, but in my short time there, he always seemed to be wearing black jeans and a black sweatshirt. Gangly, pale-faced, and shy, he usually walked past our home without any type of acknowledgement. His head was usually dropped forward, his eyes always on the ground in front of him, and my wife described him as most of the other neighbors did: creepy.

On that first night of storms, we watched as Drake walked out of the front door of his house. He had a giant duffel bag slung over his shoulder and from what we could tell, it looked pretty heavy. He opened the gate in front of his house and lugged the bag down the little gangway to his private dock. The waterfront homes in Naples Island have their own private docks, though the only things on our dock are two kayaks left over from the previous owner. I keep telling myself that I'll get down there and try one out, but exercise isn't exactly my thing.

Drake threw his bloated duffel bag into the back of his small Duffy, an electric boat, and began to untie it from the dock.

"Kinda weird to be taking the boat out just as this storm's about to hit," Darrel Paisley said, and his wife agreed.

"Devil worshipper," Marsha said. "That's what I think. Or maybe just a druggie."

After untying from the dock, Drake steered his electric Duffy down the canal and out of sight. At this point, the rain was more than just a drizzle, and we all bolted inside. My wife and I grabbed our cheese plate and our glasses of wine and headed indoors.

Chapter Three

My nine-year-old son, Toby, was on the couch, playing video games. I swear that's all that kid ever did. At least his older brother enjoyed listening to music and playing music. There was something admirable in that. But on most days, I was pretty sure that Toby would be content to spend all day in front of some video game with an IV sugar drip inserted into his arm.

"Are you ever gonna stop playing that thing?" I asked. I might as well have been talking to the wall. "Hello? Anyone there?"

His eyes were glazed over. Toby didn't even blink.

"This boy needs some professional help," I said, setting our glasses of wine down in the kitchen. For the second time that afternoon, I realized I hadn't seen Bessie for a while. I scanned the living room for a sign of her and didn't come up with anything. "Hon, have you seen Bessie? I haven't seen her in a while."

"No." She shrugged, taking a bite of cheese. "Not since earlier today."

"Well, where is she?"

"I don't know. Probably sleeping."

A flash of lightning filled the house, followed by a loud peal of thunder. The rain fell relentlessly, and by this time I was pretty convinced that something wasn't right. Bessie loves being with people. Even if she had heard the first cracks of thunder and had run into another room because she was scared, she would have come back by now. That was just the way she was.

I did a walk-through of the house and checked under every bed and behind every piece of furniture but didn't come up with anything. By the time I did my second walk-through, my wife was taking me seriously. Madison did the second search with me, and we couldn't find anything. We even looked in closets and showers, but there was no sign of Bessie. We stopped in the kitchen when we were done, looked at each other, and didn't know what to make of it.

"You did look out in the backyard, right?" Madison asked me.

"Well, no. Why would she be sitting in a rainy backyard when there's a warm house here? Plus, you know how little that yard is. And there's no shelter."

Madison rolled her eyes. Anyone who has ever lived on Naples Island knows we don't have much in the way of yards. With waterfront property being so valuable along with builders trying to maximize every square inch, residents are pretty lucky if they have a ten-by-ten patio out back. That was about what we had.

My wife, having peeled back the curtains, looked out as the rain poured down endlessly on the back patio, but there was no sign of Bessie anywhere.

Toby was still engrossed in his game, and we could hear Owen playing keyboard in his room upstairs. We didn't want to say anything to them yet, especially Toby, who had gone with us to pick Bessie up from the pound. But it seemed like the writing was pretty much on the wall at this point. The dog was gone.

"When did you see her last?" Madison asked.

"I don't know. A little before we went out front with our wine, I guess."

"She couldn't have gotten past us, could she?"

"No way. We were sitting right there. Unless she slipped past us during my momentary distraction with your boobs."

That earned a slight grin from Madison.

"They are quite distracting at times."

"Well, we have to keep looking," she said.

"But where? We've gone through the whole house. Twice. And you know as well as I do, she wouldn't last a minute out there in the rain. She'd be back in a heartbeat."

"Well, we must have missed something. You look down here."

I agreed and walked through the downstairs, opened every closet door, and looked behind every piece of furniture in the remote possibility that Bessie might be in hiding, but after a while it just became ridiculous. She just wasn't like that.

I took a seat in my leather chair in the downstairs office where I spent my early mornings drinking coffee and meeting my daily word quota. I looked out the blurred window of rain, listened to what sounded like a million watery nails being hammered into the shingles of our home, and knew that I would eventually have to go outside to look for her.

I got up from my chair and glanced out at the rain one last time, and I noticed Drake returning to his dock. The hood of his black sweatshirt covered his face. He looked completely drenched as he climbed out of his Duffy and tied up to his dock. In a hurry to escape the rain, he jumped back into his boat to retrieve his duffel bag, and then climbed back out and ran to the front door of his home.

Only now, it looked like the duffel bag was empty.

The idea first entered my head as I was about to leave my home office. I paused for a moment in the doorway and caught myself, almost unwillingly, slowly looking back toward the window and the strange dark figure sloshing forward to the front door of his house.

The duffel bag. It was carrying something before he'd gotten onto that boat. Something heavy. Something no longer in it.

Something about the size of Bessie.

Devil worshipper, Marsha had said. I'd read stories about those people before, and I remembered how I'd seen Drake walking by the house earlier that day. I'd seen him walk through the back alley behind my house on more than one occasion. And certainly he was tall enough to reach over the gate and undo the latch.

"Is it possible?" I whispered in the silence of my office. "Is it really possible?"

Chapter Four

I put in a little time writing before searching for Bessie.

I was up at my usual five o'clock, sitting at my desk with a steaming cup of coffee, all seventy thousand words of my manuscript on the screen in front of me. Writing is all about momentum. For me, even missing a day or two knocks me completely off rhythm. On a good day, I'll crank it out till about noon and then spend my afternoon doing edits. On a bad day, I might throw in the towel around ten. But spending too long away from a story is like being a blacksmith who hammers at cold metal. You have to pound on the anvil while it's hot.

But as I sat in my leather chair and watched the first light of dawn show itself, I knew I wasn't going to get much done. My wife and I had gone to bed without telling our sons because, what was the point? Miraculously, they hadn't noticed that she was missing. The rain had come down heavy that night, without interruption, and we knew it would be pretty ridiculous to start a search in those conditions. I'd thrown on my jacket and checked the houses near us before going to bed, but that hadn't amounted to anything. We figured it would be better to wait until morning when there was light and it was clear enough to see. I tried not to think of Drake and his duffel bag. My mind couldn't completely go there quite yet.

I sat in my chair for twenty minutes, sipping coffee and trying to get back into the book I'd been grinding away on for the last four months, until I realized that I just couldn't do it.

I closed the laptop, decided I'd go out, and went to the closet and threw on my jacket. The rain had stopped and there was enough light that I could at least walk up and down the island and do my due diligence. I decided not to wake up Madison. She loved that dog, but I think she loved sleeping in even more, and it wouldn't hurt for me to get outside and put in an hour on my own. If things went well, I'd find her hiding under some neighbor's bushes, and the kids would never even know she was gone. Then I could plop back down at my desk and pound away on that anvil.

But I had no such luck. I walked up and down our stretch of the island twice. The first time I was respectful of the neighbors and kept quiet, but the second time I didn't care, and I called for Bessie every ten feet or so. I'm sure many people on Naples Island sat at their breakfast tables later that morning and while drinking their coffee, wondered if they had dreamt of some madman running around yelling "Bessie!" or if it had actually happened.

After two laps around the island, realizing the futility of my endeavor, I returned home and woke up Madison. We sat on the corner of our bed and had absolutely no idea where to begin.

"Okay, why don't I make some posters to put up around the neighborhood," Madison said, finally getting out of bed. "Did you get the new ink cartridge for your printer?"

"No."

"Alright, then I'll have to use Owen's."

"Owen's?" I said, half-laughing. "Good luck with that. He

probably didn't go to bed until a few hours ago, and you know what it's like waking him up."

"Well, he can sleep right through it then, can't he?"

"*If* you can find the printer. That room of his has a way of swallowing things up and transporting them to some other dimension. What about Toby? He'll be up soon. Should we tell him? You know how much he loves Bessie. This is gonna crush the poor guy."

"I'll talk to him. Moms are good at that kind of thing. Why don't you go for another romp around the block. Bessie couldn't have gotten far. And I'll call the pound just in case somebody turned her in."

We both knew that didn't make much sense because Bessie had a nametag with both of our phone numbers on it, but neither of us mentioned it.

I turned away to resume my search, but my wife grabbed me by the tail of my shirt and pulled me back onto the bed. She leaned in toward me, kissed me on the cheek, and despite the breath—she hadn't brushed her teeth yet—I found her quite appealing at that moment. She rubbed her index finger down the side of my face.

"If you recall, you said you'd prefer to take care of business inside instead of outside, right? That's what you said."

"Yes, that's what I said, but, come on, we have a missing dog on our hands."

She was already taking off my shirt. When my wife is on a mission, she wastes no time.

"Well, then I think before we begin this search, it's important to fulfill our marital duties. Plus, and don't take this personally, but based on prior experiences, this probably won't take very long anyway." She winked.

Before I knew what was happening, my shirt was off and so was hers.

The rescue mission would have to be temporarily delayed.

Chapter Five

Having dutifully fulfilled my marital obligations, I set out on my third and final trip around the island, only this time I knew I was on a fool's quest. If Bessie really was hiding out under a patio in someone's front yard, she would have come out long ago. If some neighbor had kindly taken her in from the storm, we most certainly would have received a phone call.

By the time I returned to my front door, I knew that something strange must have happened. I admit that as I stood by the front door of my house after that search, I looked for a long time at Drake's Duffy across the way, and I felt seized by horror.

I decided to cross one of the many bridges extending over the canal and pay a visit to Drake's property. I wouldn't go up to the door and knock—I had no real reason to yet—but it might be helpful to just walk by his house and glance over things, then stop by Samantha's and ask if she'd heard anything unusual the night before.

As I made my way there, I noticed Marsha step outside. The front door to her house slammed shut. She was wearing a red apron over her muumuu with the words KITCHEN DIVA written on it in bright orange lettering. She brushed remnants of flour off her hands as she approached me.

"Hello, Mr. Dees! Speak of the devil!" she said. "I was just about to head over to your house and ask your lovely wife if I might borrow some brown sugar."

I side-stepped a large puddle and advanced toward her. "Well, I'm certain she wouldn't mind loaning you some. She should be home making some flyers to put up in the neighborhood. You see, it seems Bessie ran away last night. We can't find her anywhere. You didn't happen to see anything, did you?"

"Oh, my dear Lord," Marsha said, aghast. With her flour-caked hands holding both sides of her face, she looked like a woman who had just been told that World War III had begun and the fighting was taking place in her own backyard. "That poor, poor dog. And to think of all the rain that came down last night and the thunder and the lightning. Poor, poor thing. And the news this morning said another wave is going to hit us. Oh, that poor dog."

"It'll probably be fine," I said, and I resisted the urge to reach out and put my hand on her shoulder to console her. It didn't occur to me until after our brief conversation how unusual it was for me—the owner of the dog—to be the one consoling my neighbor. But that's how things went with Marsha Walker.

"No sign at all of her?" she asked.

"No, not yet, but I'm not too worried. Bessie could only have gotten so far. I'm sure some neighbor on another strip of the island took her in for the night, and we'll get a call any moment that she's doing just fine. We're going to put up some flyers just to be safe. I'm sure by the time you're done baking whatever you're baking, Bessie will be back to her normal routine."

Marsha nodded. Her eyes looked a little teary. "Well, I'll be praying for your family and Bessie," she said solemnly. Again, so sincere and dramatic an expression over a missing dog that was most likely alive and well in some neighboring house struck me as odd, but I knew Marsha's intentions and I appreciated it.

I thanked her for her support, chatted for a brief moment about that short story of hers and how she was going to send it my way once it was ready, and eventually headed across one of the small bridges to Samantha Wheeler's side of the water. Marsha headed to my house, where she would pick up some brown sugar and lavish more condolences on my wife.

As I crossed the bridge, I couldn't help noticing how clean and fresh the air was that morning. My wife and I, while happy to escape what often felt like the constant deluge of Seattle rainfall, had always loved going for a walk the morning after a downpour. Especially the morning after one of the first rainfalls of the season. There was always something invigorating about it.

Just as I went over the crest of the small bridge to the other side of the canal, I saw Hot-rodder come my way on his tiny BMX bike. Hot-rodder wasn't his real name; Bryan was his real name, but ever since I saw him on my first weekend living on the island, I had dubbed him with that title. Probably about twelve years old, the little rug rat was a wide-eyed, scruffy, smiley, mischievous-looking kid who reminded me of my younger brother, Alan, before he passed away at the same age. He also reminded me of a pure and good time in my life. Someone once told me that writers write to recapture their youth. I think there's some truth in that. With Hot-rodder, I felt like I was being transported to another time.

"Mr. Eddie!" he screamed, peddling toward me. He had glued a card (the ace of spades) to the frame over the back wheel of his bike so it penetrated the spokes. When the wheels turned, it sounded like a helicopter. He kicked on the brakes and skidded to a stop just in front of me, wiping sweat from his forehead. He met me with a big, voracious smile. "Word of the day!" he piped.

"Okay, word of the day," I said, thinking. It took me a moment. "Exorbitant."

"Exorbitant," he said. He scratched his scruffy mop of hair and looked up at me, squinting in the morning sunlight. "I give up. What is it?"

"Overly expensive. Superfluous."

"Superfluous," he repeated, barely able to form the word on his tongue. He seemed to chew on that word for a few minutes, quite content, and then, as if he just realized he was late to some very important meeting, jumped back on his bike. "Cool! Thanks, Mr. Eddie!"

He was gone, like the little tornado that he was. He peddled hard down the other side of the little bridge and I heard the card—his imaginary engine—disappear in the distance.

I don't think I'd ever seen Hot-rodder without his bike, but our word of the day tradition began the first time I'd met him. I had asked him for directions, and when he asked me who I was and what I did, I was immediately impressed. What eleven- or twelve-year-old kid asks an adult what he does for a living? I liked the curiosity in him, because I could tell that was why he asked it—not because he'd been taught to. He really wanted to know, and when I told him I was a writer, he told me he wanted me to teach him a new word every time we ran into each other.

And so the tradition began.

I crossed to the other side of the canal and walked past Drake's Victorian home. I thought again of the duffel bag I'd seen him carrying on and off his Duffy the night before, and I debated about walking down to his private dock to search his boat. Perhaps there would be answers or evidence of some kind. But knowing that Drake's neighbor, Samantha Wheeler, might have some information, I decided to maintain my course and start with her.

I felt a bit nervous as I walked up to the front door of her ultra-modern home. The last thing I wanted was for my impromptu visit to fuel Samantha's attraction; that wasn't my goal.

I pressed the green luminescent doorbell and, a moment later, Samantha was at the door wearing only spandex shorts and a sports bra. She had a bottle of Avian water in her hand and a workout towel draped over her shoulder. Clearly, she had just finished a round of cardio-something.

"Eddie!" she said. I think it was a greeting. It also sounded like a pleasant surprise. She took her towel off her shoulder and wiped her face, and I was surprised to notice that even with no make-up and her face dripping in sweat, she was pretty stunning.

"Hi, Samantha. I hope you don't mind me just swinging by like this."

"Mind?" she said. "Why would I mind? Of course you can. Any time."

I'm sure she thinks that about many men, I thought. Sam was lonely, plain and simple. A hundred other guys could have knocked on her door that morning and she would have been just as happy to see them.

"Well, I just had a quick question. Bessie, our retriever, is missing. I've patrolled the neighborhood several times in hope of finding her, but to no avail. You haven't seen her or anything, have you?"

"No, I'm sorry, I haven't. Would you like to come inside?"

"Thanks, but I should probably be heading back home soon. No sign of Bessie?"

She shook her head.

"Well, I did have one more question then, and this one concerns your neighbor. You know who I'm talking about?"

She wrinkled her nose and nodded. Drake was, in our little neck of the woods, the unpleasant odor everyone was aware of but didn't always want to acknowledge.

"You haven't seen anything unusual next door, have you? Or heard anything? Anything strange last night, particularly?"

Her eyes went wide. She started to say something, stopped to rethink what she was going to say, and then started again.

"You know what, I didn't really think about it until you mentioned it, but yeah. There was something kind of weird yesterday."

"What?"

"You're going to want to come inside for this, Eddie," she said, pointing toward Drake's front porch only feet away from hers. She wanted to be out of earshot.

I followed her obediently into her house. The inside continued the theme of modern décor, and I found myself sitting on a curved, steel barstool in her kitchen that looked much more uncomfortable than it was. When I first saw the row of barstools surrounding the enormous granite island, I thought they looked like NASA projects that had been converted to furniture. Strange modern stuff.

She handed me a bottle of water and began to drink some green vegetable concoction she had blended just prior to my arrival. She offered me some, but I declined. My wife had tried, just a year before that, to get me into juicing. Liquefied broccoli, kale, spinach? No, thank you. I'll stick with my One A Day.

"So what exactly did you see?" I asked.

Sam sipped her green juice. "It's not really what I saw, it's what I heard," she explained. "To be honest with you, I haven't thought much of it until now. Yesterday afternoon, before the storm set in, I was sitting here in my kitchen, going through mail, when I thought I heard something on my back patio."

"What do you mean something? Thunder? Lightning?"

"No, it sounded like a door blowing open, followed by a loud metallic sound. I assumed that something in the backyard must have fallen over, so I looked out the sliding glass door to the patio and noticed the shed door was open. My husband keeps some of his woodworking tools in that shed. It's an old hobby of his.

"I thought a gust of wind must have blown it open, but even that seemed strange to me because it's usually latched, so I went out to the shed to close it. Everything seemed normal, but I did see one thing that struck me as odd. The saw. It wasn't where it normally was."

"Saw?"

"Yes. You have to understand, my husband is a Type A personality to the max. He's always doing little projects when he's home, and he keeps those tools meticulously organized. One of the saws was missing from the sidewall, and I remembered the warbling metallic sound I'd heard, like a saw hitting our side of the wall. I imagined that weirdo next door jumping over the concrete fence of his backyard, opening the shed, taking the saw, and then jumping back over to his side. I know it sounds weird, and it was just a fleeting thought. By the time I was back inside and dried off, I'd pretty much dismissed it. But when you asked me if I'd seen anything weird going on at Drake's last night, it just all came back to me."

I sipped the bottled water that Samantha had offered me. I still didn't understand much of what was happening, but I didn't like the possibilities. *Devil worshipper*, Marsha had said. A missing dog. A stolen saw. A freak next door with a duffel bag. Was it really possible that Drake was involved in this?

"Did you ask your husband about the saw?"

"No. Like I said, I didn't even think about it again until now. I can text him, though."

"Why don't you? It might help."

"I know he's kind of a weird guy, but why would Drake want to steal a saw out of my husband's shed? I just don't get that. And what would that have to do with your missing dog? Am I missing something?"

Perhaps several points on an IQ score, I thought, but I held my tongue. Samantha Wheeler clearly wasn't the sharpest tool in the shed —no pun intended —but I really couldn't blame her for being unable to connect some of the dots. After all, she hadn't seen Drake get off his Duffy with that empty duffel bag, and maybe her mind wasn't quite as sick and twisted as mine was. Maybe all the creative writing had truly warped my imagination.

"What time did you hear all that and close the shed?" I asked.

"Not sure. A little before I talked to you and the neighbors last night. Just as the storm was beginning to make its appearance."

The timeline fit perfectly, and my heart sank because of it. I didn't want to think anybody could be guilty of something so perverse.

"I've heard some noises in his backyard recently," she continued. "He seems to be moving around in his garage a lot. You can look down from our bedroom and make out something going on down there through the trees. I've always just assumed he's been cleaning it out or reorganizing it or something."

"Really?" I said, and then I had an idea. "Can I come back tonight maybe about nine or so, and just peek out of that window to see what he's doing?"

"Sure," she said, shrugging. But I could tell she looked a

little puzzled. "Is there something going on? Something you're looking for?"

"I'll know when I see it," I said, and I thanked her for her time. I excused myself to return home to assist with the posting of lost dog signs throughout the neighborhood.

As I stepped out of her house, I realized what I'd just done. I had been in a woman's home —a ridiculously hot woman wearing only spandex shorts and a sports bra and had made an appointment with her to come back and visit her bedroom that night.

"A lot of men would be jealous of you," I mumbled to myself as I began to cross the small bridge that led back to my side of the canal. But by the time I reached the other side, I was mumbling something else entirely.

"Idiot. Moron. Fool."

Chapter Six

I spent that evening at the Captain's Room, a small haunt I'd discovered my first week living on the island. It's a dark, cozy, and relatively quiet bar on Second Street, the two-mile thoroughfare that runs through the island.

That night, the place looked as usual. Larry of the Long Island Ice Teas was sitting in his usual spot at the bar, right in the corner, dressed in a t-shirt and flip flops. I had been to the Captain's Room about a dozen times, and Larry had been sitting in the same spot and drinking the same type of drink every time I'd been there. I'd talked to him briefly a couple times, and when I did, it seemed like he really only enjoyed talking about his wife and what a horrible person she was; I had noticed that his wife's villainy seemed to increase with his alcohol consumption. Larry loved talking at times, but more often, he just sipped his drink and played on his phone.

There were a few others I hadn't seen before. I'd noticed a Harley out front, and when I went inside I saw a biker sitting at one of the back tables, drinking a beer. I didn't pay much attention to him when I first walked in. I found a place at the bar a few seats down from Larry, and Jesse threw a napkin down on the bar in front of me.

"The usual?" Jesse asked. A middle-aged man always dressed in a flannel shirt, with a grizzly beard halfway down to his belt buckle, he looked like he should be living in the back woods somewhere as opposed to working a bar here on Naples Island. He had moved to Naples several years before from Louisiana to be closer to his son and also to start the bar. His son worked there with him. I'd seen him on a few occasions running dishes and pouring drinks. With sun-bleached hair, bronze skin, and usually wearing Hawaiian shirts, his son looked like he lived in a completely different universe than his dad. You couldn't get much different if you tried.

"You got it."

"You like those Metropolitans, huh?" Jesse asked.

He turned to make my drink. It was the only thing I'd ordered there. I've never been a big fan of beer, and I had enough good wine in my own cellar back home. Not long after college, a friend had introduced me to Metropolitans. It's been my "go to" drink ever since.

As I waited for my drink, I reflected on the day. After breaking the news to Toby—who took it as poorly as we thought he would—we had taken a family hike through the island and posted missing dog posters up and down the streets. We even woke up Owen to help us. He, of course, complained the whole time, as I suppose most teenagers are apt to do if woken up before noon.

After that, we took our sons into Belmont Shore for lunch at a little Mexican restaurant called Fish Taco Cantina. We'd fallen in love with the salsa on our first visit there. We even got some ice cream cones after and went for a stroll, all of which, of course, was really an attempt to get Toby's mind off Bessie. Owen, as I suspected, was pretty unaffected by the whole matter. He was taking his new girlfriend to the movies that night, a little blond girl in the neighborhood I had met on one previous occasion. Her name was Candice. I couldn't believe he already had a "lady friend." He had wasted no time.

My wife had called Long Beach Animal Care Services earlier that day to see if a Golden Retriever that matched Bessie's description had been brought to any of the facilities, and when the answer was no, my mind couldn't help but drift to thoughts of Drake, his duffel bag, and whatever he was doing in that backyard of his. After a long day of dealing with kids and not getting a moment of writing in, Madison granted me permission to head over to the Captain's Room just as the sun was setting and just as another storm was making its way toward us. She was going to watch a movie with Toby—further effort to distract him.

It was nice to get in a little alone time. Sometimes I brought a book to the Captain's Room and found a spot at one of the back tables and read while sipping my Metropolitan. But on that night, it felt nice to sit at the bar and just unwind.

"There you go, my friend," Jesse said, placing the drink on the napkin before me. "Anything else?"

"I think I'll just stick with this for now, thanks."

"Keeping out of the rain tonight, huh?" he asked. "The weather report says the storm's gonna be worse tonight than last night. That was quite a downpour, don't you think?"

"Yeah, it was. My dog even ran away last night. Spent all day putting up fliers and everything for her."

Jesse's son, who was walking by at that moment, overheard me and said, "Oh, dude, that was you. I saw those signs on my way here. Totally lame."

"Yep," I said, and then Surfer Dude disappeared back into the kitchen.

"You and your wife going to watch the fireworks tomorrow night?" Jesse asked. "It'd probably be a good way to get to know people, being new here. It's usually a pretty good time."

"Yeah, I think we're going."

The following day was only the third of July, but Naples had always prided itself on its own little fireworks show on the third. It was a smaller, more intimate affair for the local residents, and most people living in Naples joked that it was an appetizer for the big fireworks show the following night down by the beach on the mainland. But the island had its own tradition on the Fourth as well. The central park on the small island hosted bands, food, drinks, and what was supposed to be a festive and family-friendly afternoon and evening for local residents. The Paisleys had already invited us to attend both nights with them, and we were very much looking forward to it.

"Hopefully this storm activity will let up," Jesse said. "I guess we'll just have to cross our fingers."

"I guess so."

The biker guy from the back table walked up to the bar just then and slammed an empty beer glass on the bar top. He was a big guy with a shaved head and caramel colored skin, clad in leather. He had piercing dark eyes, a goatee, and one of his eyebrows was missing a chunk of hair in the middle.

"Gimme another Guinness," the biker said, looking blankly at Jesse and then at me. He swayed drunkenly for a moment, and then went back to his table.

"Who was that?" I asked when he was out of earshot.

"A jerk," Jesse said and called his son out of the back kitchen to pour the beer. "He started coming in here a few days ago."

"Yeah, he didn't seem like the nicest guy."

"He introduced himself once as Klutch."

"Klutch?"

"Yeah, who knows? A biker name or something. But I can tell you one thing kinda weird that happened when he was here last night." Jesse leaned toward me just to make sure he wouldn't be overheard. As he did, his son, who had poured a new glass of Guinness, walked it over to Klutch's table. "Our register came up a hundred dollars short."

"A hundred dollars short?"

"Yep. Now, I didn't see anything, so I can't make any outright accusations or prove anything, but I'm telling you this register was short. And the only person sitting in here—for one stretch, at least—was that idiot. We mustn't have closed the register. He noticed and reached his greasy little fingers into the register while I was in the back grabbing something. It's the only thing that makes sense."

"You thought about confronting him with it?"

"I don't think that'd go over too well," Jesse said, stroking his beard. "And again, what evidence do I have? Could be a miscount, but I highly doubt it. I'm just watching closely for the next round to see what happens."

"I hear you."

"And I'm making sure the register is closed, you can bet on that one."

We laughed.

I stayed at the Captain's Room for another half hour or so, sipping my Metropolitan and thinking about the evening before me. I had an appointment with Samantha that night and knew I'd best start heading her way; plus, before I commenced my evening of spying on Drake, I wanted to see my son off on his date. This new era of him going to the movies with girls was a bit disturbing. I left Jesse a generous tip, thanked him again, and left the Captain's Room.

It was a short five-minute walk back to my house. On my return there, I ran into Hot-rodder, who was pumping away on the pedals of his BMX bike. This time he didn't stop and tore right past me.

"Word of the day!" he yelled.

I looked up at the dark army of clouds moving closer.

Storm and rain looked to be only an hour or so away. "Cumu-lonimbus!"

"Cumulonimbus!" he cried back.

"The type of clouds you see in a thunderstorm!"

"Cumulonimbus!" he yelled again, turned a corner, and was gone.

I smiled. I don't think that's a word I've ever used in a novel or story I've written. I'm pretty sure that one came from a science class I took in college.

I passed several of our lost dog signs on my route home, and my heart sank even more in knowing how futile it had been to post them.

When I got home, Toby and my wife were on the couch, watching *The Wizard of Oz* and deep into their second bowls of ice cream. I could tell that the little guy had spent some time crying that evening—it came out in bursts when he thought of Bessie. His hair was disheveled and his eyes were glazed over, but the visual trip down the yellow brick road seemed to be getting his mind off things. My wife gave me a quick thumbs up when I walked into the room. I took that to mean he was doing better. Perhaps they'd had a good talk.

Owen was in the kitchen, eating a granola bar, and just about ready to head out of the house.

"How you guys getting to the movies?" I asked.

"Oh, I'm just gonna walk over to her house on the other side of Naples and pick her up. We're gonna walk to the movies from there. It's just over the big bridge."

"You're gonna walk? Have you looked at the sky? It's gonna storm again tonight."

He went on chewing his granola bar. He obviously hadn't considered the weather. "I'm sure her parents will drive us back if we need them to."

"That sounds good. Or call me, okay? I don't want you to get sick out in the rain."

"Okay," he said with a slight roll of the eyes. It was strange; in the last few years, I'd seen him roll his eyes more times than I could count. It almost made we wonder if there was some kind of biological necessity for teenagers to do this; it made me thankful to still have Toby's innocence. Things are so much easier when a bowl of ice cream and *The Wizard of Oz* can cure your child's ills.

I wanted to say something more to him because I wasn't sure how many actual dates Owen had gone on. I wasn't even sure, in Owen's mind, if this was a date. I had no idea how youth went about defining these things. It occurred to me that Madison and I really hadn't ever sat down and had the whole birds-and-bees conversation. I guess we just chalked it up to the idea that he was a boy and he would pick up these things through osmosis. You can't grow up and go through school without learning these things.

Maybe I had never taken it too seriously because my own parents never sat down to have the talk with me. It's hard to sit down and do those kinds of things, I suppose, when you are beating each other up over a divorce and division of property. But standing there in the kitchen that day, I felt the impulse to tell him some things: *Go out and have a good time, and remember, I'm way too young to be a grandfather.* No, that wouldn't do. *Have a good time tonight, but remember, make sure the snake stays in the cave.* Nope, that probably wouldn't be very effective either.

So I gave up. I slapped him on the shoulder as I headed out of the kitchen. "Don't forget to wear a condom tonight, okay?"

"What?"

I looked back at Owen, and just like the night before when he saw Mom and Dad getting frisky, he looked at me in complete disgust. I'd slipped.

"I meant jacket. Jacket, okay? It's gonna get wet out there. Wear a jacket."

"Okay, Dad," Owen said, and with another roll of the eyes,

he threw his granola wrapper in the trash and headed out of the kitchen. I couldn't blame him. I leaned against the counter and gathered myself.

"Way to go, Dad," I mused. "Way to go."

I said goodbye to Madison and Toby, who were somewhere along the Yellow Brick Road and en route to Oz, grabbed my jacket—not a condom—and headed over to Samantha Wheeler's house.

The sky had darkened and the winds had picked up, and even though I saw the dark storm clouds rolling in, the air was still hot and sticky. It was very humid. I'd brought the jacket to keep dry, not to keep warm. The storm would certainly be here in an hour, maybe two. I saw the flickering of lightning and heard the low growl of thunder. This front looked bigger than the previous night.

Crossing the bridge, I realized how vacant the canals seemed. Perhaps everyone could see another summer storm front moving in and had already taken shelter. No locals on stand-up paddleboards leisurely cruising through the water. No Duffys en route to anywhere. All was silent as the sun went down that night.

Samantha greeted me at her door. Wearing low-rise shorts and a red top that bared her midriff, I wondered if she had spent a little time in front of the mirror before I'd arrived. She looked good as always, but she looked like she had spent time and energy trying to look even better.

I'll just say this: It worked.

"I talked to my husband," she told me as I stepped inside her house. It occurred to me that I hadn't told my wife that I was coming over here. "He said all of his tools should be in his shed. And the saws, especially. He says everything should be accounted for."

"Really?" I said.

"Yep."

She offered me a glass of wine and, being courteous, I accepted it. Something felt wrong about the whole situation, but all I needed was a glance at what Drake was doing and my job would be complete. I had no idea what I was looking for, but I knew that I would know when I discovered it.

We talked briefly and, before the rain came our way, I asked Samantha if I could go to her bedroom and look out the window. She agreed, and as we made our way toward the stairs, I noticed something on her dining room table: a very large bouquet of flowers that hadn't been there earlier that morning. A handwritten note lay beside them. Samantha must have seen me look at them.

"My husband sent me the flowers," she said as we ascended the flight of stairs. "His way of saying sorry for being gone so long. He thinks flowers can make up for not being here all the time. Sometimes I just wished they'd disappear and a real man would take their place."

I sensed disappointment in her voice, but I didn't say anything. I knew that even a mild attempt to comfort her could be misconstrued. It was weird enough walking into Samantha's bedroom with a glass of wine in my hand.

She invited me to the window, and once there, I set my glass of wine on a small table beside the window and hunkered down close to the window sill. Samantha dimmed the lights. I cracked open the blinds and saw the storm drawing close. Brilliant flashes of light filled the sky. Thunder rumbled in the distance.

Looking down, I could see Drake's back porch light. Someone was moving around down there, but Samantha was right—it was difficult to see what was happening because of the tree. So I listened closely and fortunately, the window was already cracked open a little. I heard clanging and movement, but it sounded merely like someone was rifling through things in his garage.

I remained there, hunkered down beside the window, for several minutes. There was more rifling through the garage— or more sorting through junk—for a while. I saw Drake's shadowy figure move across his back patio a few times, but the tree made it really impossible to see what was happening. And then everything went quiet. The noise stopped completely. I wasn't sure if he had gone inside his garage or gone back into his house, or if he was quietly standing on his back patio, working on something.

For many minutes I was still, crouched by the window. Samantha, standing behind me, interrupted the silence.

"Did he leave?" she asked.

"I have no idea. Hard to see or hear anything."

"So what exactly are you looking for?" she asked and backed away a few steps to take a seat on the edge of her bed. "I'm still not exactly sure what you hope to find."

"Neither am I," I admitted. "Remember when we saw Drake get into that Duffy with his duffel bag last night? Who goes for a ride on a Duffy in a storm? And when he came back later, I noticed his duffel bag was empty. I don't know. I guess I wondered if he might have something to do with my dog's disappearance."

I don't think Samantha knew what to say to this. She nodded, sipping her wine.

"It's probably stupidity on my part, I'm sure," I said.

"Well, it is a strange house. Living there with his father, and you never see the father. My husband passed Drake once in front of the house and he thought he heard Drake mumbling to himself and cursing something under his breath as he passed. I don't blame you for thinking it, Eddie. I don't blame you at all."

I waited there for another twenty minutes, making small talk, looking for a sign of anything on Drake's back patio, and finally the storm hit us. The rain came down violently, and it was much worse than the night before. Much more rain. And unlike the previous night, the winds had picked up as well. I could hear it out there, wailing and pounding on the sides of the house.

It was my cue to leave. Nothing more was going to happen.

"Well, thank you very much for letting me come by and take a look," I said, handing her back the glass of wine. She took it from me. I had only taken a few sips.

I began to make my way toward the door of the bedroom, and she stepped in front of me. Not forcefully, but clearly with purpose.

"Well, you don't have to leave in such a rush," she said, obviously taken by surprise at my sudden will to exit. Her hands crossed at her chest, a wine glass in each of them.

"Actually, I do. My wife thinks I went back to the Captain's Room. I really should get going."

"Are you sure you don't want to stay and chat a little? I'd love the company."

"Maybe another time," I said, and right after the words escaped my lips, I deeply regretted saying it. Would that give her too much hope? *Another time*? Was there something suggestive in those words?

Before I had time to think about it, Samantha set her wineglasses down on her nightstand and approached me. She did look amazingly beautiful, I will say that. She touched my shoulder with her delicate hand and stroked my arm. I felt the pulse in my toes and fingers. These were uncharted waters for me, because somehow in all my years of marriage, I'd never been in a situation even remotely like this.

"You seem like a good man," she said. She was still touching my shoulder. "You've done so well with your life, you love your kids, and you seem like such a kind person. I haven't seen much of that lately. My husband's never home, and all I have most of the time is this big empty house all to myself."

"I see," I said. For a brief moment her eyes flickered with hope. She wanted me to respond. This was a woman who craved the response of *any* man. I wondered what kind of father she had and could already guess the kind of man her husband was.

I took her hand, but only so I could remove it from my shoulder.

"If what you say about me is really true," I told her, "then there's something very important you should understand."

"What is that?"

"Very simple. If I am as good a man as you say, then there's probably one person most responsible for it: my wife. She's the reason for all of it, Samantha, and I should probably get going."

She nodded. I think she got the hint pretty clearly.

She sat down on the edge of her bed dejectedly, and I realized she really had thought I had some ulterior motive for this evening visit to her bedroom. And how could I blame her? I felt suddenly horrible for ever initiating this meeting and wanted out of her house as quickly as possible.

"I'll see myself to the door," I said, grabbed my jacket, and headed downstairs.

I looked at the dining room table and saw the flowers her husband had sent her. I felt bad for Samantha. Beneath it all was probably just a woman who really wanted her husband. I guess flowers can only do so much for so long. Maybe love and affection is just like food, and when deprived of it, even the best of people will seek it wherever it can be found.

Once outside, I zipped up my jacket and raced over the little bridge and toward my side of the canal. It was pouring buckets. That may be cliché, but that was what it felt like— buckets, barrels, and tubs of water pouring down from a dark army of clouds above. I crossed the bridge and trotted to the front door of my house. I tried to open the door but it was locked. I hadn't thought about that. I hadn't brought my keys.

I reached for the doorbell but happened to glance over one last time at Drake's house and saw, to my amazement, Drake walk out of the front door of his house with a duffel bag slung over his shoulder.

I froze. My finger was just an inch away from the doorbell, but I didn't press it.

Drake dashed through the rain toward his Duffy. He tossed his duffel bag into the back of the boat, got it ready, and then untied from the dock. Why was this guy going for another evening cruise in pouring rain? And why did he have a duffel bag with him yet again? Was someone else going to be roaming Naples tomorrow morning because their dog had gone missing?

Satanist, Marsha had said.

As he slowly pulled away from the dock, I wanted to follow him. But how could I? I couldn't swim fast enough to keep up with him, but I desperately, desperately wanted to know where he was going and what he was doing.

Then I realized I could run alongside the canal and follow him.

"I've already made a fool of myself once tonight," I said, ringing my own doorbell. "Why not do it again?"

Chapter Seven

"You're doing what?" my wife asked me. Normally, she was the kind of person who thought spur-of-the-moment and spontaneous things were fun. She had an affinity for going against the grain and being a little crazy. But she didn't get this at all. How could I blame her?

"I need my binoculars. I'm going to follow him." I had already been to the garage to get them.

"You're going right now?"

"Yes."

"With your binoculars?"

"Yes?"

"Hmm. Bird watching in the storm, is that it?"

"No, I'm going to—"

"Peeping Tom, maybe? I know you have a thing for Marsha Walker but, come on now, how much did you have to drink at the Captain's Room?"

"Maddie, I'm serious. I think this guy might have something to do with Bessie going missing. I'm just gonna follow at a safe distance. I just wanna know where he's going. It could be someone else's dog he's taking tonight."

Madison shook her head and laughed. She thought I was being silly. I briefly recounted what I had seen the previous night with the duffel bag and Drake's strange voyage in the storm, and although it seemed to strike a nerve in her, she clearly thought I was taking this too far. Much too far. But my wife isn't one to squelch a spontaneous impulse. In a way, I think she thought it would be amusing to watch me, a grown man, run through the rain with a pair of binoculars.

"Well, I hope you have a good excuse if the neighbors see you," she said, and considering that somewhat of an approval, I raced outside.

Drake's Duffy had already pulled away and was slowly making its way down the canal. I followed along the side of the canal and maintained a safe distance behind. I didn't want Drake to catch sight of me following him.

We made several turns though the labyrinth of canals. Nobody in their right mind would be out for a ride in this storm. After a few zigzags through the canals, I was very uncomfortable and sopping wet. I began to wonder if this wasn't such a good idea after all.

Finally I saw Drake slow his Duffy beneath one of the many small bridges in the canals. The boat idled there. I crouched down behind some bushes, where I watched, waited, and wondered as the rain poured down on me. I used the binoculars to see what was happening.

Drake was standing in the Duffy and unzipping the duffel bag. He was putting something into it. No, he was taking something out of it. Then I saw something long, black, and shiny in his hand. I steadied the binoculars and tried to make sense of it. A rifle? That was certainly what it seemed to be. Was it a rifle?

"What?" I gasped, and my hands jerked the binoculars to the side. I lost him. Now I was looking at a boat along the side of the canal. Like a camera, I panned left until the Duffy was back in my double-O vision.

Drake climbed out from under the safe canopy of his Duffy and into the bow of his boat. But why? He wouldn't get drenched, I suppose, because he was under the shelter of the little bridge, but what did he plan on doing? The duffel bag was slung over his shoulder.

I lost him again. The rain was pouring down so hard, it pushed my hands and binoculars down. I had to compensate. When I got him in my sights again, I saw him standing there, but he was looking up at the underside of the bridge. I didn't know what he was looking for, but it seemed clear that he was looking for something.

That was when my binoculars gave out. They fogged, and the sights went completely gray. I couldn't see a thing through them, and I realized that this set of binoculars, the same ones I'd bought right after college and kept around for all these years, probably weren't nitrogen-filled waterproof binoculars. I was broke back then; I never would have opted for the expensive ones. I looked at Drake with my own eyes but couldn't make out a thing of what was happening.

It wasn't long until Drake had done whatever business he wanted to do beneath that bridge, because he started coming back. I ducked low behind the bushes, and he rode past without slowing down. A few flickers of lightning turned everything—the surface of the stormy water, the row of boats, the cloud-filled sky—ghost-white for brief, popcorn moments. Following the flickering and flashing came the low drone of what sounded like giant rusty gears turning behind the clouds: thunder.

I waited behind the bushes to give Drake enough time to get back to his berth, tie up, and get back inside without noticing the crazy writer across the canal following him in the storm. I was soaking wet. Fortunately it wasn't cold, but the unusual humidity made me feel gross.

The whole time I couldn't keep the obvious questions out of my mind. Why did Drake have a rifle with him? Was that what was in the duffel bag, a rifle? Had I seen correctly? And why was he so interested in that bridge?

By the time I reached home, Drake's Duffy was tied up on his dock and he was nowhere to be seen. *Good*, I thought.

I walked to the front door of my house. My shoes squished like sponges around my ankles. I thought of running to get out of the rain, but after all that time out in the storm, there was no point.

As I neared the front door, I realized I wouldn't have to knock. No need.

The door opened, and my wife stood there. Beside her, my son, Owen. Beside him, Candice, his teenage crush. They all looked at me like a freak of nature, and I realized how ridiculous I looked.

There I was, fully clothed, soaked head to toe, binoculars around my neck. I was half-surprised my wife didn't take out her phone and snap a picture to put on social media to make fun of me. She'd done it on many occasions, and her not seizing this wonderful opportunity was my first indication that something was wrong.

"How's everyone doing?" I said.

Owen and the skinny girl just looked at me.

"I'm glad you're back," Madison said, but I didn't like the tone of her voice. I knew that tone.

"What is it? What's wrong?" I asked.

"My jewelry," she said. "It's been stolen."

Chapter Eight

"What? What happened? What's been taken?" I asked.

"My jewelry box is gone," my wife explained. We were standing in the kitchen. Toby was in bed, and Owen and Candice had gone into the living room to watch television. The movie they had gone to see was sold out, so they'd decided to watch a movie at our house. "The little jewelry box I have. The one my cousin bought for me years ago. The one I put my bracelets in."

"What do you mean it's gone? How could it be gone?"

"It's not there," she said. "I happened to look for it, and I couldn't find it. I turned the whole closet inside out."

"When's the last time you saw it?"

"About a week ago. It's usually behind the big jewelry box."

"And you looked everywhere?"

"Yes."

My wife had a tendency to be scatterbrained, and on more than one occasion, she has been known to lose things that almost require effort to lose; but she is quite tenacious, and when on a quest to find something, she'll turn over every rock in her path. I believed that if she had really conducted a search of the closet, then she had done a pretty good job. Where the jewelry box had gone, I could only imagine.

"But you've been here tonight, right? All night?"

"Yeah, me and Toby especially. It couldn't have happened tonight. We were sitting on the couch all night."

My mind worked hard to compute all the possibilities. I did have to agree with my wife: If someone really had taken the jewelry box, it must have happened at another time. No way could somebody have gotten into the house, snuck through the living room, taken the jewelry box, and gotten out without so much as stirring my wife or son. And why would a thief go right for a jewelry box tucked away in a huge walk-in closet? And why the small jewelry box? The more I thought about it, the more none of it made sense.

"Are you sure you really looked everywhere?"

"Yes, everywhere. Trust me, it's not there. I went through every inch of that closet."

And then a disturbing thought occurred to me. Who else had been in our house that week? No thief would have found his way to the master closet and that jewelry box. There would have been more signs, more obvious things taken along with it. I didn't have a degree in law enforcement, but it didn't take a genius to figure that out.

"Who has been here this week? Anyone at all?" I could tell by my wife's expression that she registered exactly what I was thinking. If the jewelry box really had been stolen, then it must have been someone who knew the house and had been let in.

She put her hands on the kitchen island, took a deep breath, and began to think about the last week, but as she did so, a completely horrific idea overcame me. It overcame me with such violence, I also had to grab the kitchen island, but more to steady myself and not fall over than anything else.

Could it be Drake? Things had been silent for a while

before I left Samantha's bedroom. Could he have possibly crossed the canal during that time and stolen the jewelry box? Perhaps that was why he'd had that rifle with him. An armed robbery? I began to think of how he could have actually gotten into the house during the storm without my wife noticing. If he went through the back door and crept alongside the laundry room wall, he could have gotten to the stairwell without anybody noticing. It was possible, though ridiculously unlikely.

I knew the backdoor was unlocked. My wife loved going out onto the back patio area and frequently forgot to lock that door. It was a relatively preposterous idea that Drake had stolen it, but I couldn't help but wonder.

We decided it would be best to deal with it the following day. My wife had no reservations about going to bed and ultimately became confused and thought perhaps she had misplaced the jewelry box. She had gone through our closet a couple weeks before and piled some clothes in the garage for a scheduled Goodwill run. Perhaps the jewelry box was part of that monstrous heap in the garage. She couldn't take seriously the notion of somebody slipping into her house that very night, into her closet, and singling out that jewelry box. Neither could I; it was too ridiculous to believe.

Candice's parents picked her up, and eventually Owen went into his teenage-cave where he would most likely sleep until noon the following day.

But I couldn't sleep well. I was restless all night. In my dreams, I imagined Drake sneaking into our house and skulking up the stairs en route to our master closet.

A missing dog?

A missing box of jewelry?

If only it had stopped with that.

Chapter Nine

The following day, July 3rd, we continued our routine and commitment to keep Toby's young mind off Bessie. The thought of a fireworks show, of a picnic in the park right along the water, kept almost everyone in a cheery mood. It was a good thing, too, because I needed it just then.

My wife, Toby, and I went for a short walk to our favorite bagel shop and talked about what a good night it was going to be. And to think, it was only a precursor to the following night and the "big" party at the central park of Naples Island. My wife and I sipped our coffee, goofed around with our son, and I was able to clear my mind.

The sky seemed quite blue for a day following a storm, but there was, in the distance, another stretch of dark clouds that could reach us by evening. I had been so consumed with everything else I hadn't taken the time to listen to the weather in detail, but my phone said another good possibility for rain that night. Hopefully, it would stay away until after the fireworks show and after we'd gone indoors.

By that point, my wife and I agreed she must have

misplaced her jewelry box. There was far more valuable jewelry right alongside it that a thief would have taken. As for Drake and his duffel bags, I began to seriously question if I had really seen a rifle in his hand. It had been difficult to see through the binoculars in the rain. Perhaps it was something else? Some tool he was using to work on the boat? I tried my best to dismiss it because at that point I didn't want to deal with it. I wanted to get back into my routine, my early mornings of drinking coffee and grinding out pages on my manuscript, and my afternoons at home with my family.

We lounged around most of the day, and I went back into my office to do some editing that afternoon. I'm not sure when Owen emerged from his room, but I'm guessing it was sometime around two or three in the afternoon.

By the time seven o'clock rolled around, we had gathered some blankets and chairs and a big cooler filled with wine, sodas, and some homemade turkey sandwiches. The walk to the park wasn't far, so we decided to share the load and make our way there on foot. We met up with our neighbors, the Paisleys, and walked with them. They were traveling quite light: just a bag containing a bottle of wine, some plastic cups, and a corkscrew.

Madison and Jenna, Darrel's wife, walked ahead of us, and Darrel and I got into a brief conversation.

"I saw you running around in the rain last night," he said, and I was shocked that someone had seen me.

"Yeah, long story with that one."

"Well, I was looking around outside, because a really weird thing happened last night."

Now he had my attention. Maybe I wasn't the only one losing my mind the last couple days.

"Jenna lost her wedding ring," he said, but I could tell there was more to it. Darrel was a quiet, stoic kind of guy, and I could tell he didn't like talking when the content primarily concerned feelings. "At least, she *says* she lost it. But she doesn't know how. But it makes a man wonder, you know? Wedding rings don't disappear."

The wives were well ahead of us, chatting. I was tugging the cooler on wheels and had a couple chairs slung over my shoulder.

"That's why I was looking out the window last night," he said, but his voice sounded distant. Otherworldly. He was troubled. It was a bit shocking to say the least, because Darrel, as I usually understood him, was the calm, older guy who seemed unfazed by most of life's troubles. "A friend of hers was picking her up to go out to a wine bar. I waited and watched. I just wanted to see, to make sure it was really Linda who was picking her up."

"And was it Linda?"

"Yeah," he said, but something about it didn't seem very convincing. "It was her. That's when I saw you running through the rain. But I saw you earlier too, Eddie. Leaving Samantha Wheeler's house."

It was a simple statement, but there was something profound in it. I didn't know what he wanted me to say. Did he want me to explain myself? My explanation would sound ludicrous, so I just kept quiet for the time being. He could think what he wanted.

"Maybe the reason I was so worried about Jenna last night is because, well, it all reminds me of what happened with my ex-wife," he said, and then he slapped me rather gently on the shoulder.

When we arrived at the park, there were still some decent spots left. We and the Paisleys made for a nice green spot near the middle of the park.

Hot-rodder peddled past us, but I didn't hear the phony motor sound of the card in the spokes of his back tire.

"Word of the day!" he yelled.

I couldn't help but wonder. "What happened to your engine?"

He stopped the bike right in front of us. "Someone stole it."

Stolen, I thought. Maybe that's when I should have realized what was really happening. A lost dog? A missing jewelry box? A missing wedding ring? Maybe I should have connected the dots just then, but I didn't.

"Word of the day," I said. I pointed to the lightning rod. "Fulmination! A violent explosion or a flash like lightning."

"Fulmination," he said excitedly. If it was possible for a kid on a BMX bike to burn rubber, I would have sworn he did so right then and there. Because all of a sudden he was gone. Just like that.

We put down our blankets and got comfortable. Owen, bored already, decided to go for a walk around the park because he was pretty sure Candice was here somewhere with her parents.

Samantha emerged from the crowd. Apparently she had set up her camp not far from us with a girlfriend of hers and just wanted to come by and say hello to all of us. Darrel looked at me knowingly, and I felt uncomfortable. I would explain everything to him later, when I had more time and more privacy.

It was very strange, really, to be chatting there about the weather and life and the coming fireworks show with a woman who had made an advance at me the night before. What was most interesting, however, was how rejuvenated Samantha looked. She seemed very happy, almost giddy, and yet she didn't seem tipsy in the way a couple glasses of wine would have made her. I wondered if it was because some other man had put a deposit in her Attention Bank since the previous night.

She didn't stay long, and all of us only talked about the kinds of things neighbors who really don't know each other all that well talk about. When she said goodbye to my wife and the Paisleys, she whispered something very quickly to me as she strolled away.

"Thank you for last night," she said. "I noticed."

And then she weaved in between the maze of blankets and chairs and back to her picnic table. I saw her flick her hair and glance back at me, a very beautiful and flirtatious smile glowing on her face. She winked.

I noticed? What did she mean? Hadn't I been beyond clear in my refusal? Or, after I left, did she somehow read between the lines of something I'd said?

We sat in our picnic chairs, ate our sandwiches, and sipped our wine as the sun began to fall and the skies turned a deep purple. It appeared that nature would be on our side that evening. While there were dark clouds coming our way, it looked as if they would arrive after the fireworks show. The air was as hot and humid as it had been, and I kept picking at my shirt at the shoulders and lifting it off my skin to cool myself down.

It wasn't long before there wasn't an unclaimed inch of green grass in the park. Lots of familiar faces were there, although I knew few of their names. But I'd seen many of these residents walking along the canals. There were also others who had driven over to watch the show. The July 3rd fireworks show mainly drew in the locals because those living outside of Naples were anticipating the big July 4th fireworks show over the Queen Mary, a retired pre-World War II ocean liner that was now a tourist attraction and hotel over on the mainland.

Just as it was getting dark, and while in the midst of a conversation about inflation with the Paisleys, we heard a loud, obnoxious motorcycle drive up to the edge of the park. Several people shielded their eyes from the blinding headlight; many more covered their ears from the noise. After seeming to get the attention of every man and woman at the park, the driver killed the engine, got off his bike, and took off his helmet.

To no surprise, it was the same guy I'd seen at the Captain's Room the night before: Klutch. He looked amongst the crowd of picnickers as if he were looking for something or someone, and he looked pretty angry. I didn't know him well enough to recognize whether or not this was his usual demeanor.

I watched as he strode slowly through the park. Amongst the crowd of what most would call "white upper-class society" picnicking in the park, he looked completely out of context—a fresh fish out of water. But eventually he discovered what he'd come for. Klutch pointed his finger at someone, and it was Jesse, the owner and sometimes operator of the Captain's Room.

Jesse, who had been sitting on a picnic blanket while munching away on chips and guacamole, stood up. The lumberjack-look-alike wiped guacamole off the beard that hung from his chin like thick Spanish moss. He wore a red-and-black checkered flannel shirt, cargo shorts, and Birkenstocks.

"What happened to my knife?" Klutch asked, but it wasn't so much a question as it was an accusation. The nearby picnickers silenced themselves. This wasn't the fireworks show they were expecting, but it was evident that a fight was about to ensue.

"What are you talking about?" Jesse asked wearily.

I remembered his complaints about Klutch at the Captain's Room. Maybe something had happened the previous night after I left, and Klutch had come here to finish unsettled business. I stood up instinctively and moved toward them. Maybe I would have to hold somebody back. I heard Madison tell me to stay put, but I didn't really pay attention. I found myself, almost without knowledge, advancing toward the altercation.

"I had a knife in my saddlebag. I take it with me every day. Spyderco Civilian. Reverse 'S' blade shape. It wasn't there this morning."

"I don't know anything about your knife, Klutch," Jesse said.

"That's what I thought you'd say. Then why wasn't it there this morning?"

"How should I know, and why should I care? Why don't you get on with whatever you're doing and leave us in peace?"

"You wanna be left alone in peace, huh?" Klutch said, and he looked at the silent picnickers surrounding them in amusement. "You all wanna sit here and drink your yuppie wine and sit on your yuppie blankets? Screw you! Screw all of you!"

"Last I looked, I don't look much like a yuppie," Jesse said, stroking his beard. It was a funny comment, and I heard a couple spectators chuckle, but Klutch didn't like that. He didn't like it at all. "And there's children and families here, Klutch. Why don't you watch your language, huh?"

"You accused me last night of taking money from the little rat-hole you call a bar," Klutch said, and I realized something must have happened after I left the previous night. "I think when you went back into your kitchen, you went out through the backdoor and broke into my saddlebag, that's what I think. You think I'm an idiot? I served this country, you know that? And I never lost a man in my convoy! So screw you for thinking you could take my stuff without me knowing."

"For the last time, I didn't take your knife," Jessie said. "And if I did want a knife, I wouldn't take it from some slimy, third-rate biker, like yourself. I'd—"

"What'd you say?" Klutch asked.

"—rather go down to Costco and buy a clean knife because—"

"Are you insulting me?" Klutch said, his eyebrows furrowing, although one of his eyebrows was missing that chunk.

"—I wouldn't want to put my hands on your nasty—"

Several people advanced to separate them. A group of men pulled them apart, and after much cursing and chaos, Klutch returned to his bike, where he turned around and yelled back at the crowd.

"I've been told there's a bunch of friendly people here on this island," Klutch yelled. At this point, I realized Klutch was drunk. "Tonight, all you guys are gonna go back to your nice homes on the water and drink your nice little wine, but let me tell you something. When it comes down to it, you all are a bunch of thieves like that guy over there. You ain't no different than where I come from. Your world starts to fall apart, you all would just eat each other alive like anyone else. You need people like me, you hear that? You need me! You celebrate your freedom because people like me gave it to you! You hear that?"

He climbed on his bike, started it up, and after a ceremonial revving of his engine and giving nasty looks to the entire community he'd insulted, he rode off into the darkness and disappeared like the leather-clad cacophonous cockroach that he was. It took awhile for everyone to settle down, and many people, including myself, advanced toward Jesse to pat him on the back and encourage him.

Even Marsha Walker marched forward in her muumuu and went on and on about what a horrible, disgusting, and appalling thing that was to witness. "Devil worshipper!" she said in full dramatic flair. "Just like that neighbor across the way! Devil worshippers! They probably get together and kill cats at midnight!"

Everyone settled down, and not long after that, the last bit of sunlight evaporated, and as the first sounds of thunder began in the distance, the fireworks commenced. Owen found Candice, and they were at the fountain, watching the fireworks show alone. Or making out. Who knew? We watched the show and sipped our wine while the heavens burst forth right above the waters of Alamitos Bay. Toby was the most impressed, of course. It made me reflect a bit, to be honest. I suppose most fireworks displays lose some of their luster as people grow older, but watching him, rapt with attention as blue, red, and yellow flower-like explosions blossomed in the sky, made me aware of how old I really was. There was still wonder in his eyes, still bedazzlement.

Maybe that saying I'd heard about writers always creating stories to recapture their youth was true after all, because I'm pretty sure that at my age the only time I looked even remotely like my son at that moment was in those early hours in front of the computer. At those times, the paper is my moonlit sky. My words are the fireworks that I control at will.

By the time the grand finale came and the last nighttime wonders had dripped down like sparkling paint in the sky, it was time to head home. Almost everyone had the same idea we had. People hastily gathered their chairs and their blankets and their empty bottles of wine and began the trek home.

Another storm was about to hit. The wind picked up, and we could see, in the distance, the sizzling of lightning. It almost seemed as if Mother Nature was sending in a fireworks show of her own, as if she was whispering: *You think you guys can put on a fireworks show? Let me show you real magic. I'll give you a show to remember.*

Even at that point, this storm felt like it was going to be bigger than the two previous nights. The air felt more humid than it had been, the thunder was louder at this distance, and electrical light strobed through the celestial expanse of broken, gray clouds that moved toward us.

Owen had caught up with us. The Paisleys, my wife, and sons, ran ahead of me in hopes of beating the storm; a very slight drizzle had begun to fall and they wanted to make it inside before it became a downpour. I ran behind, towing the cooler behind me. If I ran too fast, the wheeled cooler lost balance and tipped over, so I was forced to jog at a moderate speed.

I was only a few blocks from home and the drizzle was growing ever so slightly, when I noticed a shadowy figure also running; this person ran along a side street and into one of the alleys behind the houses. I only caught a momentary glance, but the runner was wearing dark clothing and a backpack. I wasn't sure if it was my own self-fueled paranoia at that point, but even though I had only gotten a quick, momentary glance of the person, I was pretty convinced it looked like Drake.

Leaving my cooler on the sidewalk, I jogged over to the back alley to see for myself. The runner had stopped halfway down the alley. He was on his knees, rummaging through his backpack. It was dark behind the houses. Away from the street-light and with the moon cloaked in cloud cover, it was difficult to make out much of anything. But there was enough light for me to see that this was, in fact, Drake. I had no idea why he had stopped to kneel down in the middle of an alley to fish through his backpack.

I began to walk toward him. I had to know what he was doing.

He heard me, and like a thief caught in the act, threw his backpack over his shoulder, turned around, and bolted through the alley with ferocity. I yelled for him to stop. I had no idea why I yelled and what I would have said to him if he actually had obeyed my request, but it seemed like the right thing to do. Only men who are guilty of something take off running like that. I was pretty sure he hadn't seen who I was, and to be honest, I'm not even convinced he would recognize me if he had.

I stopped when I reached the spot where he had been kneeling. I didn't try to pursue him on foot, and the reasons were simple. I would never catch him. I've never been much of a runner and judging by the speed he had bolted away, it would have been a completely futile effort. Secondly, I wasn't even sure what he had done wrong. As far as I knew, there was no crime in kneeling in an alley and looking through your backpack.

I stood for a moment in the alley, feeling my hair dampen as the rain came down, and just as I was about to turn around and head back to my abandoned cooler, I noticed something on the ground: a spiral notebook. I bent down and picked it up but knew this wasn't the time and place to look through it. I tucked it under my jacket to keep it dry from the rain and went back to my cooler.

By the time I got home, the drizzle had turned into a downpour. The Paisleys had already gone inside their home, and my family had gone indoors as well.

I ran up to the front door of my house with the cooler, but before I went inside, I took the notebook out of my jacket. Just outside the front entrance and sheltered from the rain, I flipped through it.

It was mostly blank. Only a couple pages had been written on. One page appeared to be a hand-sketched map of the park we had just left. I could see where Drake had drawn in the fountain and indicated the four cardinal directions with a large N, S, E, and W and arrows at the top of the map. A series of dashes went along the perimeter of the park and toward the fountain and then off the page. What did the dashes mean? I assumed the dashes represented some kind of path or trail, but I had no idea what it alluded to. Was this the path that Drake had walked this night while watching the fireworks? It was very odd.

Below the map, Drake had written a few notes:

- down Toledo

- into D
- to B
- Climax!!!

I looked it over for a few minutes to make sure I was reading correctly. *Down Toledo? Into D? To B? Climax!!!* I had no idea what I was reading, why Drake would have this with him, or what exactly he was doing, but, as I look back, I wonder if it was something else in the air that really unnerved me that night.

The storm hit particularly hard. I awoke several times to deafening thunder. The rain sounded angry against the roof shingles and windows, a great watery judgment.

But, again, I think I didn't sleep well because there was something more in the air that night. By the following day, I became aware that something terrible was at work, something far beyond anything I had imagined.

I don't think I was the only one to realize this either. Now, as I look back, it all makes sense. Once I learned more and put together other people's stories, it was clear. We should have seen it coming.

I woke up the following morning to rainless skies.

The real storm—I would realize later—was about to begin.

Chapter Ten

S amantha woke up at her usual time at five-thirty for yoga. She was taking classes at a little studio on Second Street, Cardio Plus, and had enjoyed the last two months with her trainer, Sandy, a blonde woman who did yoga and weights with militant passion. She certainly had the body of someone who had made yoga her religion and was quite a good trainer. Samantha had already seen and felt the results these last couple months.

She put on her workout clothes and grabbed a protein bar out of the refrigerator. She sat down at the bare dining room table, drank her bottled water, nibbled on her bar, and thought of the bouquet of flowers that had been there before Eddie had shown up. The table looked so empty now. When Eddie had left after her advance a couple days ago, she spent nearly an hour in the bathroom in front of the mirror, crying and yelling at herself.

"Why did you have to marry a man who's gone half the time?" she had said accusingly at her reflection. With tears streaming down her cheeks and her mascara blemished, she thought she looked like some kind of over-aged Goth wannabe. She couldn't remember how long she remained in the bathroom, sobbing, grieving. She felt so foolish because she'd misread Eddie's motives. Why else did a man invite himself into a woman's bedroom? She was completely mortified by his kind yet firm rejection of her.

Or had it been that firm? There seemed to be some kind of spark, some kind of attraction beneath it all.

By the time she had washed the tears and the mascara from her face and left the bathroom, Samantha wasn't sure if she would ever look Eddie Dees in the eyes again; she had made too much of a fool of herself. That wasn't a mistake she was going to make again, and she would avoid him at all costs.

But that was before she had gone downstairs the following morning, before she had noticed the missing bouquet of flowers.

She had stood beside the table, wondering. She asked herself the same question over and over again: Was it possible she had thrown them away without remembering doing it? But no matter how many times she asked herself that question, the answer was self-evident: No. The flowers had clearly been there when Eddie arrived. She had even explained what they were and who they were from.

She sat at the bare table that morning, contemplating the mystery of the missing flowers for a long while, when the answer occurred to her: Eddie took them. No one else had been in the house except for him, and the only logical explanation was that he had taken them as he left that night, right as she was making her way to the bathroom for an intense grief session.

But the more serious question remained: Why did he take the flowers?

She spent some time thinking about it, and a possible

answer swept over her like a crisp, spring breeze. He was giving her a message, a sign. By taking the flowers, he was, in actuality, giving her another message entirely. *You don't have to settle for a husband who is gone half the time*, he was trying to convey to her. *You're worth more than that. You can get rid of these. They'll be replaced with something better. Something fresher. Something closer.* Hadn't she told him that? She wanted the flowers to disappear and a man to take their place?

"Yes, I'm worth more than that," she muttered to herself while contemplating how barren the table looked. As time passed, and by slow degrees, she convinced herself that Eddie Dees was trying to tell her something by getting rid of the flowers that she herself had complained to him about when he arrived.

When she saw him yesterday at the fireworks show, she had whispered to him, "I noticed."

And she'd seen the look on his face. He knew that she knew. It was a look of understanding. Of acknowledgement. There was a promise in it.

Yes, I think he wants me, she thought. Oh, to be wanted again! To be wanted in a way that made the little hairs on the back of her neck prickle! He would come to her, certainly, again. Who knew what the excuse would be this time. Maybe he'd want to take another peek out her window, or maybe he'd conjure up some other explanation. And this time, perhaps, he wouldn't chicken out. Because as these newfound epiphanies crystallized in her mind, that was the reason for Eddie's hasty refusal and exit that night: He'd gotten cold feet. Understandable, of course. Maybe he had never done anything behind his wife's back before.

But he would come to her again, and they would make love. It would be passionate. It would make up for her husband's absence and his lukewarm appreciation of her when he was home. It would rejuvenate her and she would feel young—truly young—for the first time in what was beginning to feel like eons.

I deserve this, she kept thinking. I deserve this.

That morning, July 4th, she was in a hurry to get going. Happy that her instructor was still doing one morning class on the Fourth, Samantha was looking forward to guilt-free margaritas and chips and guacamole that afternoon. She finished her water and threw away the wrapper for her protein bar. Grabbing her keys and her gym bag, she hurried out the front door. The gym was just a short walk. No need to pull the Mercedes out of the garage.

Sam was only a couple feet out of the door when she noticed something else missing. It had been there last night when she had raced home from the fireworks show to beat the rain. Or, at least, she thought it had been there. The engraved garden stone, the one that read "John & Samantha," was gone. They'd put it there years ago, and there it had remained, right in the garden alongside the winding path to the front door. She looked at the brown, flattened earth where the stone should have been and wondered again.

"Maybe he came over here last night and took it," she whispered.

Her whole body warmed and tingled with pleasure.

It was another sign, she thought. Another message, to say that "John & Samantha" were a thing of the past. Just as new grass and flowers would grow to cover that barren spot created by the stone's resting place, so would Eddie, like a vine, wrap himself around her and pull her into a new palatial garden. Her heart fluttered with adolescent excitement.

"I think he wants me," she said giddily, and as she raced to yoga class that morning, she already wondered what secret message he would send next.

Or maybe there wouldn't be any other messages; maybe he would just come to her in the night, to her bedroom, and take away the cold loneliness that haunted that room.

Maybe it will be tonight, she thought hopefully as she jumped across puddles on her way to the gym. *Maybe any moment.*

Chapter Eleven

After nearly two hours of turning her house upside-down, Marsha Walker began to wonder if she was developing an early case of dementia.

She had come home after the fireworks show on July 3rd, and like most others, barely beat the torrential downpour. She spent that night looking over her short story, "Bedazzled," and told herself that she was finally ready to hand it over to her neighbor, Eddie Dees. She had been so nervous. He was a real writer, after all, and maybe he wouldn't like it. That had occurred to her, and she'd even lost a little sleep over it.

"I know I left it right here," Marsha said for what felt like the millionth time that morning. She was standing beside the little breakfast table in the kitchen, and this whole thing wasn't making any sense. She closed her eyes and replayed the prior evening in her mind over and over again: She had read through all twenty-one pages of the story, sipped her hot chocolate, ate two bowls of caramel crunch ice cream, and had gone to bed with the manuscript lying right there on the table.

"Right there!"She knew she had been a little out of sync these last few days and a bit absentminded. She attributed some of it to menopause. She'd had her share of hot flashes, incontinence, and mood changes. Dr. Grissom said those things would happen. Usually, it was more of a blue, dreary feeling she experienced, and she longed for nothing more than to crawl on the couch and sleep away half the day. She'd kept it hidden from most, she thought, but when alone and inside her home, an oppressive fatigue sometimes swept over her. She was still taking the same anxiety medication she'd been taking for the last ten years, but she wondered if, considering the menopause, she should talk to her doctor again about changing the dosage.

The other day, she'd felt foolish marching over to borrow some brown sugar from the Dees because she had seen some brown sugar in her cupboard just the day before that. It'd been right there in the pantry beside the tub of sugar. She had specifically made a list of things she needed at the store and had clearly checked off that item when she saw it there.

But if that frustrated her, this was even more ridiculous and upsetting. She sat down at the breakfast table in the same spot she had spent the prior evening, devouring words and ice cream, and decided it was time to make a call to her doctor. If the manuscript wasn't where she remembered leaving it, then she simply must have put it somewhere and completely forgotten. Something about that terrified her. If she couldn't even remember what she did the night before, if she was that "out of it," then it was definitely time to call the doctor, because maybe this whole menopause situation was taking away more than just her biological ability to bear children. Maybe it was taking her memory along with it.

She noticed the familiar burning in the face just as she stood up to make breakfast. She imagined someone holding a heat lamp to her forehead. The warm sensation spread down to her waist, and a thin layer of sweat, almost instantly, percolated to the surface of her skin. She fanned herself briskly with her hand, though it didn't help much. She knew how these flashes came and went. She waited until the warm sensations subsided, then went to the kitchen sink and splashed cold water on her face.

After drying herself with a kitchen towel, she decided to call her doctor's office and leave a message. She was pretty certain that nobody was going to be in the office on a holiday, but it would feel good to make the call and get it over with.

She had only taken a couple steps, when she looked out her window and saw the side of Eddie Dees' house. A thought occurred to her. She tried to dismiss it as being foolish, yet like a snowball, it picked up momentum the more she pondered it. She leaned against her stove and looked out the window.

Did Eddie sneak into the house and take the manuscript? Like another hot flash, her thoughts boiled in her mind. *He writes about people who sneak into houses, and he probably knows how to do it himself, doesn't he? Who else but a writer would want to sneak into my house and take that manuscript?*

"But why would a bestselling author want to take my short story?" she said aloud, trying to solve the puzzle.

Because he wants the idea. He wants to take it from you.

"But I was going to give it to him," she found herself saying, verbally debating the accusative speculations that, like another storm, swept through her mind. "Why steal it?"

Because he doesn't think you will. Because you've been telling him that for a long time, and he's desperate. Desperate for an idea. Have you noticed how long it's been since his last book came out? He talked about a deadline, didn't he? Some publishing deadline? He's desperate, Marsha, utterly desperate.

"Oh my," Marsha said. She didn't fully believe it, but there was a bizarre logic to it.

She went immediately to the bathroom, opened her medicine cabinet, and went for the Xanax. It had been prescribed exactly for days like this. After she took a pill and chased it with a gulp of water from the sink, she looked at herself in the mirror and wrestled with the idea that Eddie Dees was a thief, and a thief of the worst kind. Was it this way with all of his books? Maybe the first book had actually been his, but maybe all of the others had been literary quilts sewn together from the fragments he'd pilfered from other adoring fans.

What other explanation was there for it?

Her more rational, logical side fought the idea: *You're being ridiculous, Marsha. This is the anxiety talking. You know better.*

She looked at her doughy face, her deep-set eyes, her tangled mess of brown curls, and she thought she looked older than she had just last night when she stared into this very mirror. The worry lines above her eyebrows were no longer slight but appeared to be deep creases—like the lines on an EKG monitor frozen on her forehead. The crow's feet around her eyes also looked prominent. All of the excess flesh kind of drooped downward like too much batter on a spatula.

Depressed enough over the manuscript, she headed right to the kitchen.

Grabbing a spoon out of the drawer on her way there, she pulled the carton of peanut butter cup ice cream out of the freezer, wrapped a kitchen towel around it so it wouldn't be too cold in her grip, and took her seat again at the table.

Time for breakfast.

Chapter Twelve

I f Darrel Paisley wasn't convinced before that his wife was having an affair, the morning of July 4th didn't help the situation. Darrel went to his home office while his wife was still asleep, looked out over Naples Island and the home of his neighbor two doors down, Eddie Dees, and saw that the storm had broken. His immediate neighbor, Dominic, was the hermit type and barely came out of his house. It looked to be a nice morning. There were still some scattered clouds and perhaps some more coming their way in the distance, but by and large, it looked like he was going to be able to go outside today without having to put on a raincoat.

He had gone through some of his client's files the previous day, and wanting to get a fresh start for the morning, decided to clear off his desk. After this, he would go downstairs and make breakfast. Since he had gone mostly paperless for the last few years, there was little to pick up. He took Karen Welch, Fred Ortiz, and Jimmy Beck's files from the desk, glanced through them to make sure everything looked right, and opened the sliding closet door to reveal a row of his personal and business file cabinets. Already looking forward to bagels and coffee, he quickly filed the folders away but noticed, just as he was about to close the sliding door, that one file cabinet at the far end looked slightly ajar.

Those were his and Jenna's personal files. Tax returns. Passports. Birth certificates. He had gone into it the other day to double check a tax statement and perhaps hadn't closed it all the way. Not thinking too much about it, but wanting to make sure he had returned everything that he had taken out of it, he opened the drawer.

There were fewer files than the last time he'd checked. Contemplating this, he quickly sifted through the files and tried to figure out what was actually gone. It didn't take him very long to realize.

"Jenna," he whispered. Her personal files were gone. They were normally right behind his. Her birth certificate, passport, and other vital documents were gone.

He opened the adjacent cabinets and rifled through them just in case but as he had guessed, there was nothing there but client files. He gave up searching after a few minutes, took a couple horrified steps backwards, and slowly sank down into his office chair. He rocked in that squeaky chair for what seemed like hours and contemplated the meaning of this.

One thing was certain: He hadn't moved those documents. If it were other files, perhaps he would chalk it up to forgetfulness or just honest misfiling, but Darrel was meticulous when it came to organization. A possible answer slowly and terrifyingly crystallized in his mind.

He thought of Jenna's wedding ring, which she had supposedly "lost" recently. He thought of the distance he had felt in their relationship these last several months that had crept, like a mist, into their home. And although he couldn't keep the thoughts from assaulting him, and would have beat them back if possible, his mind turned to his first wife, Suzie, and how that separation and divorce went down.

Married at twenty-one and divorced by twenty-three, he remembered that marriage, so many years later, as a miserable layover on his flight to financial success and happiness. Now, it seemed like just another breakup as opposed to an actual marital dissolution. Too young, too immature, and too poor, Darrel had used that marriage as a lesson many times while his own son was much younger, and it usually went something like this: *Do some growing up before you put a ring on someone's finger.*

Suzie, who ended up running off with a guy she met in one of her college classes, had planned her escape for months. She started taking things out of the apartment, piece by piece. When Darrel came home one day after work to a vacant apartment, much of the heavy lifting had already been done. He'd seen some of the signs and had questioned her, but she always had an excuse. By the time she disappeared, she had already opened up a new bank account, had two new credit cards, and had moved all of her things into her boyfriend's apartment.

Rocking in his office chair, Darrel had to admit this didn't look good. It didn't look good at all. First, Jenna's wedding ring went missing and now all of her personal files were gone too. *She would want those if she was really planning on leaving*, he thought. Already, he imagined her starting her own bank account, maybe taking out a credit card in her own name, all in preparation for a flight out of her marriage. It was possible, wasn't it? When Suzie left him, he had been an ignorant imbecile, giddy with newly married optimism, while his wife—behind his back—was sharpening the executioner's axe. Could it happen again?

"There is a profound fear in a man who experiences tragedy," he whispered, "the fear that the same thing can happen again." That was a line he often used with clients who, once burned by the market, learned that they had to go about investing their money differently the second time. But now the quote aptly applied to him.

He promised himself that he would keep careful watch, just in case. Maybe he had misplaced the files when he had last gone through them, though he found that unlikely. Perhaps Jenna had gone through the files for some other reason, taken them out, and had simply forgotten to put them back. She was awfully forgetful at times. Yet the more he thought about it, the more he realized how unlikely a scenario that was. She rarely, if ever, stepped foot in his office.

He got up and made his way downstairs, promising himself that he wouldn't think about it for now. He would brew a pot of coffee and watch the morning weather. From what he understood, the storms weren't over yet. There was more coming their way.

"Honey, are you downstairs?" Jenna called from the upstairs bedroom.

"Yes! Making coffee!"

But as he began to brew a pot and looked over his living room, his mind couldn't help but do a silent inventory of the furniture he was sure that Jenna would want and the furniture she would allow him to keep.

Chapter Thirteen

The boy was in front of his house, straddling his BMX bike and crying. Jesse wondered if he had taken a bad spill and injured himself, but something about these cries made him think it was something different entirely. He was pretty sure the boy's name was Bryan—or Hot-rodder, as his Metropolitan-loving patron Eddie Dees liked to call him.

Jesse was doing his usual morning walk to the Captain's Room, where he would do some inventory and get things geared up for the day. The Fourth of July would bring in a lot of customers in the afternoon hours who would want to swing by and throw back a few cold ones before running off to parties and firework shows. It would be a good day for business.

He often saw the boy on his bike on his morning walks because the boy lived here. Usually, he was out in front of the house on his bike, circling in the street, popping wheelies. He'd never seen the little guy look this somber and this dejected.

As he walked closer, Jesse was pretty sure he could deduce the cause of the boy's tears. A man was screaming inside the house, cursing, in the midst of what sounded like a middle-aged man's temper tantrum. He sounded pretty drunk too.

"I've told that idiot kid of mine not to play around with my tools! I've told him a thousand times!"

A woman inside tried to calm him down.

"I didn't take your stupid tools," the boy said, wiping tears from his face. His breathing was tattered, and his whole body shook.

Jesse, who had walked up to the boy, asked if he was okay, and the boy nodded without saying anything to him or even looking at him. It didn't take much for Jesse to figure out that the man in the house was the boy's father.

"I'm gonna kick that kid's rear!" the boy's dad yelled belligerently. "I'm gonna take this belt and make his rear bleed, do you hear me, Gina? I'm sick of that stupid kid thinking he runs this place and can just take my tools without asking me."

The front screen door of the house flew open. A guy wearing a pair of checkered boxers, a white V-neck undershirt, and white socks pulled up to his knees stepped out. He held a black belt in his left hand. A moment later, a woman with blond tousled hair wearing a bathrobe ran out behind him, took the man by the shoulders, and pled with him to come back inside. Mom and Dad argued there on the front porch and eventually made their way back indoors where they continued to yell and curse at each other.

Jesse, whose own dad had been an alcoholic and walked the thin line between abuse and discipline, looked down at the child with great empathy. He'd walked many miles in those same shoes, and from what he could judge, this sort of fighting probably happened a lot at this house.

He knelt beside the kid's bike. The kid was just about done wiping tears from his face.

"Sorry you have to put up with that, kid," Jesse said.

"He always blames me, and this time I really didn't take them," Bryan said.

"Your old man thinks you took his tools, is that it?"

Bryan nodded.

"And you didn't, huh?"

"No, but I know what did. It's been taking everything. It's been—"

"Bryan, come inside now. I'd like to talk to you," his mom called. The fighting indoors had subsided, and Bryan's mother stood by the door, arms crossed in front of her, waiting for her son. At least the yelling had stopped. Maybe she had talked a little sense into her husband and would make sure that belt was used for its proper purpose.

"Good luck," Jesse said.

The boy went inside, and Jesse was reassured by the silence that followed. He didn't hear any more screaming, and he didn't hear that leather belt tearing apart the boy's hind end.

He continued his walk to the Captain's Room, and his mind turned once again to business and matters of the day. He was still disturbed by last night and his altercation with Klutch. He had the overwhelming feeling that he hadn't seen the last of him. Klutch must have been drunk out of his mind to blame Jesse for taking his knife; or, if it wasn't due to drunkenness, maybe the guy was just that paranoid. Whatever the case, Jesse hoped he wouldn't have to deal with him anymore.

Jesse finally reached the Captain's Room and was unlocking the front door when he noticed something missing. It almost didn't catch his eye, but as he opened the door to his bar, he realized that the big banner he'd hung the night before —like he did every year—was gone. In big red and blue letters, it read: OPEN FOURTH OF JULY! CELEBRATE WITH US! But it wasn't there. Jesse went inside, turned off the alarm, and then went back outside to contemplate the missing banner.

He'd been putting up banners like that for years when the

different holidays rolled around, and nobody had ever taken one down. He wondered for a moment if last night's storm could have blown it away; there had been a little wind and lots of rain, but not enough, he assumed, to take down the banner. It hadn't been a hurricane. And if it was because of the storm, where was the banner now? Shouldn't it be on the ground?

But there was nothing. Just a few puddles along the sidewalk left over from last night's rain.

It didn't take long to speculate who had taken down the sign: Klutch. He'd left the park last night, drunk and angry, and had probably driven here, tore down the banner, and cut it into pieces like some kind of sacrificial lamb. Maybe it was his way of getting even for his missing knife.

Jesse went back inside the Captain's Room, through the back kitchen, and into his tiny, private office. He unlocked the bottom drawer of his desk and took out the Smith & Wesson .38 Special. He loaded it and tucked the gun into his belt. He'd bought the gun years ago and had kept it in the back office for protection in the case of a robbery, but now it was obvious that he needed to keep the gun on him at all times. That guy, Klutch, wasn't done.

Not yet. Not by a long shot.

Chapter Fourteen

The morning of July 4th, Morgan Grewell waited for the Pill Giver. The pills always made the pressure in his head go away and replaced the aching, congested feeling in his skull with dream-like pleasure and rest. The sun had come up, and Morgan could see the sunlight behind the shutters, which meant the Pill Giver would arrive soon. Morgan thought it was morning, but he'd been wrong before. Time lost all meaning in this place.

He wondered, for a moment, who the Pill Giver was. He remembered the face: pale, sickly skin, black shoulder-length hair, and dark eyes. The Pill Giver usually sat on the edge of his bed and spoke to him about the parasites. He wasn't sure what the parasites were, but the Pill Giver always talked about them. They were the reason for all the problems, and once gone, everything would be better.

But who was he? Who was the Pill Giver?

Is he my son, Drake, who I've lived with all these years? Or maybe he's my brother, Timmy. Yes, my brother Timmy. He looks like Timmy. He has the same eyes as Timmy. He must—

His head ached, and Morgan closed his eyes and rubbed

his temples with emaciated hands. His thoughts didn't make any sense. It couldn't have been his brother Tim, because Tim had died just after college in a car accident. He remembered playing baseball with Tim as a kid. A vivid memory from long ago seized him with violent clarity. He remembered being on the beach with Mom and Dad and Tim. Dad was throwing baseballs, and Morgan and his brother were learning how to catch. Seagulls hovered over the waves. It was the perfect day, because he realized that Dad wasn't just a guy who went to the factory to work. Dad was good at throwing the baseball, and he was a good teacher, and—

Maybe the Pill Giver is Dad. Maybe? But no, Dad is dead. Dad is long dead. It can't be Dad.

The room was musty and rank. The shutters had been closed for what seemed like an eternity, and he stared mindlessly at the splinters of sunlight that broke through them.

His eyes swam drunkenly across the room to his work desk beside the window, the one that he used to sit at and pay his bills in the evening, and he noticed the shadow that had always been there. At first he thought it was the way the sunlight broke through the shutters, but now was sure it wasn't a shadow at all; there was a person crouched beside the desk. A Dark Woman. Sometimes he thought he could hear her cry in the middle of the night.

She's a guardian angel who, knowing something's wrong, sits in the shadows and weeps.

Morgan realized that his hand was up and he had been clutching at something. What was he grasping for? He only remembered reaching for the shutters and the sunlight behind them. Maybe he was trying to open them. He put his hand down, and realizing how heavy his eyelids felt, decided maybe it was time to go back to sleep. Things were easy and peaceful when asleep.

The door to his room slowly opened. It had always been

creaky, just as it was now, and Morgan turned his head as someone came into the room. It was the Pill Giver, the one who made the awful pressure in his head go away. The Pill Giver walked into the room, took a seat at the edge of his bed, and looked at him.

Morgan found himself looking at the Pill Giver's face, but he struggled to make a connection. Pale skin. Black, greasy, shoulder-length hair. Dark, sorrowful eyes. Who was he?

"How are you today, Dad?" the Pill Giver asked.

"Alright," Morgan said. "Are you Timmy?"

"No, Dad," the Pill Giver said with slight exasperation. He shook his head. "I'm not Tim, Dad. Tim has been dead for a long time. I'm your son, Drake."

"How did he die?"

"A car accident."

"But we were at the beach, with Dad, throwing baseballs."

"I know, Dad, I know," the Pill Giver said. "Are you in pain? Do you need more Oxycotin?"

"What?"

"More medicine? Would you like more medicine?"

Morgan nodded. The medicine would bring relief. The pressure in his head would subside.

"Okay, then I'll be right back. I thought we had some more in supply, but I was wrong. I'll be back shortly."

"What is happening here? To me?"

The Pill Giver looked at him thoughtfully. "You have a brain tumor, Dad. Glioblastoma. It's almost over, you don't have much longer, and I'm doing my best to make you comfortable and relaxed during this time. And, like I promised you, I'm going to take care of the parasites before you die. Every last one of them. I'm doing this for you, Dad. All of this is for you, because I promised you that I wouldn't let you slip away in vain."

"The parasites?"

"Yes, the parasites. You used to talk about them all the time after you lost your job five years ago. Remember how hard you tried to cling onto this house? You drained everything you and Mom worked for to hold onto this place. Remember how much you sacrificed? And you'd look around at all these rich, sycophantic neighbors who didn't give you and your struggles a single charitable thought. You remember all that, Dad? And even before all that, when Mom died, you didn't get one knock on the door, not one card, not one bouquet of flowers from them, did you?"

Morgan nodded, but he had a hard time keeping up with the Pill Giver's words. He clutched his blanket and looked up at the ceiling. He thought he could hear the shadowy girl weeping in the corner of the room.

"The plan is all ready, Dad," the Pill Giver said. "I'm doing it for you. These leeches are gonna pay. All of them."

Morgan noticed that the Pill Giver had a gun in his hand. The Pill Giver leaned toward him and kissed him on the forehead. Morgan looked into the man's dark eyes, at his yellowed teeth, and at the handgun.

"It's the Fourth of July today," the Pill Giver said, "and you're not gonna have to suffer much longer, Dad. But I'll still get you the Oxycotin. And tonight, I'll make sure you go out without any pain. That's a promise. No more suffering for you. And when you're gone, I'm gonna teach those punks what real pain and suffering means. I'm gonna even the score tonight, Dad. I'm gonna even it."

Morgan coughed, and when he did, his head throbbed. It felt like someone was tightening a vise around his skull.

"I'll take out as many of them as I can, but I'll be right behind you, Dad. We'll be with Mom again, and we'll be together. No more pills and pain. I love you, Dad. I love you so much."

"I love you, too," Morgan said and took hold of the Pill

Giver's hand. "Thank you for helping me, Timmy. It's so good that you come here and help me. I couldn't have a better brother."

Chapter Fifteen

I woke up very early on July 4th even though I had gone to bed much later than I should have. Whenever I take too much time off from writing a novel, the idea starts to become stale in my mind, and I remember wanting to get back into my manuscript before I lost my rhythm.

I brewed a cup of my favorite coffee, took a seat in front of the computer, pulled up my manuscript, and sat in the silence of my office for a long time before getting back into the story. It was difficult to clear my mind; my discovery of Drake in the back alley and his notebook the night before were still bugging me. And. once again, I found it difficult to concentrate.

I managed to get in an hour or so of progress, but despite my efforts, it was slow and painstaking. Sometimes the words flow effortlessly; other times, constipation of the imagination sets in, and the flat sentences and paragraphs must be painfully squeezed out. At the end of that hour, I glanced back over what I'd written, sipped my coffee, and decided I would crawl back into bed and get some sleep. Bad writing days almost always put me in a grumpy mood, and I thought it might help to get another hour or two of rest.

When I crawled back into bed, my wife reached over and put her arm around me. She moved her hand up and down my chest.

"Back so soon?" she asked, half-asleep.

"Yeah. Words didn't want to cooperate this morning."

"I'm sorry, baby. I can make you feel better."

She kissed me on the cheek, snuggled into me, and closing her eyes, fell back to sleep. I must have conked out right after her, and I felt much better when I woke up later. It was nine or maybe even ten o'clock. We hadn't moved an inch, but my wife was kissing me again. Not a bad way to wake up.

"You ready for today?" she asked. "Big day. Fourth of July."

"I guess so. The kids are gonna have fun. Especially Toby. Owen, I'm not so sure. I think if he's anywhere with that girl he likes, he'll be happy. Where's Toby? What's he doing?"

"Probably watching cartoons in his room. And Owen probably won't be up for hours, which means you and I have a little alone time. I say we put on a little fireworks show of our own. What do you think?"

"I think that doesn't sound so bad," I said, kissing her. For several minutes we lay in bed, kissing each other, touching each other, enjoying this moment of one-on-one attention that would certainly be lost once the trials and tribulations of the day began. We lost ourselves in that moment. Before long, my wife's shirt was off, so was mine, and our bare skin was pressed into each other. I completely forgot about my bad writing day and the strange encounter I'd had with Drake the evening before in the back alley. All of those concerns faded away, like the last sparks of one of those big fireworks the night before slipping down the nighttime sky.

"Why don't I put on something fun to wear," my wife said suddenly, and jumping out of the bed, raced for the closet. I already knew what she meant. Lingerie, of course. She was going to put on one of my favorites, for sure, and I put my hands behind my head, looked up reflectively at the ceiling, and waited for her return. My wife loved lingerie about as much as I loved taking it off her.

She came back into the bedroom a moment later, but she was topless and only wearing her panties. No lingerie.

"Couldn't make up your mind, I take it?" I teased.

"It's gone. My drawer of lingerie is empty. Not there."

It was difficult for me to make out if she was upset or just confused.

"What do you mean it's not there?" I asked.

"I mean, it's not there. It's like the jewelry box, Eddie. It's just gone."

"Did you ever find the jewelry box? I thought you said it might be in the garage."

"No, I didn't find it. I just assumed it was misplaced, but this is weird."

"Yeah, kinda weird," I said, sitting up in bed. "But look, it's got to be here. We've already had this conversation, right? I doubt someone snuck into our house, took that jewelry box, and then came back to take your lingerie. I'd believe Owen was a cross-dresser and was sneaking into our closet before I'd believe that. You must have misplaced it, Maddie, you must have."

She crawled back into bed, but the passion had almost been completely snuffed out, and it was apparent that our romantic rendezvous was going to take an intermission. I could tell my wife was troubled. She lay in bed next to me, staring at the ceiling, and I could almost hear the gears turning inside her head as she tried to make sense of it.

"Eddie, this is really weird."

"I know," I said.

After perhaps a full minute of just lying there thinking, she turned toward me, and I saw the fear on her face. I can still remember that look. My wife doesn't get frightened or disheveled very often but, when she does, she certainly wears her heart on her sleeve.

"You don't think that's true, do you? It can't possibly be?" she asked me.

"What are you talking about?"

"About Owen being a cross-dresser? Do you think? I mean, jewelry and lingerie both missing? It kind of adds up, doesn't it?"

I felt my face wrinkling with disgust.

"Babe, I was joking. It was a joke."

"I know, I know, but it kinda makes sense, doesn't it?"

"Babe, this is the same boy who spent last night with that blond girl at the fountain, probably making out the whole time. I doubt he's spending his nights wearing your lingerie and jewelry."

"Her name's Candice."

"Whatever," I said, but it occurred to me that maybe the reason I had such a hard time remembering her name was because somewhere inside me, I didn't want to acknowledge the fact that I was old enough to be the father of a boy who was dating. It made me feel old; perhaps ascribing a name to her actually made me acknowledge that fact on some deeper level. Who knows?

Seeing my wife look so concerned over the notion of Owen sneaking into her room and putting on her clothing seemed so ridiculous to me, I couldn't help but crack up right there. I don't think she appreciated it, and she looked upset. It was a strange reversal of roles, because usually my wife could find the humor in just about anything.

"Eddie, I'm serious."

"I know."

"Then why are you laughing?"

"Because it seems ridiculous. You honestly want me to lie

here and have a discussion about Owen being some kind of transvestite?"

"Well, you don't have to laugh at me," she said, and I knew the romantic rendezvous that seemed inevitable just moments before was definitely cancelled. "I wasn't trying to be funny, Eddie. I was trying to have a serious talk. It doesn't make someone feel good when you laugh at them."

"I wasn't laughing at you."

"Really? Well, then what were you laughing at?"

"The idea of it."

"The idea of it," she said, repeating my words. "What is that supposed to mean? Isn't that just another way of saying you were laughing at me? Do you know how that makes someone feel?"

It was the second time in less than a minute that she'd used the word *feel* and this time, it clicked in my head. I took note of the date and did the math quickly.

"Maddie, you're taking this way too seriously," I said, kissing her on the cheek. If there's one thing about my wife, it's this: she never resists genuine affection. I love that about her. "I'm not laughing at you. I think it's a certain time of the month, and you're getting a little emotional right now, if you know what I mean. You're getting a little out there, babe."

She squinted her eyes. "So you're blaming it on that, huh?"

"I'm not blaming it on anything," I said. "I just can't believe I'm lying in bed having a discussion about this. Your feelings shouldn't be hurt because I don't think our son is a cross-dresser. You're being too weird and emotional about this, okay? I'm not a cross-dresser, Owen isn't a cross-dresser, and I doubt Toby has marched into your closet to try on your lingerie in between watching *The Wizard of Oz*. This is something you should be happy about. I think you must have misplaced the lingerie when you cleared out the closet. That must have been what happened to the jewelry box too. There's no other woman in this house who wants to wear your lingerie and your jewelry."

"Maybe not in this house," my wife said, catching me off guard. I could tell she was going to drop the whole cross-dresser conspiracy theory, but now, suddenly, she had gone onto something new.

"What are you talking about?

"They seem like things a woman would want, though I'm not sure who would want to wear another woman's lingerie," she said. "What about that Samantha woman across the street? She's totally into you."

"What are you talking about?"

Looking back, I don't know why I played so ignorant. Of course, Samantha was into me. After my evening in her home, that was beyond apparent.

"I wonder if she's crazy like that," my wife said. She looked at the ceiling, and once again, I could almost hear the gears turning in her head. "If she's so into you and wants you, maybe she snuck into our house and took my jewelry and my lingerie. I've heard of women who have done that. It's their way of taking the place of the wife."

"I don't know, babe," I said. "I think I'd believe the cross-dressing theory before I'd believe that one."

"Have you talked to her recently?" Madison asked, sitting up in bed. She looked at me, and I felt her stare pin me like a butterfly. It wasn't accusative, and in all honestly, she probably didn't mean much by it, but I knew that it would require lots of explanation if I was going to answer this question. I wasn't convinced that this was the best time to go there, and when I paused, she sensed it. Her eyes squinted again and her head tilted just slightly.

"Kind of," I said. I wasn't sure if it was the truth, or a lie, or a little of both, but that was what came out of my mouth. I couldn't look her in the eyes either. If there's one weakness I have—and a weakness my wife is well aware of—it's my complete inability to look her in the eyes if I'm dancing around the truth.

"What do you mean?"

I was trying to formulate some kind of answer when, to my relief, the doorbell rang. Madison looked at me peculiarly, got out of bed, and threw on a robe. My wife and I have always been very forthcoming with each other in everything, so I don't think she suspected an affair or anything of that nature, but she knew something was askew. She went downstairs to see who was at the front door, and I lay in bed, rubbing my face, knowing I was going to have to explain my paranoid venture to Samantha Wheeler's bedroom.

Jenna Paisley was downstairs. I recognized her voice. Madison and my wife were talking, and at first, I assumed Jenna had come over to see what we were doing that day; perhaps it would be good to walk together to the park later on and enjoy some of the holiday festivities. But before long, it became apparent that they weren't just talking. Jenna was crying and sounded very upset. I threw the blankets off me, got out of bed, and walked over to the door of our bedroom. It was ajar, and I opened it a little more and tried to make sense of the downstairs conversation.

"I just don't know what's gotten into him lately," Jenna said through sniffles and sobs. She had a loud voice, and I could hear her clearly. "He just hasn't been himself. He's saying the weirdest things."

"I'm sorry, dear, would you like some coffee? Just let me know," my wife said.

Clearly Darrel and Jenna had had a bad argument, and Jenna had come over here to lick her wounds and find comfort with another woman.

I was about to turn away and take a shower before Toby was up and out of his room and the chaos officially began, when I heard something that caught my attention. I stood there, one hand on the door, the other on the wall, paralyzed.

"He thinks I'm having an affair," Jenna said. "We had an argument over something completely unrelated, and all of a sudden, it came out. He thinks I'm sneaking around behind his back. It was crazy listening to him."

"Oh, I'm so sorry, dear."

"I just don't know what's wrong with him. Sometimes I think the divorce he went through with his first marriage really messed him up. He doesn't think it did because he was so young, but it really wounded him. He thinks I'm gonna do the same thing that she did. I've tried to explain to him how ridiculous that is, but he doesn't believe me. I just had to get out of the house for a little bit."

"I understand, I understand. You're welcome to relax here for a bit if you'd like."

"He was so upset, he even mentioned your husband, Eddie."

"Eddie?"

"Me?" I whispered in disgust. Now I wasn't going anywhere. I opened the door and crept forward a few feet so I could hear better. I was only wearing boxer shorts, but they were downstairs and around the corner in the living room. They wouldn't see or hear me here.

"Yeah, he mentioned Eddie," Jenna went on. "He said something about seeing Eddie leaving Samantha Wheeler's house the other night and how there must be something in the water here that's causing spouses to want to cheat on each other. Obviously, he doesn't know what he's talking about. He's being paranoid."

I felt like someone had punched me in the gut and knew the conversation about my trip to Samantha's was inevitable. The timing of Jenna's comment was impeccable. I was going to have a lot of explaining to do.

"I'm sure he's just very upset," my wife said in response to Darrel's claim that I had been over at Samantha's, but as her husband, I could hear the restrained tone of her voice. She meant, *I don't think my husband's having an affair, but there's something he isn't telling me, and we are going to have a LONG conversation about this.*

I took a long, hot shower, and while I got dressed, I debated with myself exactly how to explain what had happened at Samantha's. Did my wife need to know everything? I wasn't entirely sure. I had clearly turned down Samantha's advances, so I wasn't worried about that, but I didn't want to add any tension between my wife and her. I wasn't sure how my wife would take the whole thing because, again, I'd never really been in that situation before.

As I threw on my shoes, I heard the doorbell ring. Now what?

On my way downstairs, I ran into Owen. He had just opened his bedroom door and was standing there in the same clothes he'd slept in.

"Finally decided to get up, huh?" I said as I walked past him.

He more or less grunted to acknowledge me.

"Why don't you come have breakfast with me?" I told him.

"Yeah, sure, but I was thinking about getting donuts with Candice."

"Didn't you see her last night?"

"Yeah. So? Didn't you see Mom last night?"

"Big difference there, buddy. I'm married to her. Last time I checked, there wasn't a ring on your finger. I'd like you to spend a little time with us this morning before you run off."

"Fine," he said, sighing, and went into his room.

"Don't get too excited about it," I yelled back as I went down the stairs.

My wife and Jenna were still on the couch, engrossed in

conversation. Madison looked over to acknowledge me but I could see her squint her eyes enough to make me aware that we were going to have that very long conversation later. Most people wouldn't even have noticed the look she gave me, but I could. I read it loud and clear.

Toby sat at the dining room table, devouring a heaping bowl of cereal. Madison must have made him breakfast while I was in the shower.

"What's up there, buddy?" I said.

"Hey, Dad, you think Bessie's okay?"

"I think she's just fine," I said.

I was surprised by the question. It wasn't the first thing I expected to hear from him that morning.

I headed for the door. Before I opened it, I wondered if Darrel had come over to take his wife back to his house where they could finish their argument. When I opened the door, Marsha stood there with a box of brown sugar in her hands.

"Oh, hey, Marsha," I said.

"Just returning what I took from you," she said rather abruptly, nearly pushing the box of brown sugar into me.

"Okay, thanks," I said, taking the box.

Marsha Walker was usually a chatterbox, but this morning something seemed different. She frowned at me and ground her teeth, and I sensed tension. I'm not great at reading any woman other than my wife, but it didn't take that much perception to determine that something was bothering her. She just glared at me for a moment, and I felt the need to break the silence.

"You gonna be at the park today?" I asked. "Looks like we'll have some decent weather today and no rain."

"Yes," she said flatly, but I could see her grinding her teeth.

"Good."

"How'd that writing go this morning, Mr. Dees?" she asked, and for some reason, it felt like a loaded question. I wasn't sure what she was insinuating, but she seemed to mean something by it. Did she also think I was over at Samantha's that morning having an affair with her? Her countenance seemed to suggest she thought something of that nature.

"Not too bad," I said. "Kind of a slow crawl this morning, but those things are bound to happen."

"Yeah, hard to come up with your own ideas sometimes, isn't it?"

Now I was at a loss. This comment was most certainly directed toward something, but I couldn't make sense of it. I had absolutely no idea what was bothering her, so like the inept social conversationalist that I was, I tried my best to gently steer the discussion in an alternative direction.

"Looking forward to reading that story of yours," I said.

"Are you being sarcastic?"

"What? No. Why?"

"You meant something by the way you said that, Mr. Dees. I can tell. What do you mean, you're looking forward to reading it? Do you mean, as if you already have it and are looking forward to reading it?"

"What? I don't understand."

"Are you sure about that? I just didn't like the way you said that."

"Said what?"

Her reaction was difficult to forget. Her eyes went wide as could be, and I thought, for a moment, that she had seen something terrifying behind me; I think I even turned around to make sure that something frightening really wasn't taking place. She started fanning herself with her hand and breathing rapidly. I thought she might pass out in front of me, but when I made a gesture to help her, she waved me away and grabbed onto the side railing of our front porch to stop from falling over.

"Are you okay?" I asked. "What's wrong?"

"Nothing," she said. "Just a hot flash. I'm fine."

I remember wishing my wife was there to say something, because honestly, I had no idea what to do.

"Would you like some water? Anything?"

"No, I'll be fine," she said, and still fanning herself with her chubby hand, she closed her eyes and caught her breath. She turned to leave but looked back at me one last time before she made her way out the front gate.

"Are you sure everything's okay?" I asked, standing by my front door.

"Just fine, just fine," she said rather dramatically. "Why don't you go back to writing your book, Mr. Author. Wouldn't want you to have to resort to stealing someone else's idea, now would we?"

She waddled back to her house like an irate penguin, and I stood on the front porch for many minutes, rethinking our conversation and trying to figure out how it went off course. I was about to turn around and go back inside when Samantha Wheeler walked by the front of my house. It looked like she had just returned from a jog or the gym and was en route to her house. She was wearing workout clothes and carrying a water bottle. She didn't stop as she walked by, but she looked over and grinned coquettishly at me as she passed.

I was afraid to say her name, because I didn't want my wife to hear. I didn't want to mention her name in or near my house until I cleared things up with Madison. But I did offer a friendly hello, and she waved back.

"Hope to see you today at the park," she said, winking. It was an inviting wink, and I was shocked that she was so bold after my refusal of her.

I remembered a conversation I'd had with a friend back in college. We were at a bar, throwing back a few drinks, and he had told me that women—while living in close proximity—

actually developed the same menstrual cycles. They all acclimated to each other.

Standing on the porch that morning, dazed and dumbfounded, I began to wonder if that was what was happening. Perhaps some freak phenomenon was taking place, and all of the women on Naples Island were experiencing synergetic PMS on an astronomical level, and I was caught in a whirlwind of bizarre emotional thinking. A neighbor angry at me for reasons unknown? A wife upset because I didn't think my son was a cross-dresser? Another neighbor who somehow heard "yes" in what could not have been a clearer "no"? Another neighbor crying on my couch?

It was too much to handle.

"I need a drink," I said and went back into my house.

It may have been early, but the Captain's Room was probably open.

And it was five o'clock somewhere.

Chapter Sixteen

I never did go to the Captain's Room. Jenna went home to make amends with her husband, and Toby finished his cereal and went to take a bath and get ready for the day. My wife sat me down on the couch to ask me what was going on with Samantha Wheeler, and I coughed up the whole story right there. I told her everything that happened that night: the glass of wine she handed me, how I crouched by the window in her bedroom to look onto Drake's property, and how she had made a pass at me as I tried to leave.

I also told her about my refusal; I made sure to include every detail of that.

Amazingly, she was grinning as I neared the end of my story. I wasn't sure how she was going to respond. I knew for certain that she would never seriously entertain a notion of me going behind her back to have an affair with our neighbor, and I was glad because of it. My wife and I trust each other to the core, but I thought she might be a little irate that I hadn't told her about what happened. We made a rule early on in our marriage not to keep secrets from each other. I wasn't sure if this qualified.

"Why are you laughing?" I asked after I finished my story. It wasn't what I was expecting.

"Because you're ridiculous."

"Great, thanks."

"You think I'm crazy because I think it's possible our son got into my jewelry box and lingerie, and yet you're running around in the rain spying on our neighbor because you think he might have chopped up our dog. And in your quest to figure it out, you've also become a Peeping Tom. So who's the weird hormonal one?"

I tried but couldn't find a comeback. Whatever writer's block had hit me early that morning was still in full effect.

She slid toward me on the couch, wrapped her arms around me, and kissed me. It was a passionate kiss, not unlike the way we had kissed earlier that morning. If we had been alone and without a little boy in the bath in the next room and a teenager upstairs who could walk down at any moment, things might have pleasantly escalated.

"Just look in the mirror next time you think my ideas are so ridiculous," she said. "You're not exactly batting a thousand yourself."

"Just don't say anything to Samantha, okay? I feel weird enough, and I made myself abundantly clear in my rejection of her."

"Oh, I won't say anything to her," she said. She grinned widely and I recognized that mischievous smile. "Next time I see her, I'll just grab you and start passionately making out with you. I'll rip your clothes off right there in front of her. That ought to teach her, don't you think?"

"Just don't make an uncomfortable situation even more uncomfortable."

"Never," she said, topping it off with another kiss.

We spent the next hour or so getting everything ready for the day. The Fourth of July would be similar to last night, only there would be even more people at the park. It was our first summer on Naples Island, so we only knew what we had been told, and the Fourth of July was supposedly a fun-filled, festive day. The park would be teeming with picnickers. Live bands would be playing all day. Bounce houses and games would be brought in for the kiddos. There were also games for the adults as well. There'd be beer and margaritas, food and festivities, and supposedly one could spend almost the whole day at the park listening to music, chatting with neighbors, and wasting the day away in good company.

The canals hosted parties of their own. From the stories I'd heard, boaters, rafters, and kayakers lazily made their way through the canals all day on the Fourth. It wasn't uncommon for water balloon fights to break out around every corner. There would be barbecues in the backs of the tied up boats along the canals, house parties, loud music, and a whole community celebrating their independence by getting outside and playing on their water toys.

There was something entirely American about it, and I had to admit, even though I was never going to win an award for being a great socialite, I was pretty excited to get out of the house with my family. Just spending some time with my wife and kids sounded fantastic.

We loaded up two coolers full of drinks and snacks and got the kids ready. Toby, asking how long it was going to be before the fireworks show, was completely enthusiastic about going. He even suggested looking for Bessie on the way to the park. Owen, as could be expected, wasn't nearly as excited.

"Can't I just meet up with you guys later?" he asked as we all stood by the front door, ready to leave. "I was gonna hang out with Candice today. I think her parents are doing a barbecue at their house, and I was gonna go."

"Really?" I said. "So you're gonna hang out with her parents and not your own?"

"No, Dad, I was gonna hang out with her."

"Didn't we already have this conversation this morning?" I asked.

"Wasn't really a conversation," he said. "More like you just telling me that I had to hang out with you and Mom."

"Exactly," I said, and opening the front door of our house, ushered everyone outside so we could begin our short walk to the park.

I probably should have noticed something was wrong during that walk, but I wasn't able to put all the pieces of the puzzle together quite yet. It wasn't exactly a beautiful summer day, but most of the clouds were gone, and it looked like we could make it through the holiday without more rain. In the distance, the sky was darker, and we hoped those clouds would empty themselves long before they reached Naples Island. With all the rain in July, I began to wonder if we should have just stayed in Seattle. They had probably gotten more sunshine than we did in the last week.

We hadn't passed more than a few houses when I heard the first of the arguments. It was a large, two-story Spanish home, and we heard a husband and wife going at it with a fury.

"Stop lying to me, Charlie! Stop lying! You know you did it! You know you did!"

Madison and I looked at each other as we passed, raised our eyebrows, and prepared to divert Toby's attention or plug his ears in case the domestic dispute became peppered with expletives, but it didn't. The woman yelled on and on while Charlie, whoever he was, said nothing. Poor guy. Usually, I've found in life, silence speaks of innocence. The guilty often feel the need to fire back. The woman was on a rampage and seemed to be accusing him of reading and throwing away her diary.

We passed that house and turned the corner, only to stumble upon another strange altercation. This time it was outside and appeared to be two neighbors. A large, overweight man wearing a sleeveless black shirt and standing beside his Ford pickup was having a rather loud discussion with another man, a thin, business-looking guy dressed in khakis and a green polo shirt.

"For the last time, I didn't get into your car last night, Ron," the overweight guy said. He had one hand on his pickup truck, and he was pointing the other hand at the skinny guy. "You really think I snuck out in the rain to look around inside your Porsche?"

"Well, then what happened to my wallet? It was in the glove compartment."

"Didn't your parents teach you not to leave your wallet in the car, Ron? Plus, you have a garage. You should have parked in there."

"I would have, but family's staying with us for the weekend and their cars are in there," Ron said. "Look, I know I should have taken it out, but it's not in there. You were sitting out here in your car when I drove home last night. I saw you."

"Yeah, I was talking on the phone to my sister."

"And then twenty minutes later I realize I left my wallet in the car, so I come back out and look. You aren't in your car anymore. And when I get back in my car and check, the wallet's not there. And you're telling me you don't know anything about it even though you were the only one out here. That's what you're saying?"

"I'm saying you're crazy," the big, sleeveless guy said.

I didn't hear much more. It sounded like it was escalating, but by the time the voices got louder, we'd passed that house and were crossing over one of the small bridges.

"Strange morning, huh?" I said, and my wife nodded in agreement.

Another thing struck me as unusual when we crossed the bridge. The stories I had been told about Naples Island made it sound like it was a virtual water park on the Fourth of July. I expected to see the canals teeming with people, boats, music, and playful laughter. Even if the weather wasn't all that great, it wasn't enough of an excuse to stay inside. This was still a holiday. But when I looked down the length of the canal, I didn't see nearly what I expected. There were a few kayakers, and I heard music emanating from some of the boats, but very little.

We continued our walk over the bridge, and after a few more turns, found the central park of the island and ground zero for the holiday festivities. We had been here the day before to watch the early fireworks show. Yet, like the rest of the island, it wasn't exactly what I expected. There were people there—several people—but it seemed quieter and more subdued than I imagined.

Lots of families sat on blankets all throughout the park and reclined on chairs. It looked like one giant picnic. Some neighborhood community organization had purchased several large bouncers along the side of the grass for the kids to play in, and before we had barely stepped onto the grass, Toby was tugging on my arm and asking to go over to jump around in one of them.

Several neighborhood shops had sponsored booths along the perimeter of the park. Kaley's Restaurant was giving away free American flags and bottles of water. South Coast Ribs Company was hosting hula hoop contests for the kids with candy prizes. The local pharmacy was doing free face painting. They had even brought in some live music and built a stage on the west side of the lawn, but they were in between sets when we showed up. I saw some guys on stage, tuning their guitars and getting things ready.

Madison directed me toward the southern part of the park and the area closest to the bay. We were to meet the Paisleys there. Apparently, they had patched up their marital issues enough that morning to venture outside and meet us. My wife instructed me not to say anything about Darrel's accusing me; she had promised Jenna that she wouldn't tell me about that. I suppose in some circumstances, a guy would be really bummed to learn that his neighbor had thrown him under the bus like that and word had gotten back to his wife, but I just didn't have it in me to be upset that morning. I knew Darrel Paisley to be a good man and I'm sure, in the heat and fire of an argument, the words just came out of him. I knew he didn't mean anything personal by it. He wasn't on a mission to destroy me or my reputation. So when we found Darrel and his wife at the very end of the lawn, sitting on picnic blankets, it was easy for me to offer a warm welcome and really mean it.

We laid our blankets next to theirs. Toby tugged on my arm and tried to pull me toward the bouncers. Owen sat apart from us, on the grass, playing on his phone. I was pretty sure he was texting Candice and trying to concoct some kind of excuse to get away from us.

"Weather says it might rain again tonight," Darrel said.

"Again?" my wife protested.

"Think so," Darrel said. "I checked three sources this morning. All of them seemed to indicate that."

Three sources? That was Darrel, the financial investor. Prudent and thorough to the core.

"What happened to the sunny California we were expecting?" my wife said.

I remember looking around the park and noticing, just as I had noticed on our walk over there, that something just didn't seem right. It was difficult to place my finger on it, and I was only minutes away from beginning to understand exactly what had been taking place on Naples Island since the storms started rolling in.

Everywhere I looked in the park, people seemed disheveled,

upset, unnerved, and if I didn't know any better, I might have believed I was sitting on the lawn in some internment camp rather than what was supposed to be a holiday gathering.

I was contemplating this when Owen bent down next to me.

"Dad, can I go over to the fountain for a little bit?"

The fountain was on the northern end of the park, and when I glanced over, swarming with teenagers. I guess that was the official hangout spot of the young at venues like this.

"Candice there?" I asked.

"Yeah."

"In a few minutes. Didn't you guys hang out last night? It won't kill you to hang out with us for a few minutes."

"Alright," he said and went on texting someone. The most likely text: *OMG my dad is so lame.*

I stood up to greet Jesse, who had walked over to say hello. Like usual, he looked completely out of place amongst the sometimes swanky, yuppie-like residents of the island. Today's wardrobe: blue Wrangler jeans, work boots, and a blue-and-black checkered flannel. We shook hands, and I reminded myself that, when I had a moment, I should properly introduce him to my wife and neighbors. Madison had never been to the Captain's Room, and it didn't seem like a place Darrel or Jenna would venture to.

"You guys enjoying your day out here?" Jesse asked, returning a firm handshake. His voice, like usual, was the no-nonsense, deep, gravelly voice of a man who was fiercely independent.

"Trying to," I said. "Kind of had a weird morning to be honest with you."

"Yeah, me too," Jesse said. "Remember that idiot biker guy, Klutch? I went to work this morning to get things going—Wilson's holding down the fort right now because my son went off to a party—and I noticed my banner's been torn down. Totally gone."

"Really?"

"Yep," he said. "It didn't take me but a moment to figure out who did it either. It was Klutch."

"You think so?"

"I know so. It's his way of getting back at me for taking his pocket knife. At least, the pocket knife he thinks I took. He wants to tangle with me, that's for sure. Just ran into him on the way over here."

"Really?"

"Yep, he's down by the fountain. Sitting on his bike and eating a burger. I stayed clear of him, but he yelled something at me for taking his whole saddlebag off his bike last night. As if the knife wasn't enough. The guy's insane. Why would I take his knife and then come back for his saddlebag? He just wants to cause problems."

"What is he doing in Naples anyway?"

"Good question," Jesse said. "I overheard a little the first night I met him. He lives in North Carolina from what I heard. Inherited a nice home here from a sister and came out on a grand road trip to check out the home and get it ready to sell. Said something about quitting his job at a warehouse and spending the rest of his life on the road. Served in the military, too."

"Yeah, he was yelling something about that last night."

"I think it messed him up some," Jesse said. "Not sure if he served in Iraq, but sounds like he was quite the leader wherever he was. Always blabbers on and on about how he never lost a guy in his command. Not sure what that means, but sounds to me like he might have come back to 'normal society' with a chip on his shoulder. He talked about his job in that warehouse like he was doing a prison sentence."

I nodded.

"Just really angered me to see him take that sign."

"That is upsetting," I said, and that was when the light bulb went on—perhaps *flickered on* is a more apt description. All of a sudden, everything sort of snapped into focus. I remembered the argument I'd heard on the way there that morning. The two guys fighting over the wallet. My wife's missing lingerie. Her missing jewelry box. Our missing dog. Jenna Paisley's missing wedding ring.

Thunder crackled in the sky overhead. The clouds, which had seemed far away just a few minutes ago, were suddenly above us. Had they slid across the sky that quickly? Was it possible?

"What's wrong?" Jesse asked. He must have seen the expression on my face. He looked up too at the sound of thunder and seemed just as surprised as me at the sudden arrival of cloud cover. The chance of rain had appeared hours away.

"Your banner was taken, huh?"

"Yeah, what about it? I told you it was Klutch."

"But you didn't actually see him take it, did you?"

"No."

"And there was money missing out of your register the other night, right?"

"Yep."

I looked amongst the crowd of picnickers, and this time, I looked closely. I looked at the faces of every man, woman, and child in our near vicinity. It wasn't that anything looked completely wrong; it was what was missing that got my attention. Where was the laughter? Where was the joy? Was it possible that everyone here was experiencing the same thing?

It made no logical sense, and in that brief moment, I imagined some thief going through Naples Island and taking things: dogs, banners, wedding rings, knives, saddlebags. Maybe there were kleptomaniac bandits skulking through the streets at night, taking all these things, because the coincidence seemed too much to ignore.

I had yet to realize the true power of the storm.

"What is it?" Jesse asked. "What's wrong?"

I ignored him. Without thinking, I walked over to a young couple sitting on the grass beside us. They were lounging on a blanket and eating homemade sandwiches. They had a little curly-haired blonde girl with them, maybe two years old, who was flipping through a picture book and babbling on and on about it.

I tapped the dad on the shoulder. He was a young guy, maybe thirty, and looked like a computer geek.

"Excuse me," I said. "I hate to ask this. I know it's going to sound weird, but you guys haven't had anything stolen from your home recently, have you? Anything missing?"

The husband and wife looked at each other. They seemed genuinely surprised and stunned by my question.

"Again, I'm sorry," I said. "I just think there may be some burglars on the island, and I was wondering if anything's happened."

"Funny you should ask," the computer geek said. "We just called the cops this morning because someone got into our back patio and took our bicycles. We think it's a neighbor because she's always telling us how much she wants to buy ones just like them, and who else knows they're back there? Were your bikes stolen too?"

"No, no bikes stolen," I said, almost in a trance, and walked back to Jesse.

He gave me a long, hard look. "What's wrong there, bud? You look like you've seen a ghost."

"I think I have," I said, looking out at the crowd.

Owen tapped me on the shoulder and asked, impatiently, if he'd spent enough "family time" and could go meet up with Candice. I could hear Toby also begging Madison to take him to one of the bounce houses. I was so consumed in my thought, I just nodded to Owen, and he began to make his way to the fountain. I think that was a strategy he'd learned several years before: wait until Mom or Dad was fully engrossed in something and then ask permission to do something. The odds greatly improved in those situations.

"What do you mean? Is something wrong?" Jesse asked.

"I mean, I don't think you're the only one who—"

My voice trailed off.

I saw Drake walking our way. As usual, he was dressed in black, and he had a backpack on. He slumped forward with his dark, greasy hair dangling toward the ground, and it was difficult to see his face. He was carrying something wrapped in a blanket. To many of the picnickers, it probably looked like he was toting around a beach umbrella. But I could tell it wasn't an umbrella. Too short for that.

A second epiphany struck me. I remembered the notebook and the crude map of the park. It suddenly made sense to me, and in that terrifying moment, I hoped it wasn't too late.

He unwrapped what police reports would later identify as an AK-47. I watched as if in slow motion. He was only thirty or so feet away from me, and it felt like all of my insides suddenly dropped out of me. I felt like a hollow shell of a human, standing there, paralyzed.

"Oh no," I said.

One thought flashed through my head: *This is going to be like Columbine. Get out of here! Get Toby, get Owen, get Madison, and get out of here!*

Drake yelled something about his father. A few people who were close saw what was going to happen, and in that moment, time warbled to a stop and everything froze. I saw the look on Drake's pallid face, the visage of an insane man, and the looks of men, women, and children who realized their lives were going to be turned upside-down in a single instant of time.

He began to fire. The fusillade tore through several people. An elderly couple crumpled to the ground before him, their chests torn apart and bloodied, and Drake slowly came our way while cutting through the crowd. The sound was nearly deafening. People ran in all directions like a swarm of startled insects, but Drake moved on, calmly directing the aim of his weapon toward helpless victims who hardly had a chance to comprehend what was taking place. I saw a few others fall to the ground as he continued on his murderous path. One of them was a bicycle cop I had seen riding by earlier.

I found Toby and scooped him off the ground. He held on tightly but didn't cry; he was still in shock like the rest of us. Madison and the Paisleys were on their feet as well. Everyone knew to run.

But I had to get Owen. My son was en route to the fountain and wasn't far away, and it looked like Drake was heading right toward him.

Amongst the chaos, with Toby in my arms, I screamed, "Owen!"

He was there, running back toward me in the madness. Like others, he ducked low as he ran—as if that would help. The AK-47 was firing in bursts. I didn't look, but it seemed as if Drake was still slowly walking and shooting where it proved the most deadly.

Owen stopped running and looked over at something or someone. I saw hesitation on his face.

"Get over here!" I screamed.

He looked at me doubtfully, blinking. My wife was pulling on me and calling for Owen as well.

Owen didn't listen to me but ran toward the gunman. I wouldn't have thought it possible to be more terrified before that moment. Why was he going toward the source of violence and not away from it? What was wrong with him? What was he thinking?

"Get down, people!" Jesse ordered, aiming a handgun toward the madman. I had no idea where the weapon came from, and I didn't know if it was a good thing. It would make Jesse a target, and I was standing next to him.

Over the screaming and fleeing of people, I don't think anybody heard him.

I discovered what Owen was running toward. The little curly-haired blonde girl I had seen just moments before was sitting helplessly between the bodies of her dead parents. Owen ran up to the little girl, scooped her into his arms, and bolted toward me. I watched him cover her with his body as he ran.

"Get down, people!" Jesse yelled again, and this time he fired.

He missed his target, but Drake noted the threat. Jesse started to move away because I think he realized he would draw fire and wanted to be away from people. Drake fired back.

Owen reached us, the little girl in his arms, and all of us started to run away. My wife was there too. I heard bullets whiz past us. How close, I don't know, but it felt like millimeters.

We didn't get far before I saw Jenna Paisley fall to the ground. Her head was blown apart, and her hair was a coagulated mat of blood and brain matter. Darrel fell to the ground beside her, howling in terror, and clutched onto her. I tried to pull him with me, because there was no use in staying. One more spray of automatic gunfire in our direction, and we'd all be joining her.

"Come on!" I yelled at him, but he remained beside the body, howling.

Jesse fired again and missed, and Drake threw down his AK 47. I think he was out of ammunition. He pulled a handgun from under his belt and fired back, and the bullet whizzed past us.

Backing away, Drake grabbed hold of a boy who had been lying on the ground, crying. He picked him up, put his arm around his neck, and held him close, as a body shield, as he backed away while waving his gun all over the place.

I recognized the kid. It was Hot-rodder. I saw his bike lying on the grass where he had been lying. At least fifteen bodies, bloodied and crumpled, lay around the bike.

"My father's gonna get his payback for all of you leeches, you hear that!" Drake shouted.

The sky crackled with thunder and flashed with lightning, and the wind picked up.

"You're all gonna pay!"

Now it was a standoff. Jesse held his ground, his gun out before him, and even though most people had run away from the epicenter of the madness, I saw a few men coming forward. A couple of them were carrying handguns. I suppose in a crowd like that, there's bound to be at least a few off-duty officers, and these were probably them. Later, I came to realize that off-duty officers really don't see themselves as "off-duty" in times of crisis.

Drake, with Hot-rodder in his grip, slowly backed away.

A massive bolt of lightning ignited the sky above us, and the thunder that followed just a moment after was so loud and monstrous, I could literally feel it in the ground. The rain started to pour. I still didn't understand how the clouds had gotten there so quickly, how the storm had virtually material-ized out of nowhere.

There were more flashes of lightning, unnatural flashes that happened in such rapid succession it appeared as if a great strobe light had been placed in the dark clouds overhead. All around us, lightning bolts showered down. This was no normal storm.

A thought even flashed through my head: *Maybe it's not light-ning. This is terrorism. A bomb of some kind.*

Still carrying Hot-rodder, Drake turned around and ran back into the neighborhood toward his house. Jesse kept his gun locked on him but didn't fire. Neither did any of the other men coming toward us. Too risky with a child in the madman's arms.

I cried out toward Hot-rodder when I saw that he was being taken away, and much later, my wife told me it was really my brother I was reaching for. Hot-rodder, even in that frenzied moment, was a metaphor for a much deeper loss I had yet to fully come to terms with. My wife has a way of doing that with me; she always has.

We were safe for the moment. I remember that thought: *we were safe.*

Shaking all over, undoubtedly from shock, I took inventory. I looked my body up and down. Was I shot? Was I bleeding? I didn't think so. My wife has always told me that I'm quite calm in moments of crisis, and I hoped that had proved true.

I checked my wife, who by now was crying hysterically next to me and on the verge of what looked like an epileptic seizure. I turned her around and checked her body, and when she tried to talk, she couldn't. I told her to just be quiet, don't say anything. Fragments of incomprehensible words dribbled out of her mouth, and I assured her that everything was going to be okay. Toby was still in my arms, and I quickly examined him. No blood. No blood at all. I held onto him as he bleated like a terrified lamb into my ear.

"You're okay, you're okay, we're okay," I said.

I looked over at Darrel Paisley, who was on his knees in front of his wife's body. He slouched forward, weeping. Drool dripped off his chin, and he had his wife's head cradled in his bloody hands. There were others around us doing the same. A tormented choir of the wounded and the groans of loved ones rose toward the supernatural display of lightning above our heads.

"I'm okay, Dad." Owen walked toward me, the little blonde girl in his hands. Amazingly, she wasn't crying. Her bright blue eyes looked up toward the lightning in sheer wonder.

I looked hard at Owen. I wanted to be angry at him for running away from me when I had explicitly called him to me, but I couldn't.

I learned something about Owen that day. There was more to this pimply-faced, overly hormonal teenager than I had ever realized.

My son was brave. Braver than his father, even.

I put my arm around him and kissed him on the cheek.

"Well done, son," I said, and he looked at me with understanding. He nodded, and he knew exactly what I meant by it. "Well done."

Chapter Seventeen

The supernatural storm—whatever it was—intensified. There was lightning everywhere in the sky; small tongues of lightning, massive bolts, and everything in between showered down from the dark clouds above us. When I looked overhead, I noticed something else too: the clouds directly above us swirled in a circle, a great, dark vortex. The wind had picked up, but the clouds swirled much faster than the wind should have allowed them to. It was disorientating to look at them.

A massive bolt of lightning struck the fountain on the other end of the park; it was an incredible thing to witness. The lightning, shimmering and blinding, had made a direct route for the fountain, as if it had been hurled at it for that explicit purpose. The fountain exploded into pieces. Bits of granite flew apart as if a great piñata had burst open, and it was followed by terrible screams as chunks of stone rained down from the explosion.

"What is this?" Jesse asked and aimed his gun toward the explosion in pure reflex.

I waited for sirens, but there were none yet. I assumed the

police would be there in a matter of seconds, but I took my phone out of my pocket to call 911 just in case; maybe nobody had called it in yet. I had no idea. There were bodies lying in the grass. Based on the wailing I heard near the fountain, I wondered if that explosion had taken more lives along with the ones Drake had already taken.

Darrel, on the ground with his wife's head in his lap, wailed like some primitive animal in the night. His hands were covered in blood and brain matter. I can still remember the sounds of him screaming, and to this day, I find it most disturbing.

My call to 911 rang once, and then it happened again.

Another bolt of lightning came out of nowhere, this time striking a jacaranda tree about a hundred feet away from us. The tree exploded just like the fountain had. My eardrums had already taken a beating from the AK-47, and this did further damage; the explosion was painfully deafening. A shower of debris swept past us, and a chunk of branch hit my hand and sent my phone flying out of it. I closed my eyes and covered my face as bits of jacaranda tree flew past me like a meteor swarm. When I looked up, there was little left of the top of the tree. The trunk remained, but the stubs of former branches were now aflame.

Then I saw another bolt strike a tree at the other end of the park. It was followed by an explosion as more people screamed. And then a bolt of lightning struck a boat in the water behind the park. It was a small Duffy and was probably filled with friends celebrating the holiday out on the water. Yet the lightning didn't stop with just one bolt; there were several more. Bolt after bolt ripped through the sky and struck the small Duffy with a fury until finally, when the electrical assault stopped, the boat was completely torn apart and nothing more than smoldering driftwood remained on the surface of the water. I had never seen anything like it; the lightning had *wanted* to destroy that boat.

I knew we had to leave, and we had to leave quickly. I suppose in most situations like that it's best to wait for the police and paramedics to arrive, but it was obvious that this was not like most situations. This was something else entirely, and I wanted to get my family inside and out of danger.

Several massive bolts of blue lightning that seemed to have originated from the very edge of the swirling clouds struck something to the east. I wasn't sure what it was, but it sounded like a building. I heard a great explosion followed by falling rubble and, yet again, the ground trembled beneath my feet. Only seconds passed before several more of those massive blue bolts struck, this time on the west side of the island. At that time, I hadn't realized what had just happened.

We were all on the ground. To this day, I can't remember if we fell to the ground to take cover or if we were thrown to the ground as the earth shook; perhaps it was a little of both. I heard car alarms going off everywhere and I thought, far in the distance, I could hear emergency vehicles.

I looked up and saw remnants of the crowd running away in terror. Most certainly, everyone was trying to find a safe place indoors. In my peripheral vision, I could see bolts of lightning everywhere whipping down from the sky, striking things all around the island. Electrical explosions and a cacophony of destruction swirled about me. Suddenly, I was in Mother Nature's war zone, and I thought the exact same thing everyone else was thinking: get inside and get inside quickly.

Toby was terrified. My wife, who had still barely pulled it together enough to utter a word, held him. Amazingly, the little girl my son had rescued hadn't shed a single tear. She looked up dreamily toward the sky as if this were all just a fireworks show put on for her amusement only.

"My house," I told Jesse. He nodded in agreement. My

house wasn't far, and once inside, we would be safe from the storm.

"Dad, what did those big bolts of lightning hit?" Owen asked. I knew he was referring to the massive blue ones that struck something on the east and west sides of the island.

"I have no idea," I said. Even in moments of crisis, I guess Owen still thought Dad had all the answers. "Run home now."

My family and Jesse began to run, and I turned my attention toward Darrel, who was still on the ground with his wife's head in his lap. He wept inconsolably.

"Darrel, let's go!"

He couldn't really talk, but I could tell by the expression on his face that he didn't want to leave his wife's body behind. It was an understandable concern but, considering the circumstances, I tried my best to reason with him as the bizarre lightning strike continued its assault.

"You have to leave her!"

"No," he whimpered while rubbing his bloodied hands through her tangled hair. I could see the fear on his face. I had seen a spark of a similar fear the day before, when he had first vocalized his concerns that his wife was running around behind his back. It was the fear of losing her, but this, of course, eclipsed that in a monstrous way.

"Darrel, you have to. We're being attacked. Something's happening. We have to get out of here."

"I'm taking her," he said, and picked up her body.

I knew that, under normal situations, it wasn't good to move the body. The couple of CPR classes I had taken in my life as well as the common knowledge I'd acquired over the years told me that, but I didn't try to stop him. Considering a large part of her face was missing, it was pretty obvious that she was dead and was going to remain that way. And none of those classes had guidelines for what to do in the event of a bizarre lightning attack.

As I watched Darrel struggle to get Jenna's body in his arms, I had the feeling he knew she was dead too. Darrel struggled with her body as more brain fluids and blood poured out of her cracked head and ran down his shirt. Even in the shock of it all, I think Darrel Paisley didn't want to let go. How could I blame him?

"Let's go," I said.

He blabbered something incoherent, and I began to run.

I heard one lone siren coming our way, and I was surprised. I had expected to hear more. When a guy shoots through a crowd of people like Swiss cheese, one expects an entire army to show up, and there was something disturbing about only hearing one. Time had lost all meaning to me, and maybe only a few seconds had passed since it all began and emergency teams would show up shortly, but, like me, nobody here was sticking around to find out.

Another blue bolt of lightning crackled down from the heavens and struck a building that might have only been a couple blocks away. The sky flashed a brilliant, blinding white, and we heard the explosion. Debris rained down like hail.

I saw Klutch standing before the open door of a large brick home adjacent to the park, and he was doing something quite impressive. Keeping guard by the entrance, he was holding a gun and ushering panicked people trying to find refuge from the chaos safely inside. Perhaps that was the house he had inherited, and many terrified people took him up on his offer. It surprised me to see Klutch, the same guy who just yesterday had stood in the same park and insulted everyone there, being so calm and collected and even helpful in that moment.

I began to understand Klutch. He was good in moments of crisis, perhaps even more poised than in times of calm and serenity; and his ego fed on the approval and need of others. As terrified citizens surged into his home, he looked up at the phantasmagoric display of light with a look of absolute control. He didn't seem afraid of the storm, not yet. If what he said about himself was true, that he hadn't lost a man when serving overseas, then perhaps this would be another challenge for him.

One police car, sirens blazing, pulled up to the edge of the park. There were no others. I didn't wait any longer to see what happened but followed Jesse and my family through the narrow streets of Naples. Others were also running indoors. I turned around to make sure that Darrel was following me, and he was lagging behind because of the dead weight in his arms. How terrifying it was to see him there, still howling in desperation, as the lightning illuminated his terrified expression and the bloodied, shattered body dangling from his arms.

He was struggling to run. Carrying the weight was getting to him.

"Come on!" I yelled.

Another burst of lightning struck a light pole right next to us. The light exploded, and a plume of sparks fell down like luminescent rain. Like the other explosions, it had been deafening, and I instinctively covered my ears. I watched as the lightning ran down the pole to the very base, sizzled there for a moment, and then ran back up to the broken light at the top.

As if everything else I had seen that night hadn't been bizarre enough, I then saw one of the most bewildering sights of nature that I ever had. A little ball of lightning separated from the sizzling pole. It was a small, green, electrical ball of energy about the size of a grapefruit, and it floated toward me. I was so shocked from everything, I couldn't move. I began to seriously wonder if the world was about to end and God Almighty had sent the first of His wrecking crew to Naples Island.

The ball slowly drifted toward me and hovered there, only a couple feet from my face. I heard some kind of soft, crackling static. I don't know if it had intelligence, but I had the strange feeling that the ball was inspecting and probing me somehow. Did it want something from me? Was it trying to communicate with me? I wasn't sure. Even in the chaos of the moment, there was a part of me that felt tempted to reach out and touch the hissing ball of green light. It was an almost irresistible urge, because there was something magnificently beautiful about it.

I began to back away from it, and it suddenly moved just a bit to the left, as if startled. Had I irritated it? Without warning, it shot to the left and burst through the window of a nearby house. Glass went flying, and the electrical orb was gone.

I was going to turn around to urge Darrel to run faster when I noticed there were more of these balls of lightning on the street. Five or six of them hovered around the electrocuted light pole like bloated fireflies, and it suddenly stank of sulphur.

Behind me, I heard Darrel drop his wife's body to the ground. He fell to his knees beside her, and it was clear he didn't have the strength to carry her anymore. I ran back and tried to reason with him.

"Darrel, let's get out of here! Follow me!"

He looked at his wife's body with what I interpreted to be a complete inability to compute the idea that she was dead—completely dead—and that Jenna was now only a corpse.

"I can't leave her, I can't—"

"You have to! We'll come back for her!"

He reached his hand toward the body and bellowed miserably, but I was able to pull him away and get him moving. We ran alongside each other and tried to catch up to Jesse and my family. I noticed two of the floating lightning balls speed away like rockets and penetrate the side of a house. The balls seemed to go right through the wall without damaging the exterior at all.

I didn't take the time to look any longer or think about it. Car alarms still wailed from every direction, and surprisingly, I hadn't heard much more in the way of emergency vehicles. As I neared the front door of my home, I saw two people running toward me from the opposite direction and I recognized them. It was Samantha and Marsha. Marsha more or less waddled behind Samantha, who was well ahead of her.

Later, I learned that both of them happened to be walking toward the Second Street Bridge and Belmont Shore. Samantha was going to her yoga instructor's get-together on Bayshore Drive, and Marsha was going to meet her aunt at Greta's Kitchen for a late lunch. They hadn't been walking together. From my observations, they had never really gotten along that well and probably wouldn't have chosen to walk together even if they had the chance.

Jesse and my family had already gone inside when Darrel and I got to my house and saw both women running toward us. There were other people behind them, and they all darted into different homes and turned down different streets.

I waved to get their attention, but I was pretty sure they had already seen me. What else had happened? Had there been another shooting on the other side of the island? Maybe it wasn't just Drake. Maybe this really was an act of terrorism, and the entire island was under attack.

"The bridge! The bridge!" Samantha yelled as she ran toward me.

I ushered Darrel inside my house, but I remained out front as the two women approached. They ran past Marsha's home and right up to me.

"The bridge," Samantha said, almost completely out of breath. She was gasping for air. Marsha was slower and still a few houses away.

"What happened?"

"The bridge. The lightning took it out. Destroyed it."

"The lightning?"

"The whole bridge is gone. Nobody can get across."

"Lightning took out a bridge? What?" I didn't completely believe it.

I remembered the colossal bolts of lightning that had struck the east and west sides of the island. If somehow the lightning had taken out all three bridges, it would make sense as to why I hadn't heard more sirens. How would the fire trucks, paramedics, and police officers get across? They would have to send in support by air, or emergency teams would have to swim across the bay to get to us. But the very idea of a lightning bolt taking out a bridge and stranding us made me more confident that what we were witnessing was not just a freak accident of nature but a very planned and very calculated attack of some kind.

"What do we do?" Samantha asked, terrified. Marsha, huffing and puffing with hands on her hips, finally caught up. Her mouth was a big O on her pale, doughy face, desperately trying to take in oxygen.

"Come inside, both of you. We stay together."

It didn't take much to convince them. They followed me, and once inside, I felt like I had stepped into a trauma ward. Darrel had fallen to his knees and was curled in a fetal position. I couldn't even imagine the pain and loss he was feeling. Toby was completely freaking out and clinging onto my wife, and she was clinging onto him; they held each other so tightly and so violently, an outsider might have had difficulty discerning who was comforting who. The child that Owen had rescued had finally burst into hysterical screaming, and my son, who hadn't had any experience holding another child since his little brother was born, tried unsuccessfully to comfort her.

Marsha and Samantha joined in the hysteria; I wondered what exactly they had witnessed when they saw lightning take out the bridge. Perhaps they had seen people die and cars go down with it. The expressions on their bewildered, terrified faces suggested a morbid tale.

Jesse alone seemed unfazed by the turmoil. He walked across our living room, pulled back the curtains, and gazed at the electrical storm all around us. As if it were in labor, the sky's electrical contractions seemed to be happening closer together, and now it seemed the sky was constantly bleached with bright light and interrupted only by brief moments of darkness. Jesse, still holding the gun, stroked his long, grizzly beard and looked up at the celestial phenomenon like a hunter trying to find a weakness in his prey.

For many minutes, we wept in that room inconsolably. It was a house of mourning, a house of confusion. For the first time, I realized we were all drenched from the rain. Nobody had any idea what to say.

"He killed my wife, he killed her, he killed her," Darrel blabbered, rocking back and forth on the ground.

"I should call the police," I said. I was shaking all over.

"I wouldn't be too concerned about that," Jesse said. "I'm pretty sure they know something's going on here. Turn on the television. See what the news says. And make sure everything's locked. That psychopath is still out there."

"Right," I said. "Owen, make sure everything's locked."

"The front door?" he asked.

"Everything!" I snapped.

With the crying toddler in his arms, he left the room and began to batten down the house.

"Do you have guns here?" Jesse asked. He turned away from the window, and he looked all business.

"Guns?" I asked.

"Yeah, guns. That guy's out there. And there could be more of them. We need protection. I only got a few bullets left in this thing."

"No, no guns."

He nodded, taking it in.

I've never owned a gun. To be honest, they scare me. That

much power in my hands just doesn't feel right. I've only been to a shooting range a few times in my life, and that was because of research for my writing. I wanted to explain what it was like to shoot a firearm with some level of accuracy, but even then, I wasn't very fond of it. Plain and simple, guns just make me nervous.

"No weapons of any kind? Nothing we can use?" he asked again.

"A baseball bat, maybe."

"Then it'll have to do."

Talk of weapons and guns didn't fall too easily on the ears of the others in the room. Marsha started completely freaking out and hyperventilating, and my wife and Samantha both had to calm her down.

"Guns? What do you mean we need more guns?" Marsha asked. "You mean there are more of them? We're being attacked, we're being attacked! Someone's attacking us. And they killed his wife. They killed Darrel's wife!"

"Drake shot her," my wife explained.

"Drake?" Marsha said, hand over her heart. Her mouth became a big O again, this time much larger than before. She started to fan herself with her floppy, pudgy hand, and her eyes rolled back in their sockets. She lost her balance, and my wife and Samantha both helped her not take too hard a fall as she passed out and collapsed onto the couch.

Toby started screaming again and grabbed onto my wife.

"What happened to her? Did she die, Mom? Is she dead?"

"No, she's not dead," my wife said. He jumped back into her arms. "She's scared, honey. We're all scared."

I fumbled for a remote control to get the television on. Maybe Jesse was right. Maybe the news would give us some indication as to what was really happening and when we could expect help to arrive. I turned it on and began flipping through stations, but the signal was terrible. We had satellite cable, and the screen was an incomprehensible blur of contorted colors and images.

Beside me, Jesse tried to call his son. He said his son was probably fine because he'd left Naples to go into Belmont Shore, but he wanted to be sure. But the call wouldn't even go through.

"No bars," he said.

I had only been flipping through the stations for a minute when I heard the largest explosion of that night. Much later, I learned that another gigantic lightning bolt took out a transformer at a sub-station on the far west end of Naples Island and this explosion, larger than the others, shook our house. Through the window, we could see a plume of fire, and it reminded me of the stories of the Old Testament I had learned about at church as a kid. I wondered if the pillar of fire the Israelites followed into the Promised Land looked something like that.

The television flickered off, and so did the lights in my house. All houselights that I could see out the window went out instantly. Now, in between bursts of lightning, our house and the neighborhood were covered in total darkness.

Only the light of Jesse's cell phone illuminated my living room.

"He killed my wife, he killed my wife," Darrel blabbered, pounding his fists on the floor. I wondered if he was completely unaware of what was happening; maybe all reality had come to a halt the moment he saw his wife's head blown off.

"Mommy!" Toby screamed. My wife held onto him. Upstairs, I heard the little girl wailing.

"Go get that bat," Jesse said in a surprisingly calm, collected voice.

I nodded and left the room. There was so much lightning, the room was brighter than it was dark. I knew why Jesse wanted me to get a bat. There might be more Drakes out there. A whole platoon of them. They had taken out the bridges, had taken out the electricity, and now they were going to sweep through the neighborhoods and take us out one by one. Maybe they'd keep us prisoner. Maybe they'd kill us on the spot. Who knew?

I got as far as my office door before my stomach cramped up. All of the images from that evening hit me at once. I saw Jenna's face, blood and brain matter rolling down her nose and into her crooked mouth. I saw the bodies of those poor people lying on the grass beneath the lightning, bloodied and lifeless.

Then I remembered. I hadn't had time to fully process it before; maybe a part of my brain didn't want to. I had seen a pregnant woman shot. Hadn't I? The last thing I saw her do was fall to her knees and take hold of her belly just before bullets ripped through her back. She fell onto her side, holding her belly as the maroon puddle she lay in enveloped her completely. A little boy had been shot too. I remembered his face. Would I ever be able to forget it? I wondered how many years of my life those images would haunt me.

And, of course, there was Hot-rodder. Drake had taken him. And now he was somewhere on this island, keeping him hostage. Or maybe it was worse. If he'd worked his way through a crowd like that and killed indiscriminately, maybe Hot-rodder was already dead.

As I thought of Hot-rodder, I remembered my brother. I remembered the last time I saw him.

"Don't let go," he'd said to me, and I'd promised him. "Don't let go."

The bat would be upstairs. I remembered my son's bravery that night and knew that I had to muster the same within myself. My wife needed me. My kids needed me. Maybe others would too. Whatever tragedy had struck had not yet fully played out. I had to be brave for my family.

I began to go up the stairs to get the bat, but my stomach

twisted again. It almost took me down. I found the office bath-room and fell to my knees. I grabbed onto both sides of the porcelain toilet, leaned forward, and vomited three times as flashes of lightning filled the room. I hadn't spent that much time vomiting in front of the toilet since I was in college.

"Be brave," I told myself, and my voice echoed into the toilet bowl. "Be very brave."

When I felt ready, I left the bathroom and headed up the stairs again, and my son was coming down. He held the toddler in one arm and the bat in his other hand.

"Got the bat, Dad. Everything's locked."

"Good, take it to the living room."

He left, and I went back into the bathroom, fell on my knees, and began to dry heave the little that was left in my system.

Bravery, it seemed, would have to wait.

Chapter Eighteen

I suppose everyone handles storms differently, whether it is an actual storm like the one that hit us that summer on Naples Island, or a storm of an entirely different nature. One man may wake up to find his car stolen and very quietly return inside, calmly call the police, and chalk it up to the fact that bad things happen in this world. Another might go ballistic and have a complete breakdown right there in the street. One woman might sit across the desk from a doctor and take the unwanted news in stoic silence and genuine confidence that she has a winnable battle before her. Another woman might collapse into tears right there in the doctor's office as her entire world is ripped out from under her.

There's a famous quote about this. Something like, *Most of life is about the way you respond to the things that happen to you, not about what actually happens.* I suppose if you've lived long enough, you recognize that to be true. It seems that the older I get, the more I realize it. Whether you're living in the ritzy neighborhoods of Naples Island or grinding out a living and spending your nights in a rundown apartment on the wrong side of the tracks, most functional people are, in the end, dealing with the same kinds of things. Whether it's keeping our kids from making the same idiot mistakes we've made, dealing with family drama, or keeping our marriages and significant relationships afloat amongst the turbulent waves of an ADHD society, the stages may change but the scripts sure stay the same.

The big difference maker, it seems, is all in the response. I haven't met a successful man that didn't experience as much failure as the most unsuccessful people I've known in my life. But there's a big difference. Those who ended up successful had the ability to get back on their feet, dust themselves off, and endure more of the same setbacks for a longer time than the other guys. Sometimes it seems maybe that's the real difference for those who have "made it" in this world. They can take defeat. They don't see it as the end. I think there are people out there who just see it as one step closer to reaching their ultimate goal.

I can't say that I'm like them, and maybe that's because I'm somewhat of an anomaly. It didn't take me long to sell my first novel, and it didn't take long for it to become a bestseller. Whenever I'm speaking to other writers about the patience it takes to be an author and the longsuffering the industry requires, I have to admit that I often feel like a phony. Sure, I received twenty-two rejection letters from agents for my first novel, but that's pretty lightweight in this field. I have to remind myself that I'm talking to people who may have written several novels and received hundreds of rejections for each of them. Comparing my situation to theirs is like a kindergartner comparing his playground booboos to a Vietnam vet's battle scars.

And it does make me feel a little disingenuous. I sometimes wonder if I had written several books and nobody had shown any interest in any of them, would I have stayed the course? I think the answers is no. I've learned to take the bad reviews—and they come in droves—but to painstakingly endure at something for years on end without any financial reward or acknowledgement would be difficult, to say the least. Would I still write? Most certainly. I can't help that. After my brother died, that became second nature to me. But after years of writing without any publishing victories, I'm pretty sure I would have given up my aspirations for financial success and reserved it solely for my private closet rather than the public forum.

They say that about writers. We can't help but write, and I agree with that. It's a form of self-therapy. A lot of people think writers are intellectual people compelled to communicate their ideas about life and humanity because they've been given a double serving of imagination and insight, and I suppose there's some truth in that. But my experience has taught me it's usually something far simpler. Most of us are just people sitting at a desk in the early hours of morning trying to deal with the junk in our heads. We work out our issues through our monsters and our villains and, if we do it well enough, we get paid for it. Not a bad gig.

I think that storm brought out everyone's inner villains and demons, and it was all in the way people responded to it. Lots of people held it together and remained indoors as the police had asked. I found out later that there were only three active officers on Naples at the time of the mass killing: two bicycle cops who were patrolling up and down Second Street and one Senior Lead Officer (SLO), Deborah Blazer, who was a long-standing officer with community affairs on Naples. There had been one other officer in Naples just before the shooting, but he had been called to a domestic dispute in Belmont Shore only minutes before the lightning trapped us on the island.

Late on that first evening of our entrapment, when the lightning and thunder had settled down, we heard Deborah Blazer's voice on the P-A of her squad car as she drove up and down Second Street. I didn't know who she was then, but her instructions were simple: "Please remain indoors until advised otherwise. All residents of Naples Island, please be advised. Remain indoors until advised otherwise. The lightning is killing anybody who sets foot in the water. All three bridges have been destroyed. Please remain indoors."

It didn't take much to convince me. Stepping outdoors into the freakish storm with a berserk gunman running around didn't sound very enticing, and I think most of the residents in Naples Island felt the same as I did.

I was able to put the following records together of some of the early tragedies that befell some residents. These are just a couple of examples. Undoubtedly, there are many more.

Ben and Julie had rented a kayak on Bayshore Drive and paddled over to Naples Island for a leisurely voyage through the canals. As the island was only a couple hundred yards across the water of the bay, they were one of many to spend their Fourth of July holiday this way. They had paddled through the canals a couple times, gawking at the luxurious waterfront homes they one day wished to own, when they decided it was about time to head back and turn in their rental. The storm clouds had rolled in with freakish haste, and they worried they'd get caught in rain.

"One day!" Ben said, pointing at one of the great manors. "Just think, Julie, one day we'll live in one!"

"You better make sure you pass that bar exam then, big boy."

They were young. Ben was in his last year of law school at UCLA, and Julie, his fiancée, had finished her teaching certification and was only a couple months away from officially beginning her career as a first grade teacher. To them, the future was full of rainbows and possibilities.

One witness, Jose Rivas, who saw them from the top of his condo building on Naples Island, said they were kissing each other when the lightning bolt struck them. It came out of nowhere, just as the others had, as the sounds of automatic gunfire erupted on the island. Jose Rivas, who happened to be eyeing them through his binoculars, watched as the lightning hit them. After it struck, they slid lifelessly off the kayak and into the water.

They weren't alone. Jose watched as bolts of lightning purposefully took out two other kayaks, three boats, and even a swimmer who had been about halfway between the bay and Naples Island. One thing was clear, and even Jose, a guy using binoculars to scope out the bikini-clad women along the bay from the private confines of his condo, had enough sense to understand it. The lightning went for anyone or anything that seemed to be leaving or going to the island.

It put a whole new meaning to the term *electrical fence*, but as it became clear to anyone watching, that was exactly what it was. He even saw lightning take out the Second Street Bridge that led into Belmont Shore. People and cars went down with it, and not long after, police cars, paramedics, and fire trucks waited on the other side of the water.

Jose even thought he saw some of the first responders try to make their way across via swimming and rafts, but they, too, ran into that electric fence. As bits of wreckage and bodies floated lifelessly in the center of the bay, it became clear that nobody was going to get onto Naples Island anytime soon.

And nobody was going to get out.

One man's death was terribly tragic. He kept a journal, and, after his uncle allowed me the opportunity to read through it, I was able to put the pieces together. They were neighbors of ours, just one block over.

Robert Pierson was a high-functioning forty-eight-year-old paranoid schizophrenic who lived with his uncle . He worked as an actuary for a small vitamin company in Carson, and when taking his medication, Olanzapine, and attending his weekly therapy, the voices were kept at bay. They were never completely gone, but they were manageable.

People who knew Robert and worked with him said he seemed fairly normal, but if you held a long enough conversation with him, there was something slightly "off." Most said it had to do with his unawareness of personal space. He leaned in a bit too close, stood a little too close, and many felt like they had to slightly move back when engaged in a discussion with him. But by and large, most people chalked up Robert Pierson as being just a bit quirky and never would have guessed that he had long ago been diagnosed as a schizophrenic.

If they had seen him off his meds, it would have been another story entirely.

Robert had front row seats in the park when the mass killing took place. I remember seeing him there. Like others, he ran away when the crazy guy tore through the crowd with his AK-47. Robert ran back to his home as the sky turned dark and weird lightning started to fork down from the swirling clouds overhead. Once inside, I imagine that he bolted all of the doors, closed all of the windows, and decided to wait it out. Something bizarre was going on outside.

Based on the journal, he had been off his meds for days; they kept disappearing. It didn't make any sense, because he knew they should have been there in his bathroom. He had gone a couple days without his meds a few times over the years and usually things were just fine until day three, when the voices became a little louder and began to break through. He was angry when he realized he was trapped inside his house and cursed himself for not replenishing his supply when the last batch went missing.

He even thought of breaking into the pharmacy a couple blocks away. He was pretty sure everyone else on the island was hiding out in their homes to escape the crazy gunman and the bizarre storm. It would probably be locked. He could break into the store, get his meds, and come back to the house.

But by July 6th, two days later, Robert had a different idea. The voices had come back with a vengeance, and they were telling him one thing: *You don't need the meds. They're trying to control you, Robert. The storm is trying to control you. You must fight it.*

It made perfect sense. He was convinced of it. They were all trying to control him, and the crazy gunman may have been a rebel, resisting the control. He was doing a good thing. He was cleansing the island of those who were trying to keep everyone under control. Maybe the gunman or someone working with him had been sneaking into his house and stealing the meds in an effort to release him from the control, so he could be truly free, and so he could join them.

He tried to resist the voices for a while. He even put on his headphones and walked around his house, listening to loud music, in an effort to drown them out, but they just made too much sense.

The voices assaulted him: *You never needed any meds. It was all a lie. All a way to control you, just like this storm. They want you quiet and sedated, and you need to fight back. They have a chip in your brain, Robert. They're controlling you with it. You must take it out. Take it out and you'll be free. When you take it out, you'll see what these people really are. They're monsters, Robert. That's what that gunman—that rebel—was able to really see. They're all monsters.*

"I must take it out," he said the evening of July 6th. He tore off his earphones and took in the voices.

He knew what he had to do. He ran all five blocks through the lightning. The rain was only a slight drizzle, but the lightning was still flashing up in the clouds. It wasn't striking things on the island as frequently as it did at first; for now, most of the lightning was confined to the clouds themselves. Cloud-to-cloud lightning, it was called. Robert could still remember learning that back in high school, right around the time the voices started.

When he reached the park, it looked like the aftermath of a small battlefield. The wet, recumbent bodies lay on the ground like forgotten soldiers. Someone had ventured out into the storm to cover them with blankets, but the winds had blown all but two of them off.

Robert stopped beside the body of the fallen officer and looked for his gun. He had seen him fall while reaching for it, but after searching the grass around his body, Robert was sure someone else must have claimed it. Maybe another officer had come back to take it, or maybe it was whatever Good Samaritan had come out to cover the corpses with the blankets.

His plan had been to find the officer's gun and use it to open his brain and take out the microchip they had planted. The voices were getting louder, more vehement, and time was of the essence. He wouldn't have it anymore.

He raced back to his home and thought he saw a couple people wandering through the streets. Maybe they were the Controllers; maybe they were the ones who controlled the storm and were keeping him trapped.

If there's no guns, there's other things you can use, the voices suggested. Yes, they were trying to help. They wanted him to be free.

I didn't need to read the journal to figure out the ending. Unfortunately, it was all to clear.

Robert went straight into the garage and lit a candle, which he placed on one of the workbenches; then he found the Craftsman nail gun. It would have to do.

He loaded it, clicked in the charged battery, and cradled it in his lap while contemplating the freedom he would soon feel. He would open his skull with the nail gun and destroy the microchip. Then they would no longer control him.

The voices oppressed him: *Now is the time, Robert. Now is the time. Take out the microchip, and they won't control you . . .*

"Now is the time," he whispered and held the nail gun to his head.

He looked at the long row of tools along the garage wall, the bikini calendar right beside the hammers, and the little refrigerator in the corner of the room where his uncle liked to keep his beer.

"You won't control me anymore," was probably the last thing he said, as he pressed down on the trigger.

Later that day, a neighbor, scouting the block to see if anyone needed assistance, supposedly saw the garage door ajar. When he walked in, the neighbor saw the body of Robert Pierson lying on the ground.

A nail gun was at his side.

It would be inaccurate to mention only the grave tragedies that struck Naples. While some neighbors didn't trust each other much during those first couple days, many neighbors banded together.

While at first many were afraid to step outdoors, there were plenty who were brave enough to venture across the street or down a few houses to offer assistance. People took food and medicine to neighbors in need, and according to one account, a group of neighbors built a fire pit in the backyard of one of their homes, rounded up all their beers and handguns, and sat around the fire for a couple nights polishing off the beers and talking about how they would put together a team to hunt down the crazy killer. But they never put together that team; when the beers ran out, it seemed their courage did as well.

By July 7th—the day after Robert Pierson ended his life with a nail gun—I think most residents were aware of a couple things:

First, help wasn't coming. All three bridges had been taken out by lightning, and even though a mediocre swimmer could have swam to the mainland in a matter of minutes, the lightning forbade it; it struck anyone in the water going to or from the island. The young engaged couple were the first of many who fried in those waters.

Large emergency teams gathered across from the island at all three of the entry points but couldn't find a way to get across. The first of the rescue teams were killed instantly by lightning as they tried to cross the water, and even later, once the governor declared a State of Emergency and called out the National Guard, they could do no better. The first two copters they sent in were struck by lightning before they reached the island. One of the pilots was fortunate and was able to make an emergency landing in Belmont Shore, but the other pilot, whose tail had been taken off by a massive bolt, spun around in the sky like a bewildered hornet and crashed into a home.

Later, I learned the government tried other things as well. They put divers in the water during one of the breaks in the storm, when the lightning had subsided, but just as the divers made it about halfway across, lightning forked down through the water and turned them into electrified fish. Some of the residents tried to leave the island too. I've learned that sometimes the affluent feel just as entitled as those who are impoverished, and some residents just didn't feel like they "deserved" to be stranded on that island in the midst of the freakish storm. They climbed into their boats and thought they could outwit the storm. Perhaps in some cases, they genuinely didn't know any better, but the result was always the same: none of those boats made it across.

We were encouraged to know there was some police presence on the island—though later I discovered it was much smaller than I had hoped. The one active police vehicle drove up and down Second Street several times a day with Deborah Blazer, the SLO, always speaking that same message through her P-A: "All residents of Naples Island, this is the Long Beach Police Department. Outside authorities are working hard to make entrance to the island. Remain indoors. Do not leave your homes. Do not attempt to leave the island. The lightning is destroying anything attempting to get onto or get off of Naples."

Her words rarely changed. Apart from that, we had little information. None of our phones worked, so we couldn't dial out. We had no electricity, no web connectivity on our laptops, no cellular reception, and we couldn't get any signal on our radios. I spent those first few days coming to terms with how technologically dependent I had become in my life; it seemed completely backwards to go hours, let alone days, without the ability to telephone or text someone or look something up online. I was one of those typically over-stimulated-and-addicted-to-his-toys Americans. Guilty as charged.

But we learned something else those first few days, and by the evening of July 7th, it became more apparent. Apart from the police, a second authority was emerging. Several times a day, we heard people running down the streets, and they seemed to be just average citizens. They were armed, which was of some concern. One of the men, a little skinny guy who looked like a marathon runner, was carrying a rifle as he passed by. A couple others—business men from the looks of them—

were also carrying rifles as they trotted by. As they ran down the street, they yelled the same message.

"Klutch offers his protection," they cried. "The big brick house by the fountain. He knows what this is! Klutch offers his protection! And weapons! Join us! Klutch offers his protection! He knows what this is!"

The first time I heard the men yelling this as they ran past my home, Jesse and I looked at each other in complete stupefaction.

"Klutch?" I said, turning to Jesse. "The crazy biker guy who thought you took his knife?"

Jesse scratched his beard and nodded.

It was difficult to believe.

"Looks like this here storm just got more interesting," he said. "Much more interesting."

Chapter Nineteen

On the morning of July eighth, four days after the mass killing by Drake, we were all becoming terribly frightened. Although we had not yet met the officer in the police car that patrolled up and down Second Street, we knew there was no help coming anytime soon and she, being stuck on Naples Island, was probably doing her best to keep the citizens at peace.

When we looked out the windows, the dark storm clouds still swirled overhead, and from my perspective at least, they seemed to be lower than even before. Perhaps the storm was descending? I wasn't sure. Less lightning struck buildings and objects on the ground by July 8th. Although the activity didn't completely cease, every few hours a loud thunderclap rattled my home. We assumed those were due to some sucker trying to make his way onto or off of the island. But by and large, most of the lightning now was cloud-to–cloud, and when I looked up, the constant electrical activity in the clouds looked sort of like a giant plasma globe.

We used candles and the lanterns in my garage to see by and made quick trips to Marsha's next door to stock up on more food and supplies. We had seen enough people running down the street to realize the lightning wouldn't indiscriminately strike anyone moving outside; it focused on people near the water. Every evening the storm intensified, and by July 8th, I wondered how bad the evening storms would become. It was a frightening thought.

Marsha and Samantha did alright coping but quarreled too much. Marsha went into episodes of paranoia, questioning what was happening and if this was God's judgment, and Samantha, exasperated, often snapped back that she needed to shut up and stop complaining because it wasn't going to help anyone. Sometimes it reminded me of the popular kid at school trying to get along with the nerd; it was annoying, to say the least, and I wondered when, if ever, the gravity of the situation might pull them together rather than push them apart.

My wife was occupied mostly with Toby and taking care of the little girl who said her name was Mia. The two-year-old probably fared better than any of us. Maybe ignorance is bliss. My wife brought out the toys and Legos from Toby's bedroom. Her strategy worked well; it took the kids' eyes off themselves, and in the end, it kept my wife sane.

Even though it was clear that we had absolutely no cell reception, Owen tried constantly for the first couple days to text his girlfriend, Candice. He was completely distraught over her and worried about what had happened to her, and I think he had a hard time focusing on anything else during those first days.

My neighbor, Darrel, was a complete mess. There are hardly words to describe him. He spent most of his time alone in our guest bedroom, sobbing, crying, wailing, and throwing things. He would come back to join the rest of us for brief moments of clarity. He would smile and talk positively about how we were going to get out of this and how everyone was going to be just fine, and then, almost without any signal for transition, he would descend back into a state of despair. Hour to hour, I had no idea which Darrel I was with. Sometimes he'd look right through me and mumble to himself and scratch his nails through his thinning hair. He was completely disheveled. I could often spot snot dripping from his nose and drool running out of his mouth. Maybe he just didn't care. Maybe it was due to all of his weeping, but he looked like a man who needed some serious help. I grieved for him deeply.

Jesse seemed unfazed, and I was glad to have him there. He didn't fall into emotional hysteria and kept a level head, and I guess I did pretty much the same. Maybe my wife was right about me. Maybe I am pretty good in moments of crisis.

Early afternoon on July 8th, Jesse and I were sitting in my office, drinking beer. We'd put some outside the night before to keep cold because the fridge had long since died.

"We need to get those weapons," Jesse said, sipping a Crescent Moon beer. He'd complained about it when I first offered it and insisted that Crescent Moon was a lady's drink, but he went on drinking it anyway.

He was referring to the weapons under the bridge. I'd looked back over the map in the spiral notebook Drake had dropped. It was clear that it was his map for his route that night, and I was pretty convinced that the big B he referred to on his map was the bridge I'd seen him under one night. He'd stashed weapons. He must have. Didn't many mass murderers do that sort of thing? Shoot up a bunch of innocents and then retreat to an arsenal nest? Isn't that what those evil kids did at Columbine?

"We really need to get those weapons," Jesse repeated.

"You really think so?"

"Yep," he said. "People start running out of food, people start getting more afraid, and they'll start turning on each other. And you have no idea what that guy Klutch is up to. We need protection. One handgun isn't doing it."

"That means we need to go back out there, down a ways," I said.

"He's still out there."

"That's a risk we're gonna have to take. Plus, I'd be willing to bet he isn't out there anymore. Guys that go crazy like that almost always kill themselves after. I'm sure he's already dead somewhere with a bullet in his head. I'd put my money on that one."

I knew that Jesse was trying to be helpful, but my thoughts were still on Hot-rodder. If Drake had killed himself, then what had become of Hot-rodder? It made me sick to even think about it, and deep inside myself, I was grappling with major guilt. I'd had the spiral notebook with the map in it, and if I'd had enough sense to look at it closely and think about it, maybe I could have prevented the whole thing. Maybe Hot-rodder would be sitting inside with us and maybe all of those dead people wouldn't be lying there in the park.

Complete nausea swept over me when I even thought about it.

"We could go into that crazy guy's house too. It's right across from you. Might have guns there too that we could use."

"I don't know," I said. "He could be in there."

"Probably would have seen or heard something, don't you think? Only one in there is maybe his dad, and he's dying. Isn't that what you told me?"

"That's what I've heard."

"We could always head there on the way back from the bridge. Look for more."

"I don't think so," I said and Jesse, nodding, set down his beer and stood up.

"I'll meet you by the front door. Let's get what we can before someone else gets those guns."

I nodded.

"And you need to get yourself some real beer," Jesse said and walked out of the room.

Just as he left, Owen walked in. He looked nervous, and he had his hands stuffed into his back pockets. I offered for him to sit down, but he didn't. He just stood there acting squeamish. I recognized his posture immediately; this was usually his demeanor before asking a difficult question involving girls, money, or anything that would most likely warrant a *no* for an answer. I took another sip of my Crescent Moon and listened.

"Dad, I want to go look for Candice."

I didn't know how to respond to this at first, so I just remained quiet.

"I want to go look for Candice," he said again. It sounded more like a statement than a question, and I didn't like that.

"What do you mean, you want to go look for Candice? You don't even know where she is."

"That's why I need to go look for her. She was by the fountain, and you yourself said that guy Klutch was taking people in by the fountain. I bet she's there. I just want to go and see her and make sure she's okay."

"Owen, you don't know if she's there," I reasoned with him. "There's a thousand places she could have gone by now and we can't take that chance. Plus, Jesse and I are going to do a quick errand to get something we need. I need you to stay here with the women and kids, okay. I need you here."

At first, I thought he had actually listened to me. I was about to get up and throw away my beer bottle, when he did something that unnerved me; he raised his voice. Almost standing over me, I felt like I was suddenly the child and he was the parent.

"Dad, you don't understand, I need to go!"

"No, you're not going," I said calmly and stood. I hated that he was nearly two inches taller than me.

"Dad, Candice might be in danger. I've sat here for days, and now I think I—"

"You're not going," I said again. "I don't care. How old is she? Sixteen? How long have you known each other? Two months maybe? Are you joking me? This is your family here."

"You and mom were boyfriend and girlfriend when you were sixteen, Dad."

"That's different."

He wrinkled his nose in disgust. "What do you mean that's different? How is it different?"

"Because that was me and your mom," I said.

He wrinkled his nose in disgust again. "You're not making sense."

"I don't have to make sense. I'm your dad. You're staying here."

My wife, hearing us bicker, walked into the office to see what was the matter.

"Is everything okay?" she asked, and Owen, knowing his defeat, slumped his shoulders and began to head toward the door. Those two inches of height didn't compensate for the decades of living I had beyond his own and my position as a father, but it was clear, storm or no storm, that all of that was changing. He had his own ideas, and I think he wanted me to treat him almost as an equal. But I just wasn't ready. Not by a long shot.

"Dad's just not listening to me," he said and walked out of the room.

I leaned back in my leather chair, sighed, and my wife sat in my lap and kissed me. She rubbed her fingertips along my eyebrows, smiled, and kissed me again on the forehead this time.

"How are the troops holding up?" I asked.

"Okay. The kids are doing well. I got them playing Legos."

"Legos, huh?"

"Yeah," she said. "You know, that little girl Mia is so cute. I forgot how cute they are that young. Almost makes me think that, maybe when this is all over, what it'd be like to—"

"Have another?" I finished for her.

She nodded.

"I think this storm has messed up your thinking. We're getting too old. How's everyone else?"

"Marsha and Samantha are driving me crazy," she said, kissing me delicately on the forehead. "They were just bickering about what to make for lunch. Samantha's complaining that she hasn't had 'real' food in days, and Marsha thinks she isn't grateful enough. That kind of thing."

"And Darrel?"

"The usual. He's in the guest room now. I'm pretty worried about him."

"Yeah, me too. Listen, we're gonna make a run to the bridge for the weapons like we were talking about earlier. It'll be quick. Hopefully they're there, and we'll be right back."

"Okay." She nodded. We'd already discussed it earlier, and the idea had settled in with her. "But how are you doing with the kidnapped boy?"

"Hot-rodder?" I asked.

She nodded.

We'd had a couple conversations about him and the guilt I'd carried like an anchor for the last several days. My wife insisted, like the others, that it wasn't my fault and that I couldn't have possibly predicted what the map was and what Drake was going to do. But the encouragement didn't help much. Guilt, I learned during that storm, is a heavy burden for a soul to carry around.

"He's not your brother, Eddie," she said softly in my ear. "You don't have to save him. It won't bring him back."

"I know," I said, but I didn't completely believe her.

No matter how hard I tried, I couldn't stop thinking about my kid brother, Alan.

He was only ten years old when he died, and I was twelve. My parents took us on a trip down to the Kern River in California for white water rafting. It was the first time we'd done a trip like that, and when I think back to those memories, it is the last I can remember of my mom and dad being happy together. I remember them laughing, and I terribly miss that sound. I never heard it after our trip on the Kern, and sometimes when I daydream and wonder what it would be like to have anything I want in this world, I think my parents' laughter is what I would ask for.

It was the afternoon of our first day, and my brother, Alan, and I were in one of the six rafts. My mom thought we should have gone in one of the oar boats carrying the food because we'd be safer in them, but we'd begged and begged, and our father eventually caved in and let us ride in the rafts with some of the older teenagers.

I don't remember the exact name of the rapid where the accident happened. A tree had fallen into the river, and the first boat in our troop didn't see it coming, couldn't get out of the way, and flipped over. The second boat did the same, and so did the other five boats behind it; like a chain of watery dominoes, we all went over.

It was complete pandemonium. I managed to climb back into my raft as everyone screamed and flailed through the water. Once I had climbed back into the raft, I heard Alan scream for me. He was still in the water and reaching for the raft. I leaned over and grabbed his hand, but I could feel something pulling him. Maybe it was an underwater current. Maybe his foot had caught on some of the vines and branches along the side of the river. I wasn't sure.

"Don't let go!" he screamed.

I can still remember his face. I had never seen anyone so

terrified. His face was ghostly white, his eyes wide and frightened, and he looked right at me.

His grip started to loosen, and even though I tried with all of my strength, I could hardly keep my grip. "I won't let go!" I cried. "I won't let go!"

"Don't let go!" he screamed, and then his hand slipped through mine like wet fish and he went under for good.

His body was found later the next day.

But I lost more than just my kid brother that day. I lost my parents' laughter. They were divorced within two years, and by the time I graduated from college, my mom had taken her life with sleeping pills and my dad, who became a roaring alcoholic in the years following Alan's death, developed lung cancer. All of it could be traced back to that day on the Kern River. That was when I learned that this world is one cruel villain and it'll take everything from you if given the chance.

I dove headfirst into writing. At first, it was just journaling my feelings; my therapist told me it was a good way to work through my thoughts. But it wasn't long before those turned into stories, and my wife has told me on more than one occasion that behind all those stories is a little boy trying to get his kid brother back. In every story I wrote, it seemed, there was a brother saving another brother from something terrible. The funny thing is that I didn't even see those things when I wrote the books; it took my wife to point it out.

I stayed in my office for a while and held my wife in the silence of the room, but knowing that Jesse was waiting at the front door for me, I decided to get going. I kissed her passionately, told her how much I loved her, and reminded her that this would be a real short trip. We'd go to the bridge, get the guns—if they were there—and come right back.

"Remember, he's not Alan. You don't have to prove it to yourself," she reminded me as I left the room.

"I know," I told her and headed to the front door.

Jesse was outside, and I was surprised to find him leaning against the wall of my house with his head down. With his chin touching his chest it looked like he'd nodded off while standing there.

"You asleep?" I asked.

He looked up at me immediately. "Asleep? Why do you think I'm asleep?"

"I don't know. You're leaning against the wall with your head down. Looks like you're sleeping."

"Nah," he said. "Just praying. We can use some praying."

"Praying?" I said. "Really?"

"Yeah, what's wrong with that?"

"Nothing, nothing at all. I just . . . I just didn't think you were the praying type, that's all."

He shook his head as if he'd heard this before. "Why do all of you Southern California folks think God fearing-men are pansies?" he said. "You ought to get out a little bit."

He took his revolver out from under his belt and led me into the street.

Chapter Twenty

There was little rain that afternoon. As I followed Jesse along the canal toward the bridge, I only felt a little drizzle coming down. I looked up at the sky and saw the dark and bloated clouds oscillating just above the island. There wasn't a single gap in them through which I could see blue skies; the only blue skies were beyond the island, where it appeared to be a beautiful summer day in July. The cloud-to-cloud lightning was still a constant flicker up there as well; at any given moment, there appeared to be a countless number of lightning bolts electrifying the cloud cover.

And the clouds still looked lower to me than they had days before. Significantly lower.

Jesse had brought a very long orange picker that he'd found in my garage; I didn't understand at first why he'd brought it, but then it made sense. Once we got under the bridge, we would need something to reach up and get the weapons with if Drake really had stashed them there.

As I ran behind Jesse, the storm was the least of my concerns. I couldn't get my mind off the reality that Drake might still be out here somewhere. Maybe Jesse was right;

maybe he'd committed suicide after the mass killing, but something in my gut assured me that he was still alive and he was still running around out here. It terrified me.

We reached the bridge quickly and found a small dinghy tied up alongside one of the docks. It was wedged in amongst the Duffies and cruisers. This was one of the many small bridges connecting the canals—not one of the main bridges leading off the island and onto the mainland.

"It's perfect," Jesse said, pointing, and he didn't even have to explain his idea.

We climbed into the dinghy. Jesse kept his firearm in his hand the whole time, alert and ready. I could find only one paddle lying amongst some ropes on the dock, and sitting in the back, I dipped the paddle into the water and pushed us forward the short distance to the bridge.

Once we were under the bridge, it was much darker than I would have imagined. Jesse, who had been wise and conserved the power on his phone when we all realized there was no reception whatsoever, used his flashlight app and probed the underside of the little bridge. There wasn't much of interest there. Just lots of concrete and some graffiti that, unlike the type you may have seen in some other areas of downtown Long Beach, was mostly benign. These were the marks of high school teams, friends, and lovers immortalizing their journey through Naples Island, not gang members claiming territory.

I kept the dinghy centered under the bridge while Jesse moved his spotlight along its underbelly, and we both saw it at the same time: a duffel bag wedged behind some piping. I was thrilled and horrified at the same time because, in a way, it made the mass killing that much more real. A wave of sickness washed over me when I saw it; a part of me wanted to lean over the side of the dinghy and hurl.

"There it is," Jesse said. I paddled closer. The bag was stashed close to the bridge's edge and was not difficult to reach.

It was a black bag and larger than the other ones I'd seen him with. Once I brought him close enough, Jesse stood up and used my orange picker to reach up and dislodge the duffel bag. He handed me his phone to keep the light on him so he could see what he was doing.

It freaked me out at first. If there were firearms in the bag —and it was hard to believe we'd find anything else in it—then would dislodging it make them accidentally fire? It would be completely ironic to think I had survived a mass killing only to die there, sitting in a little boat under a bridge. *Death by Duffel Bag* didn't seem a very noble epitaph for my tombstone.

Jesse poked and prodded the bag with the orange picker and was able to hook it and gently lower it into the dinghy. When it was down, he unzipped it, and sure enough, our suspicions were accurate. The bag held two rifles, a shotgun, handguns, knives, and ammo. None of the weapons were loaded.

It was sickening. What had Drake planned to do? Hide out after the killing in some back alley because someone might track him to his house? And then what? Come here, resupply, and do the same thing over again? It was disturbing to say the least. He must have made numerous trips to this place, unloading his supplies and transferring them to this one duffel bag. I don't know why he hadn't done it all at once. Was he even sane enough to know? Maybe he was stealing weapons from someone or changing his plan and how many weapons he thought he needed. Like a wicked bird, he'd returned again and again to build his dark nest.

Now that we had retrieved everything, I paddled back to the dock, and once the boat was tied up, we began to walk back to my house. Jesse stopped for a moment and took the twelve-gauge shotgun out of the duffel bag. He loaded it, showed me how the safety worked, and handed it to me. It was a strange feeling. I'd never fired a shotgun, only handguns, and those had been at a shooting range.

"It's got a shoulder pad that will keep your shoulder from getting all purple and bruised," Jesse said, carrying the duffel bag. "But hopefully you don't have to shoot it that much, or at all. And remember, it sprays. You're gonna hit everything in front of you, so be careful if you do have to shoot."

"Okay," I said weakly.

We hadn't walked far when we both looked across the canal at Drake's house. Almost instinctually, we both came to a stop. We didn't have to say anything because we both knew what the other was thinking. If these guns were under the bridge, then there could easily be more weapons in that house, and there might be more clues as to where Drake had taken Hot-rodder. It was pretty obvious that Hot-rodder's kidnapping hadn't been premeditated, but maybe there would be more notebooks in that house with crudely sketched maps of hideouts. He could easily be hiding out in one of those. We were sure he wasn't in the house; we'd kept an eye on it for days and hadn't seen anything. No candles or flashlights. Nothing.

"It might be worth it," Jesse said.

"I know."

When he said that, I'm pretty sure he was talking about the weapons, but honestly, all I could think about was Hot-rodder. If there was anything in that house that might offer some kind of clue as to where he was, how could I live with myself if I didn't at least make the effort? I owed him at least that. I'd felt one child's hand slip through my own as it was pulled into the depths of death, and I wasn't going to let another—not when I had a chance to do something about it. And so much of it was my fault. I'd seen the notebook with the map and should have put it together. I should have called the police. Jenna would be alive, Hot-rodder would be indoors with his parents, and I'd have a burden the size of Texas lifted off my shoulders.

So in the end, it was guilt that led me to Drake's house.

"Let's do it," I said.

Jesse didn't say a word, but nodded knowingly.

My wife probably wouldn't understand and would most likely be irate when we returned home. I'd promised, hadn't I? I'd told her that I would go straight to the bridge, get the weapons, and come right back.

But she would have to understand—at least, I *hoped* she would.

Chapter Twenty-One

A thought seized me as I climbed through the bathroom window of Drake's three-story Victorian home: What if we were wrong? What if Drake had come back and had been holed up here ever since the afternoon of the killing? We hadn't seen any sign of life or movement, but it wasn't like Drake was going to advertise the fact that he was hiding out here.

After I slid through, Jesse handed me the shotgun. He had gone in first, and I'd handed him his gun and my shotgun through the open window; we had stashed the duffel bag in the bushes along the perimeter of the house until we were done with our search.

I realized, as I took the weapon into my hands, that I was shaking all over; my whole body was trembling. The fear I'd felt in going outdoors and searching the underside of the bridge for weapons was absolutely nothing compared to this; this was downright terrible.

"You okay?" Jesse asked in a hoarse whisper. He probably saw that I wasn't doing well.

"What if he's here?"

It felt good to vocalize my fear, even if it was a hardly audible whisper.

"Take it off safety," Jesse whispered, pointing to my gun. "Just in case."

Not encouraging words. I looked for the pin along the gun and couldn't find it. Flustered as well as overcome with trepidation, I couldn't even remember if it was on safety or if it was off. How was I supposed to know? Jesse, noting my confusion, took it off for me.

"It's hot," he whispered again. "Watch where you point it. And keep your finger off the trigger."

"Got it." Sweat dripped into my eyes and stung.

Jesse slowly opened the bathroom door and looked into the living room. Things were dark with all the cloud cover, and it was hard to see. It was eerily quiet, which was mostly a good sign. Chances were that Drake wasn't here.

Jesse looked across the dining room and into a long galley kitchen, gazed left into a large, vacant sitting room, and— seeing nothing and hearing nothing—stepped forward into the room and waved for me to follow. The oak floors creaked loudly beneath the weight of his work boots, and Jesse stopped instantly the moment the sound reverberated through the house. We both stopped, anticipating some kind of flustered response somewhere in the house, but there was nothing. This was a good sign. I felt some of the tension dissipate throughout my body.

There was a rank odor. We weren't sure, at that point, what it was.

The living room was beautiful yet somewhat ostentatious for my tastes. Antique couches lined the walls as well as bookshelves with large portraits of English castles and manors hanging above them. The books' bindings advertised the fact that they were all important and the property of a learned family. A massive brick fireplace—the centerpiece—greedily drew attention to itself, and a row of antique vases sat atop a great wooden mantelpiece. The room, like the rest of the house, was thick with humidity. It was difficult to breathe.

Jesse motioned for me to get behind the couch. He had something in mind, but I wasn't sure what. I followed his command and took refuge behind the couch while he crept over to the front door. He loudly knocked three times, listened closely, and waited. We didn't hear the sound of anything stirring within the house. At that point, I realized what his plan was: imitate the sound of a visitor, wait to see if someone came down the stairs or moved in the house, and then shoot him. Fortunately, there was nothing.

After the third time knocking, Jesse looked at me and nodded. We were pretty convinced that the house, as we had presumed, was empty. Drake was out there somewhere, and Hot-rodder too.

Walking a little more assuredly, we peeked into two other downstairs rooms. One was a guestroom that looked like it hadn't seen a guest in quite some time. A wooden sleigh bed, an empty nightstand, and an empty closet were the only things within. A second room, which was completely barren, was the only other place of interest downstairs.

I think we both assumed that if we were to find more weapons, and if I was going to find anything that might give insight as to where Drake had taken Hot-rodder, it would be in Drake's room. I imagined it would be a cluttered, dark, gloomy room, because that's what bedrooms often are—a reflection of the mind that inhabits it.

Jesse pointed upstairs, and I followed closely behind. Even though we'd knocked on the front door, the shotgun was heavy in my sweaty hands, and I was still shaking. We had only gone halfway up the flight of steps when both Jesse and I noticed that foul, terrible smell emanating from one of the upper rooms. We didn't have to say anything, but we both knew exactly what it was: a corpse. Could anything else account for that acrid, decomposing vapor filling those upper chambers?

We looked at each other with grave understanding, because both of us knew exactly what this meant. Perhaps Drake *was* home, or at least, his body, because he'd already taken his life as Jesse had predicted. Maybe he'd looped back around during his flight away from the mass murder and ended his life at his house. It was entirely possible—likely, even. In all of the crazy thunder and lightning that afternoon, who would have noticed another gunshot or two?

With this revelation came a harrowing second question: If Drake had come home to put a bullet through his own head, had he brought Hot-rodder with him?

An image, as terrible as the stench I found myself in, assaulted me. I imagined Drake's body lying in a puddle of blood in one of these upper rooms, the gun he'd killed himself with by his side, and next to him and in a smaller puddle, the body of Hot-rodder. It took me a long time to get the image out of my head. The thought of Hot-rodder, who should have been out in the sun, pumping the pedals on his BMX bike, covered in blood churned my stomach in a way that was most terrible. I hoped against all hope that the image in my mind would be anything but prophetic and that the smell would be Drake's body and his body alone.

Knowing well what we might stumble upon, Jesse and I looked at each other, nodded solemnly, and finished our climb up the stairs. We found ourselves in a grand hallway with several doors, the largest of which was ajar. Two things became clear to us: the large open door, based on its enormous size, was most likely the grand entrance to a master bedroom, and we were confident that the smell was emanating from there. Although there were hardwood floors up here as well, we walked along a blue oriental runner that led directly down the hall and to the doorway of that master chamber. On the walls, portraits of men and women—family ancestry, perhaps—glared at us as we made our morbid trek down the hall.

When we stepped into the master bedroom, I was happy to discover that my suspicions weren't true; I didn't see Hotrodder lying dead on the floor, and I didn't see Drake either. Instead, the smell was coming from the corpse of a man lying in the bed. He appeared to be asleep, though his face was nearly as pale as the white sheets covering him.

I assumed this was Drake's father, the one nobody had seen for months. Several prescription bottles were on the nightstand beside him, and some had fallen onto the floor. Perhaps he had killed himself several days ago, just as the storms began, and had drifted to sleep under the influence of the drugs. Maybe Drake overdosed him just before he began his killing spree that afternoon. We had no idea.

We took a couple steps into the room and silently took in the reality of what we were witnessing, then suddenly heard a noise. The front door of the house unlatched and slowly opened, and there were footsteps along the creaky floorboards.

"No," I whispered.

Anxiously, we looked around the room for somewhere to hide, and I found myself crawling under the bed with my shotgun. I can't remember if Jesse ushered me that way or if I, in that terrifying moment, found shelter there of my own accord. The stench was horrid, and I covered my nose with one hand and tried to keep a steady grip on the shotgun with my other. I tried to position myself in a way that I could get a decent shot at Drake if he discovered me, and I tried, unsuccessfully, to ignore the fact that a stinking corpse was only inches above my head on the other side of the mattress.

Jesse hid behind the door, where he waited for Drake to make his entrance.

That minute seemed to be the longest in my life. I found myself shivering under the bed while I listened to Drake slowly make his way up the stairs. One by one, the steps creaked as he drew closer and closer, and I wondered if I was going to pass out. Even though my heart was pounding furiously in my chest, I felt completely weakened with fear. I wondered, if the moment came, if I would even have enough strength to pull the trigger.

After Drake ascended the stairs, I watched, from below the bed, as the black shoes and the bottom of the black jeans walked into the room. They stopped maybe five feet from the bed. I was terrified, and I wondered if he would hear my beating heart. Or maybe he'd hear me shaking.

Then he started to kneel down. Was he going to see me? The shotgun was too long, and I wouldn't have time to swing it around and aim properly before he saw me. And in my panic, I still couldn't remember: Was the safety on or was it off? Why couldn't I remember?

The air went completely out of me. I closed my eyes and prayed for Jesse to shoot Drake and stop him before he did anything.

But Drake only bent down to pick up the prescription bottles on the floor. When I opened my eyes and saw the hand that had taken Jenna's life that close to my face, a grotesque chill enveloped me.

"Get down!" Jesse yelled. He stepped out from behind the door and Drake, clearly flustered, dropped onto the floor beside the bed.

Lying there, he looked right at me, and if seeing the hand that killed all of those people was terrible, looking directly into his dark eyes was that much worse. He didn't look shocked to see me under the bed; instead, he just looked angry—like a spoiled child who was having a toy taken away. I was most amazed by what I didn't see in his eyes: fear. You expect to see fear in the eyes of a man who has been ordered to the ground by a gun-wielding stranger in his own home, but when I looked into those eyes for the briefest of moments, I didn't see a single ounce of it.

I crawled out from under the bed and saw Jesse, gun drawn, standing over Drake. Not quite knowing what to do, I aimed my shotgun at Drake as well. I was still trembling so much, I wondered if I would be able to hit Drake if I needed to fire my weapon, even at this point blank range.

"You're gonna just lie there and stay calm, you understand?" Jesse said.

Drake said nothing.

"Where's the boy?" I asked.

He still said nothing.

"You heard him," Jesse barked. "Where's the boy?"

No response.

Jesse hunkered down beside Drake, his gun aimed right at his head, and said, "I'm gonna give you one more chance. Where's the boy? We can make this mighty painful, if need be."

Drake lifted his head just a little off the floor and tried to look at Jesse, and for the first time, I thought I saw some of what had been missing flash across his face: fear.

"The storm," he said. "It took him. The storm took him."

Chapter Twenty-Two

J esse and I decided we would have to personally escort Drake to the police. The island was cut off from all outside help, but we'd heard, every day, that cop car drive through the streets and a woman ordering people to remain indoors until further advised. Usually, we heard the announcements in the mornings and in the evenings. It was still only afternoon. We would wait until we heard the announcement that evening, and we'd take Drake right to the source.

We both found his explanation of Hot-rodder's disappearance troubling. He explained how the kid had wriggled out of his grip and started to run away, but then, out of nowhere, a big ball of lightning floated down from the sky and took him. It literally wrapped itself around him like some kind of electrical cocoon, and even though he fought against it, the ball shot back up toward the storm clouds with him in it.

I imagined Hot-rodder screaming and kicking in his spherical cage as the storm reeled him back up, and it was a horrifying image—almost as bad as the one I had of him bloodied and dead beside Drake. Maybe just as bad.

I wished I could have been there when it happened. I wished I was there to reach out and hold him back.

I imagined Alan's hand slipping out of mine and into the waters of the Kern River.

Maybe I could have stopped them. Maybe I could have held onto both of them.

Drake said little more than that. Most of the time, he was stone faced, and knowing his defeat and imminent return to the authorities, he looked down at the floor and avoided eye contact at all costs. It amazed me to think that this man, who had evoked fear in so many people at the park during his killing, was really, beneath it all, just a coward. Maybe that's simply the nature of those who are willing to senselessly take the lives of men, women, and innocent children. Take the weapons out of their hands and innocent people out of their path, and they are exposed for what they really are: spineless, worthless cowards.

It repulsed me to even be in the same room with him.

Before I went down and searched the garage for something to shackle him with, we briefly discussed just putting an end to him right there. Jesse commented that we should just drag him out into the backyard and put him out of his misery, and even though I didn't know if he was that serious when he said it, we looked at each other and contemplated it. Would it really matter? Would anyone really grieve Drake's death, and by doing so, wouldn't we save the court a lot of money for what would be an inevitable verdict? But we decided against it. I'd like to think that's because, when standing next to one of the true evils of this world, I felt a need to be unlike him. What terrified me even more than what he'd done was the idea that I could do something similar. A horror writer I knew once told me that what makes evil so frightening is the fact that we can see ourselves in it. I've always remembered that, and I didn't want to see any of myself in Drake.

I was able to find some rope and duct tape in the garage while Jesse kept the prisoner under guard. We may have gone a little overkill with it, but we bound his hands, his legs, and duct taped his mouth, and together we carried him back over to my house with the duffel bag. We were exhausted from carrying our prisoner. I had his feet and Jesse had him by the shoulders, and fortunately we didn't see anybody on the streets, because I don't know what people would have thought. From a distance, we probably appeared to be two grown men lugging around a corpse.

When I looked at the clouds, I would have sworn they looked even lower than they had just an hour or two ago, and they were certainly darker. What was happening to them? Why were they descending so rapidly?

It is difficult to describe, but it felt like the storm was about to intensify again. Every night was worse than the one before. Perhaps it would soon be raining again, and the cloud-to-ground lightning would resume. I wondered if I would see those lightning balls again. Was that what had taken Hotrodder? Would the lightning start taking out buildings? If it could take out bridges, what would be next? Maybe the storm was an extermination of some kind: a big can of Raid spraying down on us ants.

We had gotten close to my house when the obvious occurred to me. I stopped for a moment and put down our psycho baggage, both to catch my breath and to talk to Jesse.

"We can't let Darrel see him," I said, panting.

Jesse got my drift. He nodded in his quiet way.

"Or my boys, or the others. Especially Marsha. She'll probably have an aneurysm if she lays eyes on him."

"Go inside first and open the garage," Jesse suggested. "Tell them to stay out of the garage. We'll bring it in from the outside."

I liked how he called Drake *it*, because that's what *it* was. It was hard to think of Drake as even being human.

I went inside the house and to the garage. I bumped into my wife, of course, as I was coming through the hallway, and I'd seen that look on her face before; in all my years of marriage, I've never been able to get anything past her for very long. Madison has a gift for catching onto me. Whether it was stealing one of her favorite wine coolers that she likes to hide in the back of the fridge or the chocolate-covered raisins she hides in her nightstand, I always got caught. It was inevitable. So there was no way I was going to bring a mass murderer into my garage without my wife picking up on it. She has too good a radar.

"What happened?" she asked. She was happy to see me, I could tell that much, but she was worried. We'd taken too long. I told her we were going to the bridge and would come right back, but that stop at Drake's added a good forty-five minutes to our excursion. She had been worried sick, and I felt terrible for it.

I couldn't lie to her. I believe in my heart that the truth is always better than a lie—that's certainly what I taught my sons —but this was one pill that was going to be very, very difficult for her to swallow.

"We stopped at Drake's house on the way back to get more weapons," I said.

"Eddie, you told me that you were going to come right back. You promised."

"I know, I know. I'm totally in the wrong here, but we were already outside, it was basically on the way, and I felt it was the right thing to do."

"You felt it was the right thing to do?"

"Yes."

"Was it worth it? Did you find any weapons?"

"No weapons," I said, but I knew I had to deliver all the

news. I tried to brace her and took her by the shoulders. I had no idea how she was going to take this. "But we have Drake. He's outside."

Her eyes fluttered in incomprehension, and I felt that she was searching my face for some indication that I was lying.

I was about to explain myself even further when my son walked around the corner of the entryway. He didn't waste any time in getting right back into his petitioning.

"Dad, I'm telling you, I need to go to Klutch's house," he said, and I didn't appreciate his demanding tone. "I think Candice is there, and I wanna see if she's okay. You yourself just went outside, and look, you're fine."

He must have noticed that I was holding his mom's shoulders, and with our faces close together, assumed we were in the midst of an intimate encounter. He mumbled something about us being gross and went back into the living room, where I could already hear Marsha and Samantha bickering about what they could forage out of the food supplies to make a snack. The way I heard it, Marsha wanted to make peanut butter and jelly for everyone, but Samantha thought they could find something better.

My wife's eyes never left my face, and she was speechless, an incredibly rare phenomenon in our house.

"He's completely tied up and bound," I explained. "Trust me, he can't move a muscle. We were gonna keep him in the garage until later tonight, until we hear the police car telling people to stay indoors, and then we'll take him there."

"You brought him here?"

"Where else are we going to take him?"

She pressed the open palms of her hands on her forehead. "I can't believe you did this. This is crazy, Eddie. Really crazy. What's going on?"

"He won't be here long," I explained. "And we need to

keep everyone out of the garage, especially Darrel. Where is he now?"

"Still in the guest room, sleeping, I think."

"Okay, if anyone needs to stay away, it's him," I explained. "I don't want to see Darrel get an up-close and personal look at the guy who killed his wife. I'm gonna open the garage, but everyone needs to stay out of there."

"Okay," she said, but was quick to remind me: "Don't do that again. Don't make me worry like that, Eddie. I can't do that again."

"I know, I'm sorry."

I went through the house and opened the garage door, and then I helped Jesse move Drake into the garage. We placed him along some boxes near the side wall. Even if he was able to exhaust himself by wriggling a few inches, there was nothing of any interest that would help him get out of his binding. He seemed to know resistance was futile, because he hadn't tried to say anything or force his way out of the ropes. Maybe the duct tape over his mouth was unnecessary, but I wasn't taking any chances.

We left him there and went back into the house to rest. But I kept a close eye on the door so nobody would accidently stumble upon our neighbor.

I felt like I needed to sleep, and outside I heard more thunder. I plopped down on the couch, and Marsha and Samantha brought everyone a plate of peanut butter and jelly sandwiches and bananas. Apparently they'd compromised and gone for half fruit, half sandwiches.

We had all barely taken a bite of our food when I heard a knock at the front door.

Chapter Twenty-Three

When I looked through the peephole, I saw my quiet and rather hermit-like neighbor, Dominic, standing outside. I mentioned him before; he's the guy I had only briefly seen on a couple occasions and a resident who, according to most of my neighbors, nobody really knew. Every neighborhood has its own Dominic, I think—the guy you might live next to for decades without hardly ever saying hello to or crossing paths with. We had only lived in Naples for a few months, but I had the feeling that if we spent the rest of our lives in that home, it would have pretty much been that way.

I opened the door and was immediately struck by his complete imperviousness to the situation at hand. My wife, standing beside me, was too. Nothing about his demeanor, posture, or words conveyed the reality that he—like us—was stranded here amidst a horrifying, supernatural storm. He carried himself lightly, almost playfully, like a child in the midst of a disaster he could not fully comprehend. Carrying a hand-held radio in one hand and eating a Twinkie with the other, Dominic, with his pear-shaped body, his white beard, and those big rosy cheeks, always reminded me of Santa Claus. I've read that there is an actual world-wide club of Santa look-alikes, and though I never got around to asking Dominic about it, I wouldn't be at all surprised to learn that he was a member.

"Hello," he said, waving the hand with his half-eaten Twinkie in it. "I'm Dominic, your neighbor."

I was still struck by his demeanor; he sounded like a neighbor swinging by to invite us over for a leisurely glass of wine.

"Yes, I've seen you once or twice. I'm Eddie, and this is my wife, Madison."

"Oh yes, pleased to meet you both," he said, waving hello again with his Twinkie.

"How are you holding up?" I asked. "Are you okay?"

"Me?" he said, almost surprised by the question. "I'm great. Doing superb. Wonderful, actually."

"Good," I said, and then there was a brief yet awkward silence. He didn't announce why he had come over, and judging by his appearance, it didn't seem that it was due to him being in need of anything. "Is there anything you need? Would you like to come in? We have plenty of food if you need some."

"Oh, I'm just fine," Dominic said, indicating his Twinkie. "I have enough food to last me a lifetime in there, trust me. I stocked up years ago just in case of some kind of natural disaster like this. One can never be too careful, you know."

"Well, good," I said, but I hoped Dominic had done more than just stock his pantry and garage with boxes of Twinkies, or else a heart attack might take him out before the storm ended.

"Oh yes," he said. "I didn't come over because I needed anything. I just came over because I had to tell somebody what I discovered. It is most exciting, and I just had to share the news with someone. I hope you don't mind."

"No, not at all."

"What did you discover?" my wife asked.

"The storm is talking to us," he said. With eyes glittering, he lifted up his small handheld radio as if it were evidence of his great discovery. My wife and I glanced at each other and were both in silent agreement that Dominic might not be playing with a full deck.

Dominic, who I sensed wasn't the best at picking up on social cues, thought we were somehow sharing in his joy, because he didn't register the incredulous looks that must have been evident on our faces.

"The storm is talking to us, you say?" my wife said slowly, over-enunciating each syllable as if talking to a man who was hard of hearing.

"Yes, the storm is talking to us," he said, in equally slow pronunciation.

"It's talking to us?" she asked again.

"Oh yes, it is," Dominic said and then, appearing flustered, addressed me: "I'm sorry, am I not making myself clear? Does your wife have difficulty hearing?"

"No," I said, and caught myself laughing. The conversation just seemed a bit ridiculous to me. "We're just not sure how your radio has anything to do with the storm talking to us. We're just confused."

"Oh," he said. "I'm terribly sorry. Perhaps if you'd let me sit down and explain it to you, it would be helpful. I'm sure you'll both want to hear this, actually."

"Of course," I said, and invited him in.

I introduced Dominic to Jesse, Owen, Marsha, and Samantha, who were all sitting in the living room and eating sandwiches. Toby and Mia were in my office, playing Legos, and my wife ran to quickly check on them while Dominic took a seat in the leather chair in the living room. Darrel still hadn't come out of the guest room, and that was probably good, because his body probably needed the rest. I didn't think he had gotten this much uninterrupted sleep since Jenna was shot.

Dominic, I would learn, was more than just the aloof, eccentric, hermit-like neighbor he appeared to be. He had worked as a physics instructor at USC in his earlier years and had also worked as an engineer; by the time he was forty, he had made a small fortune on various patents and inventions. He tried to explain them to me but, for the most part, he lost me after the second sentence. Never married and never having children, he spent much of his life tinkering in his garage and experimenting with his electrical gadgets. I think it is safe to say that Dominic had probably forgotten more about physics and science than I had ever learned in my entire life.

"Now, I'd like everyone to listen," Dominic said and turned on the small battery-powered radio he had come in with. "I'm going to turn it down to the very low AM frequencies, and all of you can listen very closely."

Like a magician about to perform some kind of magnificent illusion, he flexed his fingers and began to adjust the radio's tuner. He had a natural gift for showmanship; I caught myself leaning forward, rapt, waiting for something to happen. Finally, I could hear a little something, but it sounded just like electrical interference, the kind of static and glitching you might hear on your radio if someone was running a hairdryer in a nearby bathroom.

We all waited for something more to happen—perhaps some kind of sound to emerge—but that was all there was. He had turned to a station with no broadcast signal, and all we could hear was the intermittent static, but I could tell, by the proud expression on Dominic's jolly face, that this was exactly what he wanted us to here. I didn't get it.

"Dominic," I said, seeing how everyone else in the room was just as confused as I was, "all I hear is interference."

"Exactly!" he said.

I waited for him to say more, but he didn't. *Great*, I thought. *I have a killer in the garage and I just brought a nutcase into my living room.*

"But it's not just static," he said proudly. "You're listening to the lightning. The lightning in the clouds. It's right here. Right in these speakers."

This, of course, was met with even more silence.

Dominic went on. "What I've done here is tune to a low station on the AM band," he said. "AM radio makes an excellent lightning detector. The static crashes you're hearing right now are actually the lightning in real-time, because the radio waves and the lightning are both traveling at the speed of light. The lightning creates radio waves, and that's what you're hearing."

"I know all about that," Jesse said. "We had storm interference on the television and radio all the time in Louisiana, but what does it matter? How does that help us?"

"Well, I doubt you ever heard storm interference quite like this," Dominic said. "Have you listened closely, all of you? Have you listened really closely to the static that you hear?"

Everyone nodded.

"You're not listening close enough," Dominic said and turned the volume up. The blipping and blitzing static interference grew louder and filled my living room. "Now listen for a pattern in it. Can you hear it? It's not just the random interference you would expect in a storm. There's a definite, intentional pattern to it, but you have to listen closely. Try to focus in and hear it."

I remembered an optical illusion painting I'd seen several years ago back at the Seattle Center. When I looked at the painting and let my eyes lose their focus, a three dimensional image popped out of it, but I had to wait for a while and be patient before I could really make out that image. That was kind of what this felt like; only, instead of waiting for my eyes to adjust, I was waiting for my ears to somehow acclimate to what I was supposed to hear.

All of us sat quietly in my living room for many long minutes, trying to discern whatever it was we were supposed to hear in the static. Darrel, who must have just woken up, walked into the room. He didn't look surprised or confused to see all of us sitting in the room, quietly listening to the virtual nothingness on our neighbor's radio. I was pretty convinced at that point that Darrel had mentally checked out completely. With his hands buried deep in his pockets, he leaned against the wall and looked off into nowhere. Frozen between grief and anger, Darrel was pretty much a walking zombie.

I kept listening to the static, and while I couldn't make out something concrete, there was a pattern to it. There was some definite rhythm and orchestration to it, and it was, so far as I could tell, not the interference that randomly occurring light-ning would generate.

"I think I hear it," I was the first to say. Maybe it was because I'm a writer and I painstakingly work with words every single day. "It almost sounds like language or something. Like it's some kind of communication."

"I hear it too," Marsha said. "It almost sounds like Morse Code."

My wife also thought she could hear something, but Jesse and Samantha said it just sounded like a bunch of static to them. Owen was too concerned about finding out where his girlfriend was to offer his opinion, and Darrel, of course, wasn't much aware of anything going on around him. I thought it was amusing that my wife and Marsha could both discern the language in the static; they were both talkers, natural communicators, and I wondered if that had something to do with it.

"Oh yes, just like Morse Code," Dominic said. "It sounds

an awful lot like that. I think it may be possible, perhaps likely, that the storm is trying to communicate."

"You're telling me this storm is trying to talk to us?" Jesse asked.

"Yes, that's exactly what I'm saying. It's quite possible. It sounds like some form of communication, and this clearly isn't a natural storm. I take it that none of your cell phones work, am I right?"

Everyone nodded.

"Well, they should work just fine. Cell phones use microwave frequencies, and a storm—even a big storm like this —shouldn't take out every cell phone beneath it. This storm isn't playing by the rules of science as we know it and I think, when you spend a little time listening to it, you can hear some kind of communication."

"I don't know," Jesse said. "I think if you listen to any kind of static long enough, you can probably hear whatever you want in it. Kind of like when you're a kid and you look at the clouds and see animals and things in them. If you look at something long enough and want to see something long enough, you'll see it. Know what I mean?"

"How is this going to help us?" Samantha asked, clearly frustrated. "How do we get off this island? I want off now. How is static going to help us get off this island?"

"Well, let him finish explaining," Marsha said. "He can't magically take us away now, can he?"

"I'm just tired and sick of being stuck here, and I was hoping to hear something more than just static, alright?" Samantha complained, folded her arms in front of her, and looked away bitterly. I thought it was interesting that my son, despite his preoccupation with his girlfriend, was more selfless than this grown woman during a time of disaster.

"Oh yes, the woman brings up a very good point, which is the second thing I'd like to share with you," Dominic said. He set the radio at his feet, rubbed his hands together, and took a rather long, dramatic breath. "The communication—whatever it is—stops occasionally. It completely ceases, and it seems that it does so according to some kind of pattern. I believe that, during these times, the electrical activity stops."

I think it took everyone a moment to translate what he was saying, or at least, to contemplate the significance of it; even if the static on the radio stopped occasionally, why would it matter? Who cared? It seemed like a completely irrelevant detail in regards to our situation.

Dominic reached into the pocket of his pants, pulled out another Twinkie, and began to unwrap it. Other than the static-like language emanating from the radio's speakers and the sound of Dominic unwrapping his Twinkie, we were left in silence.

"What do you mean the electrical activity stops? What does that mean?" I asked.

"Let me explain it this way," Dominic said. "The evening of July fifth, a little more than twenty-four hours after the storm hit our island with a vengeance, the electrical activity briefly ceased. It went down at precisely three minutes after eight o'clock at night for thirty minutes. I was monitoring on my radio at the time, and the electrical activity stopped. No static. No communication. Just emptiness. I monitored it visually, as well. When I verified what I heard by looking outside, I noticed that there was no cloud-to-cloud lightning or cloud-to-ground lightning then. The clouds were dark and swollen, but there wasn't a single flicker of activity in them."

What he said was interesting, and I knew he was going somewhere with it, so I listened attentively.

"But a funny thing happened," he said. "While I was monitoring the following night, July sixth, the same thing happened. At exactly three minutes after eight o'clock, the communication on my radio stopped. Dead silence. Only that night, the electrical activity ceased for exactly twenty-five minutes, five minutes less than the previous night. Strange, isn't it?"

"Strange," Jesse said, "but what does it mean?"

"Oh yes, I suppose I can only speculate at this point," Dominic said. He took another bite of his Twinkie and leaned back in his chair in reflective thought. As the relatively eccentric science type, he might have looked somewhat dignified leaning back in my leather chair with a pipe or a cigar in his hand; holding that Twinkie, he looked a bit silly. "Last night, the cloud 'shut down' for exactly twenty minutes. Every night it's shutting down and losing five minutes. It is hard to imagine that to be coincidence, don't you think? And something else happened too. The clouds, after that, seemed much lower than before. Much, much lower."

Jesse and I looked at each other. We had been outside and had seen the low-hanging clouds. They had been lower than before; there was no questioning that.

"But what does this mean?" my wife asked. "Does it mean we can get off the island? Does it mean we can finally leave?"

Even Owen, who was standing next to Darrel and leaning against the wall, seemed to take genuine interest. Dominic was building to some important point.

"I think it means this," Dominic said. "I think the storm is in some kind of pattern. I don't know exactly. During those intervals, when my radio went dead and when I looked up at the clouds, I think it was possible to get through. I think someone could cross over the water then without the lightning taking them out. In theory, I think those are the times that the storm is recharging. It's gathering energy, whatever it's doing. And interestingly enough, the storm intensifies just before each of these breaks. Haven't you noticed? Each night the storm is getting worse. And each night, following the worst of it, there are these small, narrowing gaps of inactivity."

"So we could have gotten out?" Samantha asked, her voice

full of defeat. I thought she might completely break down into tears right there. "You're telling us that we could have gotten out and we missed it? We missed it?"

"Yes and no," he said. "I think we could have gotten out during those windows of time, but I'm not certain. It's all a hypothesis, really. It can't be proven until someone actually attempts it, right? But I think the same thing is going to happen tonight, and that's what I'd like to verify. Tonight, at exactly three after eight, I think there's a good chance the same thing will happen again. Only this time, I'd be willing to bet that it'll shut down for exactly fifteen minutes, five minutes less than last night. And I'd be willing to bet that, just like before, the storm will rage just before the pause."

"So you're saying we can get out tonight?" Jesse asked.

"Or tomorrow night," Dominic said. "If the pattern continues, it'll be too narrow after tomorrow night. I don't think anybody would be able to get out in so short a time period after that. Even tomorrow night, at ten minutes, would be pushing it. And remember, it's all just a theory at this point. It would take someone to actually test it to see if it's valid, and I think tonight will prove whether it's just a freak coincidence or whether there is really a pattern to the storm."

"But what is it?" Owen asked. I was surprised to hear him speak up amongst the adults in the room, but he was as attentive as ever. "What is this storm?"

"Oh yes, that's a question I can't answer," Dominic said, shrugging. He finished his Twinkie, crinkled up the wrapper, and shoved it into his pocket. "There are many possibilities, but I guess, if I had to make a definitive answer, I would say it is somehow alive. It's not just a storm. It's alive, and I think, like lots of organisms, it's trying to destroy us. Those clouds are getting lower and lower. I say we have a couple more days, perhaps, before it completely wipes us out. I do remember in college once reading about a strange historical incident. The Carrington Event?"

"The what?" I asked.

"It was the largest solar flare in recorded history. 1859. Made the sky glow, but geomagnetic disturbances brought down telegraph systems across the globe and some of those same telegraph machines sparked and went up in flames. Caused terrible fires. If we make it through all this, you should look it up some time. There was one small town that was hit particularly hard—somewhere in Virginia—and the people became paranoid. I think it was called Rockville, but I could be wrong. Strange geomagnetic phenomena happened and prevented people from leaving. A terrible storm entrapped them, much like what has happened to us. And the residents turned on each other. I think nearly ten people were killed. But they had issues before all that, at least, according to some articles."

"What kind of issues?"

"Trust issues," Dominic said, grinning. "That was two years before the civil war, you know. The country was divided and dealing with all kinds of issues. Lincoln would, of course, become president in 1860. It was a time of tension, change, and division. And even more, a time of fear."

I waited. What was he getting at?

"What I'm saying is this," he said. "There are people out there—conspiracy theorists, I suppose—who think the Carrington Event wasn't just a freak solar flare. There's been other events, too. Lots if you study them. But some think that it was a monster, for lack of a better word. A monster that we've fed and that we've nurtured. Hatred. Bigotry. Division. Those are the things it feeds on."

I considered this. Suddenly, I felt like we were talking science fiction.

"The timing couldn't be better," Dominic said. "Have you

watched CNN? Have you watched Fox News? Makes you feel like the world's coming unglued, doesn't it? Maybe it found a hole here—in our little community—to try again. To gather strength. To make its entrance into the world."

"What happened to the people in that town? What did they do?"

"That's the thing," Dominic said. "They were in a remote area, and they had little help. As they ran out of food and supplies, they turned more and more on each other. They became paranoid and hoarded food and supplies, until one guy, I think his name was John, was credited for being the leader to help them survive. He's the guy who talked sense into the town, got them working together again, and brought justice. It's what he said that was so interesting and what caused all of the stories."

"What did he say?"

"Well, when asked what they did to survive the storm, he answered simply: We starved it."

"We starved it," I said, trying to make sense of it.

These words brought contemplative silence, and I found myself agreeing wholeheartedly with Dominic. I didn't know if the storm was "alive" in the way that he meant or if it was some freakish entity sent from another world, but I was more than convinced that it was trying to destroy us. It began with all of the things that had gone mysteriously missing; I thought of Jenna's wedding ring, Bessie, and my wife's lingerie. I remembered the solemn faces on the Naples residents before Drake unleashed his fury and before the crazy lightning struck.

Yes, it was clear to me that the storm was trying to destroy us; but it had been trying to destroy us even before the lightning took out the bridges and before the dark, swirling storm clouds settled solely above Naples. Maybe it was alive and had some kind of intelligence, because it was clearly trying to turn us against each other even before it trapped us there. I hadn't yet talked to Marsha, Samantha, or any of the others about the things that had gone missing from their homes, but I knew the storm had been at work before Drake went on his killing spree. I was totally convinced by Dominic's observation: the storm was trying to destroy us, through whatever means available, and this might be our only ticket off the island.

"I was kind of hoping you would be able to help," Dominic said, directing his comment toward me. "I heard you're a writer, right? What would you do? Aren't you guys good at coming up with creative solutions like this? What would you do if you were writing a story and your characters were in this situation?"

"What would I do? What would I write?" I asked and contemplated it. A little neighborhood community trapped on an island in a storm that sizzled anybody who tried to get on or get off it? A mass murderer tied up in my garage? A widower who had turned into a zombie since his wife was slaughtered right in front of his eyes? A high-maintenance flirt and a menopausal woman constantly nagging each other in the midst of all of it? "I think only a complete idiot would attempt to write something like this."

"Really?" Dominic said. "Why?"

"Because it's an antagonist that you can't beat," I said. "You can't fight a storm. You can't win against a storm. You have to just sit and wait it out. It wouldn't make much of a story, and it wouldn't give a protagonist a fighting chance. So I think we have no choice. We have to see if you're right. Maybe we can get out of here."

"We can try it tonight." Samantha said, suddenly alert. She stood up and began to pace back and forth hurriedly. I don't think Samantha was used to this much discomfort. I think she felt it was *unfair* for someone of her social class to be subjected to it. Marsha, who had been sitting next to her, almost looked like she was going to hyperventilate. She started to fan herself with her hands.

"Hold your horses," Jesse said. "First, we need to test it. And I don't know who is gonna want to swim or boat across the bay as the guinea pig, 'cause if it don't work, you're gonna be fried pork before you reach the other side. And we need to tell others about it. What about everyone else who's stuck on this island? We can't just leave them."

"So we just sit here and die with them, is that it?" Samantha asked.

"No," Jesse said. "We do our due diligence. We test your neighbor's theory and we do our best to let the rest of the island know as well. There are more than just us in this room."

"Whatever," she said and shrugged resentfully. "When did it become my responsibility to care about everyone else on this island? You're telling me there's a chance to get off this island and you're not willing to try?"

"He didn't say that," Marsha said.

"That's right," I said. "He didn't say that. He just said we wait. We can test it out, try to let others know, and we can—"

I stopped mid-sentence at a terrible sound: something fell in the garage.

Chapter Twenty-Four

The way Jesse and I reacted must have looked completely ridiculous to everybody else in the living room. Something falling in a garage might elicit fear, especially to people who were in a situation like us, but nobody would have expected Jesse and I to respond the way we did.

We were both on our feet in a second, and Jesse had already pulled out his gun before he rushed out of the room. Marsha and Samantha both screamed, but I don't think it was necessarily due to the sound of something falling in the garage; I think our reactions conveyed that something was wrong in a most serious way, and that terrified them.

I followed Jesse to the garage, and he barged right in. My wife stayed back with the others to make sure they didn't follow, or even worse, open the front door and try to run away.

Fortunately, we didn't see what most feared when we stormed into the garage. I had imagined that Drake had somehow gotten free of his bindings and had found something in the garage to use as a weapon. Maybe he would be standing in the middle of the garage with a saw in his hand; maybe he'd found something even more deadly.

But Drake hadn't even come close to getting out of his fettering and had simply rolled into a box of Christmas ornaments along the perimeter of the garage and knocked it over. He wriggled on the ground like a worm, but it was clear that he wasn't going anywhere.

Breathing a sigh of relief, Jesse lowered his gun and we looked knowingly at each other. We felt like we'd dodged a bullet, and we both knew that we had to get him out of there quickly.

We made brief plans while my wife kept the others back; I wasn't sure what she was telling them, but nobody came into the garage, and the hysteria died down. Jesse and I made plans quickly. It was evening, and most likely, the police car would make its nightly trek up Second Street, the main thoroughfare through the island, and the officer would give her nightly admonitions to remain indoors, to remain calm, and not to make any attempts to leave the island.

Our mission was now twofold. We would deliver Drake to the Powers That Be and tell the police what Dominic explained to us. Everyone else would have to be told. We couldn't just leave the island without making some attempt to notify the others, and I had no idea what was in store for us on the other side of the water. But not to make some effort to bring others with us felt inhuman, and even if it meant we had to wait until a narrower window was available to cross the water, then so be it. I wanted to cross the water with two things intact: my family and my conscience. If I could get across with those two things, I would be alright.

We decided to make our exit. There was no use of waiting until later. I was about to run inside to tell Madison when, suddenly, the garage door opened and Owen stepped in. His mom was right behind him.

"Dad, you brought that guy to our garage?" Owen asked. He looked completely disgusted, far more disgusted than he usually did when he walked in on Mom and me making out on the couch. "Are you kidding me? You're kidding me?"

"You told them?" I asked Madison, completely ignoring my son.

"I tried, but I didn't know what else to say," she said. "I think Marsha just passed out. She completely hyperventilated."

"Wonderful," I said.

I heard Toby crying for his Mommy around the corner and the little girl, who had been so quiet up until then, began crying too. My greatest concern, however, was Darrel. I didn't want Darrel to see him. I didn't know what he would do or how it would affect him to lay eyes on the man who had murdered his wife. But it wouldn't be good; I knew that much.

"We're gonna take him to the police, okay?" I said. "We're gonna go right now and take him to that police car that rolls through here every night. And we're gonna tell them everything Dominic told us. They need to know."

"This is crazy," Owen said, looking down in awe at the gagged and bound figure of Drake. "I can't believe you have him."

"You need to watch over everyone here," I told my son. Jesse left the garage to go into my office and get the duffel bag. "I'm putting you personally in charge, okay? You need to keep everyone calm and relaxed and keep an eye on everyone."

"Dad, I think you should go see what that guy Klutch is doing. It sounds like people trust him. He might know something too."

"Don't worry about Klutch, okay? He's not the police. He's an obnoxious biker. We don't need to get involved in that."

"But Candice might be there. She might—"

"Forget about Candice," I said. "You need to worry about your own family now, okay? Your brother's depending on you, your mom's depending on you, and I'm depending on you. Understand?"

"Yeah, Dad," Owen said, shrugging. "I just think our neighbor's kinda weird. How do you know any of that's even true? It sounds like he's just making it up."

"Then that's something we'll have to see as time plays out," I said.

Jesse came back into the garage with the duffel bag in his hands. He mentioned that everyone was fine in the living room and even Darrel, now aware that his wife's murderer was in the garage, seemed at ease; surprisingly, Jesse explained, he seemed more at ease than the rest of the group and was even trying to relax and calm everybody down.

Jesse unzipped one of the bags, removed a nine millimeter handgun, loaded the mag and handed it to my son. Owen took it but looked at it incredulously before glaring at me in confusion. I'd seen that look on him just a month before when, while we were out to dinner, a waiter accidently put an empty wine glass in front of him as he poured wine for the table. The expression simply conveyed: *Dad, am I allowed to do this? What do I do?*

"Jesse will show you how it works," I explained.

Jesse did a quick walkthrough of the handgun, and I watched silently. Drake, lying on the ground, looked up at me, and it made me most uncomfortable. I looked forward to getting him out of the garage.

"We'll leave the guns here in the garage," I explained. "Don't let the others know they're here. Not yet. Not unless you have to."

"Are you sure you have to go?" Madison asked. "Are you sure you have to go now?"

"Yes," I said. "I'm sure."

I knew what she was thinking. If the storm kicked up and started throwing down lightning bolts again, what would happen this time? What if I started seeing those weird balls of lightning, and what if this time, they did something far worse?

I believed Drake's story because I'd seen the genuine fear in his eyes. If the storm had taken Hot-rodder, then it could certainly take me. I imagined one of those lightning balls enveloping me like a bubble and levitating me toward the clouds overhead. What a horrific way to die, I thought, and I hoped Hot-rodder hadn't suffered much.

I wondered if it would have been less frightening if Drake had just shot him and killed him before the lightning took him.

"I love you," I said and hugged Madison. She was on the verge of tears because she knew the risk of stepping out into the storm. She didn't want to let me go, and I almost had to pry her arms off me.

"Come back quickly."

"I will," I said. I walked over to Owen and hugged him. "You're in charge, okay? You're almost a man now. Keep everyone calm, and more importantly, keep an eye out for anything wrong. Got that?"

"Yeah," he said. He scratched his head and looked down at the gun that still looked awkward in his hand.

"I love you, Son."

"I love you too, Dad."

We opened the garage door, and as it rolled open, Jesse cut the ropes that bound Drake's legs. We had several blocks to go, and it would be too far to carry him this time. He would have to run alongside us.

Outside, there was just a slight drizzle, and the street looked empty. The dark clouds still oscillated slowly above the island and flashed with lightning. If Dominic's calculations were correct, that cloud-to-cloud lightning would soon become something far worse, only to be followed by fifteen minutes of silence. Hopefully we would be able to make it to the police, drop off Drake, and inform them of what we knew.

The garage door closed behind us, and Jesse and I began our trek to Second Street with Drake in front of us.

Even though I didn't realize it until much later, and with much regret, something terrible happened while Jesse was explaining to my wife and son how to use the guns. Even though I wasn't aware of it at the time, it seems to be the only explanation for the tragedy that happened later.

Around the time Jesse was giving my son a crash course in handgun use, I believe Darrel was standing just outside the garage door, listening. I can imagine him standing there, with his ear pressed against the door. He must have gone into the garage later, after my wife and son had gone back into the living room to join the others.

I can imagine him kneeling down beside the duffel bag, removing one of the other handguns, and hiding it in his pants.

That must have been when he came up with his plan, and maybe that was why Darrel seemed "better" from that point forward. He was, according to my wife, more helpful, more alert, and more present in the current circumstances. We attributed it to the notion that he had finally snapped out of the spell he was under, but in hindsight, it must have been because of what he planned on doing.

And one thing was for sure: none of us saw it coming.

Chapter Twenty-Five

W e made our way to Second Street with Drake and kept him in front of us by prodding him with our guns. We hoped we didn't cross anyone on the street, because we weren't sure how someone would react if they saw us with him. What would they think? There were people out there who would probably want to take him from us and execute their own form of justice.

Nobody was out. The streets were as empty as ever, and we pushed Drake along in front of us. The wind had picked up though, and a slight drizzle was coming down. The air was humid and sticky, and overhead the clouds were a great, dark beehive of electrical activity. If Dominic's theory was correct, it was about to get worse. Much of that cloud-to-cloud lightning would turn into cloud-to-ground lightning, and the storm would once again assault us. But at least this time, we knew when it would end. Just after eight o'clock, the sky would become a graveyard, and the clouds—dark, massive tomb- stones overhead—would cease to throw down their electrical spirit.

The window would open, and people would be able to get

through. At least, they *might* be able to get through. It was possible, and my heart clung tightly onto that one hope. Even though we wouldn't be able to test it tonight—there probably wouldn't be enough time—we would certainly be there tomorrow, and we'd show up on the edge of the water with as many residents of Naples as we could.

We didn't pass one person on our short journey, but we did hear one of Klutch's ambassadors running through one of the neighboring streets, delivering the same message: "Klutch offers his protection! The big brick house by the fountain. He knows what this is! Klutch offers his protection!"

There were also voices in several of the homes as we passed, and I suspected that we were one of many homes in which neighbors had gathered together to pool resources and wait out the storm. I was confident of it. I could see candlelight in many of the windows, but almost never in two homes that were side by side. It amused me. Was it possible that the storm's attempt to take things from us and turn us against each other had backfired? Wouldn't that be the greatest of ironies?

Once we reached Second Street, we sat Drake against the edge of a building. It was a hair salon. Jesse and I stood sentinel beside him and looked up the dark, empty, silent length of the main strip and decided that we would simply camp there until the police car made its normal dinner-time rounds while warning all residents to remain indoors and to resist making attempts to escape the island.

We didn't wait very long. Just as Jesse was checking his watch and letting me know it was closing in on five o'clock, we saw two lone headlights on the other end of the island begin crawling their way toward us; soon after, we could hear the same announcement that we'd heard the previous days: "All residents of Naples Island, please remain indoors until otherwise notified. Do not make any attempts to leave the island. All bridges have been destroyed by lightning. The lightning is striking anybody attempting to leave via water."

As the police car neared us, I noticed the first of the cloud-to-ground lightning. The hot, humid wind picked up, the rain began to increase, and the lightning began to lash down from the clouds. The storm was heating up. If Dominic's prediction was accurate, this would be the first of another wave of rain and lightning, and it would be worse than the last violent episode the previous night. I wondered if the lightning would take out homes this time, and if I'd see more of those weird lightning balls floating around. What would they take with them this time? If they took Hot-rodder, then those lightning balls would certainly take others.

Jesse and I stood in the street and waved, and the police car stopped about a block away from us. Its lights were flashing. I had buried my shotgun in the bushes nearby, and Jesse had pocketed his handgun, and we had done so because it wasn't exactly inviting to see two gun-toting strangers standing on the corner of the street, waving; yet, it seemed the vehicle was still apprehensive about moving forward. I didn't blame the officer. For all they knew, the crazy gunman was still running wild through the island, killing people.

The door to the vehicle didn't open, and none of its windows slid down. It waited silently down the street as the sky filled with plumes of white light and peals of great thunder. Finally, we heard the woman's voice through the P-A: "Please return to your homes. Remain indoors until otherwise notified."

"We have Drake!" Jesse screamed, and I joined him.

"We have the gunman," I cried and, nearly jumping up and down, pointed to the tied up figure leaning against the wall of the hair salon.

This was terrible. I hadn't come all this way to have the

police completely ignore us and assume us to be nothing but a couple of trouble makers.

But something we said must have gotten her attention, and I'm sure she saw Drake leaning up against the wall. From her perspective, I imagined that she thought we had brought someone wounded to her. The vehicle suddenly drove forward. The headlights were blinding. Another spotlight on the vehicle blinded us as well.

"Get down on the ground and spread your hands and legs!" the woman's voice commanded through the P-A.

"What?" Jesse barked. "Are you looking over here? We have the killer! He's right there!"

"Get down on the ground and spread your hands and legs!"

"Are you kidding me?" he asked angrily.

"She doesn't know who we are," I explained. "Just do it. She's just being safe."

Grunting in disagreement, Jesse hit the deck along with me. I lay on the ground with my cheek against the wet asphalt as the rain came down. I heard the car door open and footsteps approach, and when I looked up, I saw the woman who would later introduce herself as Deborah Blazer. Two other people had gotten out of the vehicle with her. She was a tall, gangly woman with a fiery crop of short red hair. Her face was an asteroid field of freckles.

She slowly walked toward us with her gun drawn. The two other people remained behind her.

"He's over there," I said as she stepped near me.

"Who is he?" she said.

"His name's Drake," Jesse explained, lying beside me. "He's the guy who killed all those people on the Fourth. That's why we came here, to hand him over to you."

She took a moment to register this and asked, "Who are you two?"

"Jesse Davidson."

"Eddie Dees," I said.

"Eddie Dees?" she asked. "The writer, Eddie Dees? I knew he lived here, but you're him?"

"Yep, that's me." It felt strange addressing her while lying on the ground.

I've never been one to take advantage of my pseudo-celebrity status, and the fact of the matter is that being a writer hardly qualifies. It's a strange profession; the imaginary people in your head are the ones who become famous. Most people couldn't pick me out of a lineup, even those who've read the books. The characters are the ones people want to meet and talk to, not me. I'm just the boring guy who gets up early in the morning and sits at the computer in his pajamas.

I remember once, while on a book tour in San Francisco, my wife convinced me to "use my name" to get us past a long wait at a very nice restaurant she'd been dying to go to, and it did work. Somehow, miraculously, we were seated within minutes, but I felt bad about it after.

But lying on the asphalt with Deborah Blazer standing over me with a gun in her hands, I had never felt more elated to "use my name."

And it worked. Officer Blazer, who always insisted on just being called Deborah, even reached down to help me to get up. She put away the gun and crossed her arms in front of her and stared at the bound and gagged figure leaning against the wall of the hair salon. The rain was coming down heavy, and all of us were drenched.

"So that's him, huh?" Deborah asked.

"Special delivery," I said. "A long story, and I'll tell you about it later, but we wanted to get him to you. He took a kid with him after the killing. I don't know if you know about that. I thought he killed him, but apparently he didn't. He said the storm took him. Cocooned him in a ball of lightning and pulled him right up to the clouds."

I remember the look on Deborah's freckled face; it was the grim, familiar expression of someone being reminded of something she most desperately wished to forget.

"I know," she said. Her blue eyes rose toward the clouds in fear and awe. "I've seen."

Chapter Twenty-Six

We rode in the front seat with Deborah and laid Drake in the backseat. The two men, both volunteers in Deborah's band of community servants who had ridden with her, followed on foot.

I was pleasantly surprised to discover that, even though it had only been a few days since the storm stranded us on the island, Deborah had been able to set up a "control center" in the auditorium of Naples Elementary School. She took us straight there, and when we rushed into the auditorium to escape the storm outside, I saw about thirty people within. A few sat at tables set up on the stage and were looking over papers, but most sat uncomfortably in the kid-sized auditorium seats and talked amongst themselves. There were candles set up throughout the auditorium, which did a poor job warding away the darkness; I had to squint to make things out.

After Deborah explained why she had come back with Jesse and me and who the bound and gagged prisoner was, the men and women cheered, clapped their hands, and broke out into genuine celebration. Many of these people approached us and shook our hands. One short Asian woman even kissed me on the cheek. I had never been much of an athlete in school, so I can only guess this was the kind of celebration a home run hitter comes back to outside the dugout after he's rounded the bases.

But after I learned who all of these people were and why they were here, their excitement made perfect sense. Deborah knew many of these people and personally fished them out of their homes to help her set up this makeshift command center in the storm. She had explained to us, on our way to the school, what had happened to the two other on-duty officers who had been on the island. Drake had shot one of them, and I thought I remembered seeing that. I hadn't remembered it until she spoke of it, and perhaps a part of me didn't want to. The other officer, a fellow by the name of Pete Sanchez, had been taken just like Hot-rodder. Two nights ago, during one of the flare-ups, a ball of lightning had materialized out of nowhere, bubbled itself around him, and hoisted him up into the madness.

Several of the men and women here were officers who were off-duty when Drake went on his killing spree, but it didn't take me long to realize that they didn't see themselves as off-duty. Many had come because of a commitment they felt to keep the community safe and under control, both from the storm and the crazy gunman in their midst.

Deborah quickly explained what they had been doing for the last several days. She emphasized the word *control* many times. Their sole mission had been to keep the situation in control to the best of their ability, and for now, that was to keep residents inside and out of the storm and out of the path of the gunman. That was why she made her nightly rounds up and down the main streets, urging residents to remain indoors.

Much more had been going on behind the scenes as well. I noticed maps spread across many of the tables on the stage. They had established quadrants for the small island and had designated a team for each section. I think everyone knew a time would come when residents would have to be notified what to do after food supplies ran out and the true chaos began. They had already thought this through and were prepared, so far as I could see, to mobilize when this was necessary. I also learned that they had already quietly gone into these areas to look for any injured, gather more qualified recruits, and get a sense of the situation in general.

Deborah's team had broken into an Urgent Care a couple blocks down on Second Street. From what I learned, two doctors Deborah had rounded up were stationed there to deal with the injured. Fortunately, there weren't many. The wife of a middle-aged man suffering a heart attack had flagged down Deborah's vehicle the night before, and he was taken there. Another of Deborah's scouts, while assessing the situation in his neighborhood quadrant, had come upon a house with lots of hysterical voices within; upon investigating, he discovered that a despondent young man had slashed his wrists in an effort to escape the storm once and for all. He was also taken to the facility.

Communication with outside authorities had been as futile for them as it had been for everyone else on the island. Their cellular phones had been equally uncooperative, and Deborah couldn't pick up anything on police dispatch. Nothing but static. What most surprised me, however, were her futile attempts at making verbal contact with the emergency crews gathered just on the other side of the water.

She had gone with others on her team to the very end of Second Street to the base of the crumbled bridge. That bridge, which had previously led into Belmont Shore, was the smallest of those that had once connected Naples to the mainland. Now that it had crumbled beneath the lightning, there were only a hundred or so yards of water between her and safe land. She had looked through the rain and the flashes of lightning upon the virtual ocean of flashing emergency crew lights where the storm wasn't falling; most likely, she assumed, they were just as desperately trying to find a way onto the island as she was trying to find a way off it. She had begun to make verbal contact with them through her P-A when the lightning began to strike the water just before her.

Her small team retreated from the water and returned on two subsequent occasions in an attempt to make some kind of verbal contact, but it seemed clear that the lightning wasn't going to allow it. The storm *wanted* the island to be isolated from the outside. In Deborah's opinion, even getting close to the water's edge was just as dangerous as getting into it because the storm was somehow intelligent and had learned what they were doing. It would thwart anyone's attempt to leave. After the last two attempts to return to the water's edge and initiate some kind of communication with the authorities from the other side, she and all of her crew had given up hope of making any real contact with the outside. The only alternative now, it seemed, was to wait it out and maintain control and trust that this storm, like all storms, would eventually pass.

Deborah ordered a big Samoan and a guy with a Dodgers cap to deal with Drake. These were the two people who had also been in the police car when Deborah found us. I'm not sure if I ever heard the big Samoan's name, but the twenty-something guy wearing the Dodgers cap was Mickey. Full of vitality, Mickey was always smiling and always seemed helpful. He had the funny habit of nicknaming people, so much that I wondered if he actually knew people's names. I was Mr. Author. Jesse was Paul Bunyan. He simply referred to Deborah Blazer as Big Chief. It could have been an annoying quality in a person, but there was something so playful and upbeat about him, I don't think it bothered people all that much. They let him have his way.

They took Drake into a small room to the side of the stage,

and I delivered the second part of the news; I started to explain to Deborah everything Dominic had told us, that there might be a possibility of getting off the island.

I had barely began my explanation when she stopped me in mid-sentence and told me to come up on the stage. They were about to have a scheduled meeting, and she preferred that I share with everyone. But I had the impression that she, like the others here, had contemplated lots of different ideas and ways to get off the island in the last several days. Would Dominic's observations just be another wacky theory?

The big Samoan and Mickey came back onto the stage.

"Got him locked up for ya, Big Chief," Mickey said, wiping his hands. "That's one less piece of trash Naples Island has to deal with."

"Very good," Deborah said.

"Locked up in the principal's office. How's that for irony?" he said.

The thirty or so workers pulled over some of the folding chairs and took seats facing Deborah. I had the feeling they had done this several times, perhaps to take instructions, report the findings of the quadrants they had explored, or to simply brainstorm ideas. In the dim candlelight of the auditorium, it felt like I was joining an AA Meeting. Jesse sat alongside me.

Deborah stood in front of the group, thanked me and Jesse for delivering Drake to them (which won another round of applause), and spoke to the group for a few minutes about the quadrants they had sectioned off and whether or not any of the recent scouts had anything new to report. Nobody did.

The storm outside was raging violently. We could hear the rain pounding on the roof, and the thunder outside seemed unending and unrelenting. Occasionally we thought we could hear explosions. Perhaps the lightning was taking out trees and light poles—I think that was what most of us assumed—but what if it was taking out more? What if the storm was now taking out houses? What if it took out the auditorium I was sitting in, or even worse, my family? *I should go home*, I thought. *I should go home and be with them.*

We all listened silently for a moment, and even though nobody said anything, I'm pretty sure we were all thinking the same thing. The storm was getting worse. This was another wave—another spasm—in what would inevitably destroy us, and we had no means by which to fight it. That was the most sobering realization.

But if Dominic was right, then there might be one possibility. It would all depend, of course, on what happened when a few minutes after eight o'clock struck. If the lightning continued to rage on, he was just a crazy Santa look-alike with a radio in one hand and a Twinkie in the other. But if the storm ceased and the lightning faded, he would be much, much more. He would be a prophet, like Elijah, calling out to people in the desert.

Seeing that nobody had anything of particular interest to report, Deborah asked for us to come up in front and speak to her and the whole group about what we wanted to share. I looked to Jesse, but he shook his head. I'd been in this situation before. For some reason, when you're a writer, everyone assumes you're a good public speaker. What a lie. He wanted me to get up there on my own.

So I did, and Deborah took her seat in a folding chair up front. I was greeted again by applause. Once again, I felt like I was at an AA meeting and had just rattled off an impressive number of "days sober" before this thin, candlelit crowd. I had gone to AA meetings a couple times years ago, when researching for one of my books. I hadn't told them I was a writer. I just sat in the back, sipped my coffee, and made small-talk, but it reminded me of this.

The applause was understandable; after all, I was one of the two guys who special-delivered the "bad guy" to their doorstep. When the applause faded away and I saw all of these men and women looking at me eagerly, my hands went clammy and I felt a knot in my throat. I had no way to prove what I was about to tell them, and it was just one eccentric guy's theory. I wondered how many bizarre theories they had discussed and debated over the last several days.

"A lot of people think because I'm a writer, I'm pretty good at making speeches, but in all honesty, I'm not," I said.

This won some laughter and a bit more clapping.

"Tell us what you got," Mickey said cheerfully.

The big, beefy Samoan sitting next to him folded his arms across his chest, looking kind of angry. I think he always looked angry. In fact, I think the angrier he looked, the more at ease he was.

"I didn't really expect to see so many people here already pulling together, and it's pretty encouraging to see," I said, not knowing exactly where to begin. "Earlier tonight, my neighbor, his name is Dominic, talked to me about some observations he's made in relation to the storm. I wanted to come here and share them with you, because I think it's important. And I think he might be right. There may be something to this."

I don't remember how long I talked, but I got into my groove and explained Dominic's entire theory to them as best I could. I discussed the cessation of cloud-to-cloud lightning and how such gaps occurred directly after the fiercest moments of the storm and the possibility that, during those times, we might have a chance of actually getting across the water and off the island; and of course, the possibility that others might get in.

As I talked, the building shook with peals of thunder, and I occasionally stopped and listened somberly to the destruction occurring outdoors. It was electrical warfare out there. It were as if I was standing in some large, candlelit bunker in the midst of a violent battle. As I listened to what must have been street poles, telephone poles, and roofs exploding all around us, my thoughts and my heart turned toward home. I hoped my wife and children were okay. I wished I could be there with them.

Car alarms sounded everywhere. Those that had gone off during the first and subsequent waves of the storm had long drained their batteries dry and been silenced, but now a new choir of sirens howled during the gaps of thunder.

I don't know how long I stood there babbling on. Along with Dominic's theory, I explained how we had apprehended Drake, and I also included everything that had happened prior to the storm hitting us. I theorized that the storm had been "taking things" from us and trying to turn us against each other before it actually struck. Those little balls of lightening had permeated our homes, cocooned our belongings—just like Hot-rodder—in the storm's effort to exterminate us. When I was done offering everything I had on the subject, I noticed several people whispering to each other, and for some reason, most turned their attention toward Mickey. I didn't know what I'd said that put Mickey in the spotlight, but I must have struck some nerve.

Deborah got up, gave me a manly slap on the back, and thanked me for sharing. "Mickey," she said. "What time did you get through to the island?"

That was when I learned that Mickey wasn't on the island when the storm hit; he had gotten in after. He was probably the *only* person on the island who hadn't been here when the storm struck, because his story was one in a million. He had worked the night of July 4th as a paramedic and instead cele-brated Independence Day one day later by getting drunk with friends in his apartment not far from the bay. A friend dared him to swim to the island and back. They had seen all of the emergency crews lining the bay and knew something seriously funky was going on with the storm and the lightning but at that point didn't realize the full magnitude of what was taking place. Being young, drunk, and stupid, it seemed like the perfect opportunity.

Mickey ran over to the bay with his buddies, found a break in the front lines that rescue workers and the authorities had established, and swam his drunken self all the way to the island without one bump in the road. The story outright amazed me. This twenty-something accomplished more with a six-pack of Guinness than the National Guard had been able to do with all of the resources at its disposal.

I had the feeling Mickey was just lucky in that way. I guess some people are like that. He was the kind of guy who could probably go to Vegas every weekend and come back in the black. I think everyone had chalked Mickey's experience up to blind luck and hadn't understood the timeframe.

"What time did I come over?" he asked, thinking about it. He took off his Dodgers cap, scratched his mop of hair, and placed it back on his head. "I don't know. Probably a little after eight, I think. A little after eight."

"Really?" Deborah said, and everyone in the room connected the dots at once.

I noticed that it was silent outside. I had talked longer than I thought, and we were now in the gap. Someone mentioned that it was 8:05, and two people, a man and woman, ran to the front doors of the auditorium to look outside. Both affirmed what everyone knew: the clouds were lower, darker, and thicker, but there wasn't a single spark of electricity in them. They were recharging, sleeping, and waiting for the next round, just as Dominic had predicted.

"Should we test it?" I asked. "Maybe we should get out there to see if it works."

"I think we already have," Deborah said. "I think Mickey here has pretty much proven your theory, don't you think? You say it'll kick back up at 8:18, huh?"

"Yeah. And tomorrow night, we'll have 8:03-8:13, if it keeps the pattern."

"Good," she said, in thought.

The man and the woman stayed at the front doors to the auditorium, keeping watch. They were as anxious as everyone else to know what 8:18 would bring.

Deborah was in serious thought, her freckled face wrinkled in concern. "We'll have to spend all night tonight and all day tomorrow going to the neighborhoods and alerting everyone of where to meet," she said. She paced and seemed to be talking more to herself than everyone sitting there. "We'll have to be organized and efficient. We'll have to form a sort of parade right along Second Street, and at 8:03 sharp, swim across. Maybe even a minute or so later since its watch might be slightly off ours. We'll have to gather something for those who can't swim, the very young, and the elderly. We'll have to be prepared."

"What about that Klutch guy?" someone asked. "Doesn't he have some people following him? He thinks this is all weaponized weather and we're under attack from the outside. That's what I've heard."

"Weaponized weather?" I said, in disbelief. "Yeah, right. I don't think the storm is weaponized. It's more like the storm is trying to weaponize us."

"One other problem we'll have to contend with," Deborah said. "We don't have a drunk guy—at least at the moment—to send across the water to make sure we can really make it all the way without the lightning getting us. So we need a guinea pig. I don't know who, but we need someone to swim out ahead to make sure it won't come down and nail us halfway across."

This brought a contemplative silence, but it didn't last long. I think Jesse was the first to turn in his chair and look toward the room Mickey and the Samoan had ushered Drake into. I heard the creaking of the folding chairs as one by one everyone turned to look in that direction: the principal's office. It was a unanimous vote made without a single word.

"Alright," Deborah said, rubbing her hands together and getting everyone's attention back up front. "Then let's start talking details and make this plan happen."

Chapter Twenty-Seven

J esse and I left shortly after Deborah and her volunteers began looking through their maps to devise a practical, efficient plan of going through the neighborhoods and alerting all of the island's residents. The lightning started again at exactly 8:18, proving that Dominic's theory was accurate. There was no discussion after that as to whether or not the theory was valid; from that point on, the only discussion was how the thousands of residents currently on the island were going to be mobilized in an orderly way to get across to the water.

The plan was fairly simple, all things considered. Deborah's team would begin at midnight. They would hit every quadrant they had established, knock on doors, yell from street corners, and do whatever it took to deliver one simple directive: all residents were to meet at 7:00 pm the following evening on Second Street, begin their line at Toledo Avenue, a block away from the Second Street Bridge, and wait in an orderly, peaceful fashion until given the order to cross the water. Deborah's volunteers would be there to help keep the residents calm and to establish some form of order. I wasn't sure what Deborah was going to do about the very elderly and those who couldn't swim, and I had the feeling she didn't either. We were all going to have to wing this on some level, but the most important thing was to help as many people off the island as humanly possible.

Not everyone would make it. We all knew that.

I didn't like how we would all be lined up along the street. It would slow people down and afford less possibility to get across, but there were few options to spread out. Deborah said she would consider this and look into it. If people wanted to swim across from another point on the island, she certainly wasn't going to stop them.

At seven o'clock, Deborah would pick up my family, and we would go with her to the front of the line. She wanted Dominic, the brains behind the theory, to be up front with her.

The most troubling part of the plan, however, was the reality that the storm would be worse than ever the following night, and all of those people—including my own family—would have no choice but to stand outside in it and wait. There was no time to remain indoors and wait for the storm to cease. We only had ten minutes. Ten minutes! We had to be outside, lined up, and ready, so that we could begin to cross the very moment the last flicker of lightning died out. That meant we would have to stand out there in the midst of the wind, the thunder, and the lightning and endure the tempest until it subsided. There was no other option and no time for anything else.

The neighborhood had taken a beating from the storm that night. Three light poles had been blown apart by the lightning, and as we walked through the concrete rubble in the street, my heart feared what the following night would bring. Two wooden telephone poles were struck as well; both looked charred and were now leaning, electrical wires twisted all about them. The clouds were lower, so low, they hardly even looked like clouds. Instead, they appeared to be more like some mystic, black vapor that hovered there, waiting to suffocate us.

The lowering of the clouds and the lessening of peripheral lights from beyond the storm brought on a thick darkness. We used our flashlights to get back to my house and would have had a tough go at it without them.

My wife was ecstatic when she opened the door to see Jesse and me standing there. I had been gone longer than expected, but she knew that it would take some time to explain Dominic's theory to the authorities, so she didn't give me too much grief over it. She nearly jumped on top of me in her excitement and Toby, right behind her, embraced me as well.

"Daddy! Daddy!" he said excitedly. "That storm was scary! Do you think Bessie is okay out there?"

He was still worried about Bessie. Little Mia was with him, holding a paper of something she had sketched with crayons. The proud artist, she held the drawing up for me to see, but I really had no idea what it was. I think moms, in general, are better at that kind of thing; they have the innate ability to decipher toddler hieroglyphs.

I had barely stepped foot inside when I noticed a new expression—a troubled one—appear on my wife's face. She didn't have to say anything. I knew something was wrong.

"What is it?" I asked.

"It's Owen."

"What happened? Where is he?"

"He's not here."

"What do you mean he's not here?"

"He left a note and took off not long after you," she explained, on the edge of tears.

Samantha and Marsha came around the corner, grave expressions on their faces. Perhaps Darrel had snapped out of it, because I thought I could hear Dominic talking to someone in the living room; I could only assume it was Darrel.

"He wants to make sure that Candice is okay, and in his letter, said he was going to go to Klutch's house," she said. "He said he wants to hear what they think the storm is, too. I'm not sure he really believes Dominic."

"What do you mean he doesn't believe it?" I said, aghast. "It proved itself tonight. Right after eight, the storm shut down."

"I know, but he was already gone by then."

"So he just left?" I said again, completely dismayed.

My wife nodded.

"How could he do that? I told him to stay here. I told him! When he agrees to stay here, then he needs to stay here. I'm going to get him."

I turned to leave, and Jesse grabbed me by the arm.

"I'll go with you, buddy" he said. "You don't wanna be out there alone."

"No, I'll be fine. Really, I'll be okay," I said. "I'd rather have you here looking out for my family. Stay here, please. Just keep them safe. I'll be right back. It's only a few blocks away."

"Alright," Jesse said, handing me the flashlight. "You just be safe, okay? And remember, don't be a pansy."

"I'll remember."

I kissed my wife goodbye as she started to cry, but I was far too livid to be much comfort. I was seeing red. I was going to walk into that home, grab my son by the collar, and pull him into the street before he even knew what had happened. I hadn't spanked him since he was a little boy, but tonight, as the storm raged on, I questioned whether I should resume that practice.

I was just stepping outside when Darrel approached me. I was surprised to see him looking so alert. Standing before me, I saw a cognizant, aware, and concerned man, not the zombie that had wandered about the house for the last several days.

"Eddie, I wanted to talk to you before you left," he said. "I just wanted to say I'm sorry for being so out of it for so long. It's been rough, but I think I'm better now. I wanna help."

"Darrel, it's more than understandable. You have every right to be upset. Who wouldn't be?"

"I know, I know," he said. "But I just want you to know that I'm here to help. Me lying around isn't going to help anyone. Let me know what I can do."

"Okay," I said. "Start out with just keeping everyone calm. Keep the kids from being too scared. That would be a good start."

"Alright," he said. "I can do that."

"We'll get through this," I said, and slapped him on the shoulder.

And then I was off into the darkness with my flashlight. The oppressive clouds hung low and sizzled above the rooftops, and I was terrified to be out there alone. What if the lightning started coming down again? What if those electrical balls wrapped around me like they had Hot-rodder and pulled me up?

But I had more determination in me than fear. It could have been Hell itself that I had to travel through. It would have made no difference.

I was going to get my son, and nothing was going to stop me.

Chapter Twenty-Eight

I quickly reached Klutch's house. It was brighter inside the house than many of the other adjacent homes, as Klutch and some of his followers had rounded up lots of lanterns and candles. I was surprised to find the door ajar when I arrived. It almost appeared to be an open invite.

Inside, I could hear Klutch speaking to his small group of storm disciples. I walked right up to the front door but hesitated on stepping inside quite yet. I assumed, since people had been running through the streets advertising this house as a safe haven, I would be welcomed if I walked inside. But I had a shotgun in my hands, and I wasn't quite sure how they'd respond to that. I stood silently on the porch and listened.

"As I've been telling you, we don't have to guess what this freak show in the sky is," Klutch said, and even though he was probably only speaking to a very small crowd, he spoke as if he were addressing an entire nation. He was passionate. "This is the last frontier of warfare. Weaponized weather. I've been saying that since this storm first hit, and now everything this boy has told me only proves my theory. The sounds they heard on the radio? That's machinery, my friends. They don't like talking about it, but our own military has been experimenting and working on ways to weaponize weather for years now."

The boy? Owen? What did my son tell him, exactly?

"We need to stay together now, no matter what," Klutch said. "This is an invasion. I don't know what country got the guts to mess with America and has this technology to back it up, but you better believe our boys are doing everything they can right now to deal with it. But we need to stay in here and fortify. You have no idea what is going on past those waters, and it's probably worse out there than it is in here. We need to stay here, maintain our provisions, gather weapons, and wait this out."

Weaponized weather? Sit here and wait it out? This guy had to be kidding, right?

"There's a reason I didn't lose one man when I was a platoon leader in Iraq," he said, almost yelling at this point. "I was the Convoy Commander for over 180 Convoys. I've been up and down the roads in Iraq and through the Valley of Death more times than I can count. This ain't any different than going down those roads and looking out for IEDs. I know how to lead men, okay? I know how to make decisions, okay? And I'm telling you, if those people try to cross that water, a couple bad things are gonna happen because of it.

"Maybe the machinery does have gaps like the boy says, and maybe they will get through, but that's just going to let the enemy know that there's a whole community down here that's still alive. We don't need to advertise that fact; it's better if they think we're dead and we find a way to survive. There's a time to act and there's a time to lay low, and right now it's time to lay low. Do you all understand?"

A few "amens" followed his brief speech, and I realized Klutch was a good speaker. He was probably a great leader, as well. I understood why he always walked around with a chip on his shoulder. It made perfect sense. When in the military, serving as a platoon leader in Iraq, he had been admired, respected, and feared. Here, in society, he was a *nobody*. But now that he was back in a position of wartime leadership, with lives depending on him, it had awoken that part of him.

I understood perfectly why the residents who had gathered in this home were so enamored by him. In a time of peace, they would have dismissed him as a common dreg to society, or worse, ignored him completely. I think that would have been the worst kind of insult for Klutch. Yet in a crisis, Klutch was an easy man to follow. That was what concerned me about Owen. He was going to get sucked in by all of Klutch's fiery words and bravado. I worried for him.

I poked my head inside. Klutch paced in front of a massive brick fireplace like a preacher at a pulpit. There must have been twenty or so residents sitting in the room, some on couches, some on chairs, some on the floor, soaking up every morsel of falsehood this guy was throwing out. It was Jim Jones all over again.

I hadn't scanned the room very long when my gaze fell upon Owen. He stood in the very back, not far from me, his arm around Candice, listening like an obedient disciple to the man on stage. He must have sensed my presence, because he looked over just then and saw me. I didn't have to say anything; the enraged look on my face conveyed plenty.

He whispered something to Candice and walked over to me. As I motioned for him to come outside, Klutch got wind of what was happening. He stopped talking for a moment, assessed what was taking place, and then launched back into a tirade about the weaponization of weather.

Owen followed me outside, his head slightly lowered. He knew what was coming.

He followed me all the way to the front sidewalk, and I stood there looking at him for a good minute, planning my words, thinking through everything I was going to say. I switched the shotgun to my left hand as thunder crackled in the sky overhead and placed my flashlight into my pocket with my right hand. There was no need for it at the moment; there was enough light coming from the windows and open door of the house to see by.

"You have no right to leave your home and family when I asked you to stay and watch over them," I said firmly, pointing an accusing finger at him. "You completely disobeyed what I asked you to do, and even worse, you didn't keep your word."

"Dad, everyone was fine. I just wanted to see what was happening here."

"Really? Well, now you've seen. It's time to go."

"Dad, I think he might be right," Owen said. "He's served in the military. He knows about this kind of stuff. He thinks that we might be making a big mistake if we leave because we could be under attack out there. It'll be even worse if we cross over."

"Yeah, I heard his ridiculous little rant myself," I said. "Come on, Owen. How old are you? Sixteen? You're not a little kid anymore. You can't get sucked into this guy's nonsense. Didn't I teach you better than this?"

"You and Mom always taught me to question things. You said being a writer means you use your mind and you don't take things at face value. You look at the other side, you see where the other guy is coming from. Isn't that what you always said?"

"Yes, I did."

"Well, that's what I'm doing!" he said, raising his voice. I was shocked. My son was raising his voice at me? This wasn't supposed to happen like this. "I'm doing the very thing you taught me to, Dad. I'm questioning things. I think this guy may be right."

"But you're not supposed to question me," I said. "I'm your dad! That's different!"

"But, Dad, you're not—"

"I've heard enough," I said, pointing a finger toward home. "This entire island is meeting tomorrow night at seven o'clock on Second Street to get across that water when the path clears. We need to get ready. Let's go."

I took a couple steps away from the house and noticed Owen hadn't moved an inch. I turned around in disgust and disbelief. Owen wasn't following. His feet were firmly planted on the sidewalk, his arms crossed in front of him, defying my command. This just wasn't possible. What was happening? Why was I losing control?

"I said, let's go!"

"Dad, I'm not going."

"What did you just say?" I asked.

"I said I'm not going," he said, in a voice that was half-child, half-man.

"What?"

"I'm not going."

"That's not an option. Get home right now."

"Dad, no," he said, and his voice cracked. In the light emanating from the brick house behind him, I thought I could see tears in my son's eyes. His voice warbled. He was afraid. "I want to stay here. Candice hasn't been able to find her parents since the shooting, and Klutch promised to do a search tonight and tomorrow to find them. And I want to hear more about what he's saying. He thinks it's a mistake for us to cross over."

I was completely out of words. I even contemplated raising the shotgun I was carrying, pointing it at him, and forcing him to move away from the house. But I couldn't point the gun at him; I couldn't even remember if it was on safety or not.

I felt assaulted by terrible, monstrous visions of my little brother's hand slipping into the cold waters of the Kern. I remembered screaming when the hand slipped out of mine and into the deep.

That was what this felt like again. I was taken back to that place and time that seemed so long ago, and I was sickened by the feeling of someone else I loved—my own son—slipping through my grip yet again. I couldn't let him go. I wasn't ready; not even close.

"Don't do this to me, Owen," I said. "Don't do this to your mom and your brother. You can't do this."

"Dad, I love you," he said.

The vision of my son defiantly standing there blurred as my eyes welled with tears. I felt myself shaking all over, and I was breathing hard.

"You know I love you," he said again. "But I want to stay. I want to hear more, and I'll come back. I promise, Dad, I'll come back."

"Owen . . ." My voice trailed off.

I always knew I'd have to let go of my son, but I thought it would be later than this. I thought Madison, Toby, and I would stand at an airport and hug Owen goodbye as he boarded a plane to college. I always imagined I'd go home afterward and have a long cry about it with my wife and contemplate the silence in my home.

But this? I never imagined I would have to let go of my son while standing outside in a storm with a loaded shotgun in my hands. I never would have guessed it.

"I'll come back, Dad," Owen said again, and he went back into the house.

I reached for him, and I felt droplets of rain fall onto my outstretched fingers. I thought of Owen, and then I thought of my little brother and almost fell to my knees right there. This storm had taken too much from me. Now it was taking my son.

Klutch walked outside and strode toward me. His hands were buried in the pockets of his leather biking jacket, and his boots clicked on the pavement as he walked. He stopped a few feet in front of me and looked me up and down. I wondered if he had a gun in one of those pockets; he could clearly see the shotgun I was holding.

"You got a bright kid in there," Klutch said. He looked nervous and fidgety, as always. "Very bright kid. Just told me you're really gonna try to cross the water tomorrow night, huh?"

"Yeah," I said.

"Not a good idea." He had little pupils with lots of white around the periphery of his eyes, which made him look a little paranoid. "You go to the other side, and you're gonna be walking into a battlefield, my friend. You're also gonna advertise the fact that we're here."

"Look," I said. 'I don't care what you do. Stay here, for all I care. Don't come with us. But I want my son back. When he's heard enough, you send him right back."

Klutch shrugged and shifted his weight back and forth a few times. He had the nervous demeanor of a chain smoker, only without the cigarettes. "He's old enough to make his own decision, don't you think?"

"No, he's not. He's *not* old enough."

"Could have fooled me," he said.

I turned and walked away. I felt so defeated and crushed, I had nothing more to say. I would go home, break the news to my wife, and try to make sense of it. I didn't know if that was possible, of course. I wasn't convinced there was a way to make sense of all of this.

I had only taken a few steps when Klutch spoke up again. What he said troubled me, and I wouldn't understand it until later.

"You mobilize people to cross over, and you endanger all of us. You know that, right?" he said.

"I don't agree with you. Someone could look across the water and tell there's no war happening. Have you seen anything?"

"Looks can be deceiving," Klutch said. "The reason there might be emergency crews on the other side of the water isn't because they're waiting to help us. They might be waiting to cross over and get away from what's behind them. You ever think of that? And even if there are crews on the other side supposedly trying to help us, how do you know what side they're really on? Nobody can be trusted, especially someone on the other side of that water."

"I don't agree."

"I don't care whether you agree with me or not," he said. "What I care about is all of the civilians here on this island. I never lost a man when I was a platoon leader."

"Yeah, yeah, I heard that part. Why do you care about everyone here so much?" I asked. "Weren't you insulting all of us in the park the other day? What happened to you?"

"This is my public service," he said. "This is what I've been trained to do. You all need me, and that's the truth. The reason I didn't lose a man is because I was careful and strategic in everything I did. I would hate to have to take steps to make sure you guys don't cross over, so you need to think real carefully before you attempt it, my friend."

"Tell my son I'll be waiting for him," I said, and went home.

What else did I have to say? I certainly wasn't going to stand there in the darkness and debate weaponized weather with some paranoid biker, and I assumed Klutch was much more bark than bite. I didn't see how one guy and a few middle-aged Naples residents who were under his spell could possibly be successful in stopping us.

When I got home and walked inside, I didn't want to talk to anyone. The gravity of the situation fully set in. Everyone was in the living room, chatting by candlelight, but I stormed right past them and into my bedroom.

I collapsed onto the floor by the window and looked up at

the dark clouds overhead, and I hated them. I hated them with everything I had in me, even more than I hated Drake.

"You took my son," I said.

My wife came in to see what the matter was, but by then I was crying hysterically. I completely lost control.

"You took my son!" I screamed at the clouds. "You took my son! You took him! You murderer! You took him!"

I pounded my fists on the floor, and saliva flew from my mouth. I was a raging animal. Madison joined in my suffering as I explained through tears and muddled sentences what had happened. We held onto each other beside the window and wept endlessly, but the whole time I held her in my arms and stroked my hands through her hair, I looked disdainfully at the swirling mass of darkness above the rooftops.

Oh, how I loathed that storm!

I don't know how long we knelt there on the floor, but eventually, as I was starting to feel fatigued from my grief and anger, I heard something outside the window. It sounded like a bike with a playing card stuck in its wheel spokes. Then a dog barked. It sounded like—

No. It just wasn't possible.

I crawled over to the window, wiped the tears and saliva from my face, and looked down.

I was right.

It was a golden retriever. Bessie! She ran toward my house, barking, and I saw a little boy ride up on a BMX bike behind her. Hot-rodder!

He stopped his bike right out front on the lawn, cupped his hands around his mouth, and yelled, "Word of the day!"

It was real. They were here.

"Word of the day!" he yelled again.

"What the—" I whispered.

Those were two words, but it was all I could think to say.

Chapter Twenty-Nine

Hot-rodder, whose real name was Bryan McMichael, told us exactly what had happened to him after Drake kidnapped him. We brought him into the living room, sat him down on the couch, and eagerly hovered over him to hear every last detail of how he came back. I soaked up every last word.

It was amazing to see him sitting there, all in one piece, looking happy and chipper as ever. Marsha even found a Coca-Cola in the fridge, which was no longer cold with the electricity out, but he happily took it, thanked her with a nod of his scruffy head, and gulped half of the can down in a matter of seconds. I could hear Toby and Mia playing in the other room with Bessie. I think Toby was so excited that his dog was back, he had forgotten about the storm entirely.

We listened as Hot-rodder explained what had happened to him, and Jesse and I, exchanging glances as we listened to the story, both realized that his account perfectly matched Drake's version of events.

Hot-rodder broke free from the crazy man's grip not long

after leaving the park, ran like crazy as lightning forked down from everywhere, and then suddenly, he felt like he was trapped in a big, sizzling bubble of electricity. He tried to break out of it but couldn't. The shell of the lightning ball was flexible in a weird way, and when he pushed and wriggled and fought to break out, it simply stretched and contorted with his movements. He hovered up toward the clouds while he screamed, cried, and pushed against the inner-wall of his prison, until—

"Until what?" Marsha asked. She was completely engrossed in the little boy's story. "Oh dear, please tell me it didn't hurt."

"Not really," Hot-rodder said, grinning. I think the little rug rat thought his story was cool. He didn't seem nearly as afraid as he should have been. "It just felt kind of staticky, if that makes sense."

"Oh yes, electrostatic!" Dominic said. He said it with such enthusiasm, I could only assume that it somehow correlated with one of his theories regarding the lightning. "Like when you touch the screen of a television, right? Felt kind of like that?"

Hot-rodder, who was growing up in the age of flat-screen televisions, just looked at the Santa lookalike peculiarly, and I urged him to finish the story.

There wasn't much more to tell. He unwillingly rode the lightning bubble toward the clouds, where he was suddenly blinded by a massive white light. He covered his face, screamed, and assumed he was going to die, but suddenly there was a very loud noise. Louder than the thunder, even. He felt the static cocoon instantly evaporate, and then he was falling—but he didn't fall far. Maybe just a few feet.

He landed with a thud in a back alley. There was a bunch of junk lying in the alley. He saw some tools, a couple paintings, keys, wallets, and clothing, all scattered about. He got his bearings and was trying to make sense of what had happened to him when he felt something racing toward him.

Scared that Drake had followed him, Hot-rodder said he put his hands over his eyes, screamed, and prepared for the very worst as he lay on the asphalt, anticipating what would happen next. Maybe the crazy guy would pick him up and run away with him again, or worse, maybe he would just kill him right there on the spot. Who knew?

But all his fears were alleviated when he experienced what was, in his own words, *assault by a slobbery weapon*: Bessie's tongue. He was a witty little kid to come up with that phrase on the spot, and the writer in me was impressed.

He recognized Bessie the moment he saw her, and her nametag only substantiated it. Hot-rodder was a dog lover, and he had stopped outside my house on more than one occasion to give her attention while I was taking her for a walk.

He knew exactly where to go. He crossed through the park on the way over, and even though he was freaked out when he saw the dead bodies lying in the grass, he grabbed his bike anyway. His own home wasn't far, so he stopped by home on the way over, but nobody was there. Perhaps his parents had taken refuge in another home.

"Wait a minute, wait a minute," Dominic said, intrigued. "You're saying you just came over right now? As in you just fell onto the asphalt?"

"Yep." Hot-rodder finished off his soda. "That's what I'm saying. Pretty much came right over."

"Strange," Dominic said, considering this. "You were taken days ago, on the Fourth. And you just got free? Right now?"

Hot-rodder, who probably thought Dominic was some old guy who was hard of hearing, spoke much louder than necessary: "Yes, I just got free and came right over!"

"How strange," Dominic said. He put his hand to his

white-bearded chin and looked off in deep, contemplative thought. "You skipped ahead in time somehow. It only lasted a little while for you, but to us, it's been days."

"So everything dropped in that alley, huh?" I asked. I wasn't sure if I was actually asking Hot-Rodder or just making the point out loud. "You saw clothes, wallets, that kind of stuff? So the storm just held all of it and then dropped it right in that alley?"

"I saw a lot of junk."

"How much?" Dominic asked.

"Dunno. A pile of it, I guess."

"It's probably one of many drops," Dominic said. "It would probably be a massive mountain of junk if it was really everything that's been taken from everyone on the island."

"I don't get it though," I said. "Why would the storm drop everything right now? What would be the point of that?"

"Probably no need in holding on to 'em, when it's about to wipe us all out," Jesse said. "It makes sense if the storm's going to wipe out this island, don't you think? It's dropping all the things it's been holding onto and winding up for a last round or two."

"So it really has been taking things?" Marsha said. "How strange. Did you see a short story there? Pages all stapled together?"

Hot-rodder shrugged, and we all took that as a "no."

"Can we be the first to leave?" Samantha said despondently. "Can we get there early and be in the front lines? There are so many people. What if we don't have enough time to get across? What if something happens to me? I can't die out there, I just can't."

Jesse shot me a knowing grin; it might be a little difficult escorting Mrs. High Maintenance to the Promised Land.

I was genuinely happy that Bessie and Hot-rodder had returned, but in some strange way, it made it that much more evident to me that Owen was gone. I slapped Hot-rodder on the back, told him he was welcome to eat anything he could find in the house, and excused myself from the room. Madison alone understood why I had to leave; sometimes, when things get overwhelming like that, I just need to be alone. It's the way I'm wired.

It drove my wife crazy our first couple years of marriage. She misinterpreted my "needing some space" as somehow being angry or giving her the cold shoulder, but it wasn't that at all. She'd follow me around the house, yapping away like a wiener dog in her effort to make things better. It took her years to figure out that she just needed to leave me alone for a while.

So I knew she wouldn't follow me outside when I walked out the front door and took a seat on our front patio furniture. The rain had let up. It was dark outside, but I didn't mind all that much. I wanted the solitude. I sat back in my chair, looked at the flickering lightning clouds above me, and realized I hadn't written in days. Maybe that was another reason I was having such a difficult time thinking straight. For several days now, I hadn't written a word, and my mind hadn't been able to process.

The front door opened and someone came outside. Maybe I was wrong; maybe Madison was going to try to yap at me to make things better. I almost told her to go back inside, to make the others comfortable, because I really just wanted to be alone for a little bit, but then I realized it wasn't her. It was Jesse.

He took a seat in the chair across from me. "You doing okay out here, buddy?"

I understood why he'd come; he didn't know me as well as my wife and didn't understand that I was like a boomerang in my grief. I may retreat into myself, but I always returned.

"Doing alright," I said.

He nodded. It was hard to see him fully in the darkness, but I heard him scratching his beard. He didn't say anything more, just sat there listening, and it had a strange effect on me, because it actually made me want to talk. My wife, in those early days of marriage, came at me with too many words and questions. It only made me want to retreat more. But Jesse, who was naturally silent, had the opposite effect on me.

"I'm just so angry at him," I said, after a very long but not uncomfortable silence. "He's only sixteen. I've done so much for him. His mom has done so much for him. And he wouldn't come back with me. I'm gonna have to restrain myself from killing him even if he does come back."

"You won't kill him," Jesse said, matter-of-factly. "In fact, you won't even be upset at him."

"Really?" I said. "And why's that?"

"Because you're too good a man for that, that's why. When Owen comes home, you'll run to him, embrace him, and it'll be like he never left. Because that's what daddies do. Good daddies, at least."

"Not sure about that," I said.

"Well then, you must have forgotten the whole point of parenting. Don't forget what you signed up for."

"And what'd I sign up for?"

"An unspoken agreement to get kicked in the groin for years on end, day after day, and still reach out and love the person doing it. Don't you forget it. If you wanted someone to love you perfectly every day and worship the ground you walked on, you should have just gotten yourself a dog."

I laughed. Jesse had a funny way of putting things.

"I'm still not sure I'll be able to restrain myself when I see him," I said.

"You just wait and see," Jesse said, "and I'll bet you a beer that everything I'm telling you will make sense then. You've never really had your kids rebel against you yet, have you?"

"Well, not really. Owen's only sixteen—and a pretty good kid, all things considered—and Toby's only eight."

"I didn't tell you about my daughter, did I?"

"No," I said.

Jesse was silent for so long I began to wonder if he was going to tell me the story. Maybe it was painful for him. I wasn't entirely sure.

"You've met my son at the Captain's Room," he finally said, "but I have a daughter who's a few years older than him, and I . . . well . . . I wasn't a very good man when I was younger. There are lots of things I wish I could take back, and I didn't blame their mom when she left me. I would have left myself if it was physically possible."

We laughed, but when the laughter faded, I sensed that Jesse was reaching into some deep, painful place.

"The divorce really hurt both kids, but it took the biggest toll on my daughter, Virginia," he said. "She eventually got involved in the wrong crowd—you know, drugs, that kind of stuff. Once I got my own life in order, I reached out to help her and staged an intervention with some others, but she walked away. But before she did, she spat in my face, cursed me, and told me that I was a loser of a father and wished me dead."

"Wow," I said. A few streaks of lightning lit the sky, and I saw Jesse in those brief, momentary flashes, looking down at his boots. I couldn't imagine what that would be like.

"Yeah," he said, "it was a hard thing to go through as a parent."

"When did you reconnect with her?"

"I haven't. But I wait every day for that phone to ring. Every day, Eddie. So when Owen comes back soon, you make sure you pick him up in your arms and thank God you haven't had to wait as long as others. And don't forget, you'll owe me a beer."

We might have said more, but we were interrupted when Dominic opened the door and stepped onto the front patio. He cradled the little handheld radio in his hands, and he had a troubled, bewildered look on his face.

"What is it?" I asked. "What's wrong?

"The static crashes," Dominic said, motioning to the radio in his hands. "They've changed. Something's happening."

Chapter Thirty

W e all huddled together in the living room to listen to Dominic's explanation of the lightning crashes. Once again, he turned on his radio and tuned to a very low AM station, and we heard the interference. This time, everyone in the room could hear what he was referring to, even Samantha, who wasn't able to discern anything before. The interference was louder, but it was repetitive and rhythmic. It sounded like a fire alarm drenched in static. If I had just happened to be scanning stations on my AM radio and heard it, I would have assumed it was some kind of emergency alert barely getting through due to weak signal.

"Can you hear it?" Dominic asked.

"Sounds like an alarm to me," Jesse said.

"Exactly," Dominic said, seeming rather pleased that we were able to discern it so easily.

"But what does it mean?" Samantha asked, and she seemed a bit annoyed to be sitting around having another discussion about the sounds of lightning. "Does this mean I can get across the water soon?"

"I'm not sure what it means," Dominic admitted, "but I would assume that perhaps it means the final sequence of the storm has begun. I think this only validates our hypothesis that as the gaps shorten each night by five minutes, the storm is really shutting down. Maybe our ten-minute window of time tomorrow night really will be the last chance. Maybe the island won't make it to the following night. It's like a final stage alarm, or something of that nature."

"You don't really know that," Darrel said, and I was shocked to hear him speak up. He was still a walking anomaly. At times, I felt like he was the old Darrel—alert, aware, and helpful; yet at other moments, I felt that his mind was somewhere else entirely. I couldn't really blame him for this, of course. If I saw Madison's head blown apart with bullets, I'm pretty sure my brain would be toast as well. I tried to give him lots of grace and patience. "We don't even know what this storm is, really. We don't know if we're going to get through tomorrow night. For all we know, the static could be things you're hearing beyond Naples Island. Maybe that Klutch guy is right. What makes us so sure? Maybe there's a war going on out there and we'll be going out of the frying pan and into the fire when we leave here."

"I don't think so," Dominic said. "It's only a hundred yards across the water. Someone would have seen and reported that by now you would think."

"I told Klutch the same thing," I said.

We didn't talk much longer about that, probably because we all knew there was no point. We wouldn't know if our plan would work until we actually crossed over, and even though I was more than convinced that there was enough evidence to suggest that our plan would work, nobody felt like debating it. Why snuff out the little hope we had?

We all sat in the room for hours, and our conversation

eventually led to the things in our homes that had gone missing prior to the worst part of the storm. In all of our fear and trepidation and plans to escape, we had never really sat down and talked through everything that happened before being trapped on the island.

Dominic began the conversation by explaining how some electrical equipment in his garage had gone missing. When he had first realized it was gone, he only assumed some neighborhood thief had broken into his garage at night and stolen it. Why else would it have disappeared?

Everyone followed Dominic's example. Marsha, in tears, told me about the morning she had realized her manuscript was missing and how she'd assumed I'd stolen it. She apologized profusely for thinking so wicked a thing of me and demanded a hug to make things better, and I obliged. She was a strong woman; the wind almost went out of me when she embraced me. At least now it made sense why she had acted so weird that morning when she came to my house.

Even Samantha, to my surprise, admitted that she thought some of the missing things in her home were because I had a crush on her. She skewed the story quite a bit and left out the whole part about her making a pass at me in her bedroom, but I didn't feel the need to correct her. I was just impressed that she was as honest as she was; I hadn't expected her to say anything.

I think it was most difficult for Darrel to talk about this. He talked about the missing wedding ring and the morning he went through the files and found some of his wife's papers gone. He was convinced she was going to leave him high and dry, just like his first wife.

He didn't talk very long. I think it brought great pain to his heart to realize that he had believed utter lies about her during her last days on Earth. It didn't resolve well in his mind, and once again, almost in mid sentence, Darrel excused himself, went into the guest room, and probably collapsed onto the bed in tears.

"My dad's been really mad because he thought I've been taking things from him," Hot-rodder said. "I've tried to tell him it's not me. I saw one of those ball things before, kinda like the one I got stuck in. Before all this happened, I was out in the backyard, and I saw one of them shoot right out of the garage. I think it had a hammer in it or something. It went right up to the sky like a backwards falling star. Weird!"

"Did you tell your dad about it?" Dominic asked.

"I tried, but he didn't believe me," Hot-rodder said, shaking his scruffy head. "He said it was just silly kids' talk. That kinda thing."

"Not so silly anymore," I said.

We talked for several more hours, and in the midst of that storm, I found it therapeutic. Maybe we all needed a little bit of that. I learned a lot more about Jesse's family and even about Marsha and Samantha, and I promised myself that when this was all over—when the storm was long behind us—I would make it more of a point to turn off the television, the cell phones, and all of the noise that seemed to so often get in the way. I couldn't even remember the last time I sat down with my family without a television, a tablet, or a cell phone being on.

What happened to just sitting down and talking? Why couldn't my kids—or even Madison and I—just sit on the couch and engage the people in the room with us without some kind of electrical device in our hand? When did all that happen?

Before long, I grew weary and needed to be alone. My thoughts were utterly consumed by thoughts of Owen.

I don't know if anybody actually slept that night, but we

tried. Toby and Mia slept in the bed with Madison and me, but I spent most of the night staring up at the dark ceiling and listening to the thunder outside. Dominic had said the static crashes had changed, and though not everyone agreed, I was convinced that the alarm in the clouds was an indicator that this freak of nature was in its final stages. I only hoped that we would be able to survive the storm's uptick that would precede the ten-minute window we would be afforded to make our way across to the mainland.

The next day was filled with anxiety. We had nothing to do but wait around until Deborah pulled up to the house to pick up Dominic and the rest of us at seven o'clock that evening. My eyes were constantly on my watch, and I debated many times about whether or not I should go back to get Owen. He shouldn't have taken this long. He should have been back already. What was the problem? Had something happened?

Madison was equally a mess, and Jesse restrained me several times from running back to the brick house and getting my son. He insisted I be patient and reminded me that, short of holding a gun to Owen's head and forcing him back to the house, I had done all I could.

But by the time two o'clock rolled around with no sign of Owen, even Jesse agreed it was time to do something. He agreed to go with me. I grabbed my shotgun, just in case, and Jesse and I headed to the front door. I was pretty convinced as we left, that this time, I really would use the gun to threaten Owen if that was what it took to get him to follow me. I was at the very end of my desperation.

I kissed Madison, who was in tears, before I stepped outside with Jesse. We had only taken a few steps away from my house when I noticed two people running toward us.

My heart nearly stopped. In the flashes of lightning, I recognized the skinny blonde girl as Candice, and next to her was Owen. I was so overcome with emotion I nearly dropped my shotgun and found myself running toward both of them. They were scared. I could see that.

"Owen!"

We wrapped our arms around each other, and I didn't want to let go. I couldn't believe he was here. After a sleepless night and a day plagued with fear and doubt, my son was right here, in my arms. Jesse tended to Candice to make sure she was alright.

"What happened?" I said, seeing how shaken he was.

"It's Klutch," he said, voice trembling. "He's going to try to stop you guys. I don't know how, but that's all he could talk about. We escaped. We did the search for Candice's parents this morning and didn't find anything, but he started acting really weird after that. He was drinking, I think. Kept talking about how you guys are gonna mess up the whole thing for him and how it'd be better if you were all dead. I got scared, Dad."

"It's okay," I said. "We'll figure it out."

"But what if he comes to our house? What if he comes here and finds us?"

"Did you tell him where we live?"

"No," he said, sniffling. He wiped his nose and shook his head.

"Then he won't find us here. We're safe."

"Okay," Owen said.

"What about his followers?" I asked. "What were they doing? Do they want to see us dead too?"

"They think he's been acting weird too," Owen said. "A few were talking about leaving, because they're not so sure anymore. And something weird happened this morning. He had stored some weapons, I guess that some of the people there had donated in case everyone started to riot or something like that, and they went missing. He thinks you took them, Dad. He thinks you and the group organizing this escape stole them from him. I think that's why he got so upset and drunk today."

"He thinks *we* took his weapons?" I said.

Owen nodded, and it didn't take me long to figure out what was happening. I looked to the clouds overhead. *You're still trying to do it to us,* I thought. *You're still trying to turn us against each other.*

"Let's get back inside, okay?" I said, and Owen agreed.

We walked toward home, and Owen was still troubled. There was something eating at him, and he stopped me a few feet from our house. Jesse and Candice waited by the door for us.

"Dad." Owen looked down shamefully, and I knew what was coming. "I'm really, really sorry Dad. It was wrong for me to stay there. I should have listened to you. I made you and Mom worry, and that wasn't right."

He was on the edge of tears. I hadn't seen him cry in years, and it reminded me of when he was a little boy. I found myself looking at him, wondering where the time had gone.

"I'm sorry," he said again. "Please forgive me."

I waited to respond. I had a feeling that Owen, who had never really rebelled in any meaningful way in his young life, would always remember this moment. Perhaps years from now, he would even sit down with his own children and talk to them about it. More than anything, I guess, I just wanted to get this right.

"Owen." I placed my hand on his shoulder. "I forgave you sixteen years ago when your mom and I brought you back from the hospital. That's a question you never even have to ask me, son. It's already been done."

He didn't say anything, but he hugged me.

I hoped I used my words well. I hoped he would remember those as the words of Eddie Dees his father, not Eddie Dees the writer.

Owen went inside with Candice to see his mom, but Jesse

stopped me at the door. He looked at me with a knowing grin and slapped me on the back.

"Looks like you owe me a beer, my friend."

"Looks that way," I said.

"And none of that pansy beer you keep in your fridge, okay?"

"Consider it done," I said, and we walked inside together.

Chapter Thirty-One

Deborah arrived at exactly seven o'clock that evening, and we were all ready to depart when she pulled up in front of my house. The storm intensified just as we had expected, and we wondered exactly how bad it would get that night. Although we talked little about it, I think we all worried that increased rainfall, wind, and lightning would reach cataclysmic proportions that evening. Whatever the case, we knew that we and all of the other residents of Naples would have to stand out on the streets and endure it if there was to be any hope of escape.

We bundled the littlest kids, Toby and Mia, up in raincoats. The storm had never been very cold, but they were going to get wet. Maybe the coats wouldn't help much, considering how bad the storm would get, but we wanted the kids to feel safe; if keeping some of the rain off them made them feel even a little more at ease and a little less afraid, it would be worth it.

While rummaging through the garage, Jesse and I noticed the duffel bag loaded with guns had disappeared. It was no surprise. Under normal circumstances, I suppose Jesse and I would have been alarmed and wondered who had snuck into the garage and stolen them, but we knew better at this point. When we noticed them missing, I walked back into the house, looked out the window at the storm clouds, and put my middle finger up against the glass. I wanted this storm to know exactly how I felt about it, and I hoped it understood me.

"It's not gonna work this time," I said. "We've had enough of you."

By the time Deborah arrived, the rain was heavy, the wind was strong, and the lightning was constant. Dominic rode shotgun along with Mickey, whom Deborah brought along with her. I think she wanted both of them close to her. Dominic, of course, she wanted there because he was the "expert" on what the storm was doing. She probably just wanted Mickey along because she hoped that some of his dumb luck would rub off on her.

Drake was in the backseat, tied up and bound, waiting to be thrown ahead of us into the water. I wasn't sure exactly what Deborah was going to do in order to motivate him to swim across, but I was sure I'd find out. Maybe just the possibility of escape was enough incentive to get him swimming.

Because the car was full, and nobody really wanted to ride in the backseat of a police car with Drake, we all walked behind as it moved forward at a snail's pace. The car's lights were flashing, throwing blue, yellow, and crimson light across the rain-drenched houses along the block.

Owen, Jesse, and I walked side-by-side behind the vehicle, each of us armed. I didn't like what Owen had told me about Klutch wanting to stop us. Maybe it was just the drunken blather of a man who was slipping from reality, but maybe he would actually act upon it. We weren't taking any chances. I still had the shotgun, and Owen still had the nine millimeter we'd given him in the garage.

My wife was to my left, and she managed the kids. She carried Mia, who was crying horribly due to the wind and rain, in utter confusion as to what was happening. I felt bad for the little girl, and my heart sank when I thought of her parents lying dead in the park. Toby walked by his mom's side, and even though he was afraid, I could tell he was trying to keep it together. Owen had a good talk with him before we left, and if there's one thing I've learned raising boys, it's this: little brothers idolize their big brothers. I think Toby wanted to be brave for Owen. He wanted to make his big brother proud.

It made me think of Alan. Oh, how I wished his hand hadn't slipped out of mine. How I so dearly wish the river had given my little brother back to me.

Hot-rodder rode next to them on his bike. We all told him it wasn't necessary, but he insisted. He thought riding in the rain and lightning was cool, and seeing no harm in it, we acquiesced. It was kind of fitting. It would have been strange for him to be out there without the bike; it was kind of like Samson's hair. The bike was where he got his strength and bravery, and none of us felt like being a Delilah and taking it from him.

Darrel walked alone, behind the rest of us, in the twilight world of his grief. He seemed unaware and unaffected by the storm.

Samantha and Marsha shared an umbrella and walked on the right side of the car. Candice walked behind them. They quibbled over who was hogging the umbrella more, but fortunately, the rumbling booms of thunder made most of their gabber inaudible.

Marsha was towing Bessie on a leash, and the poor dog was clothed in a plastic doggie raincoat we received as a gift years ago from my wife's aunt, a woman who probably treated her cats and dogs better than her own kids. We laughed when we received the gift, boxed it away in the garage, and forgot about it. White elephant gift exchange, here we come! I promised myself that I would never lose enough of my manhood to actually put a jacket on my dog. It was just *wrong* in every sense of the word.

But desperate situations called for desperate measures. Toby knew about the jacket, and in his love for Bessie, he cried, pleaded, and insisted that I find it and let Bessie wear it, because she might get scared out there in the cold. So while in the garage, just before noticing the missing duffel bag of weapons, I found the ridiculous doggie raincoat and put it on Bessie.

It was a short trip. Deborah stopped the police car about fifty yards from the water's edge, where the Second Street Bridge once stood. Rain began to pour down relentlessly, and I could see flashing lights on the other side of the water. There were emergency crews over there, probably doing the same thing we were. I wondered if they had a Dominic on their side who had cracked the storm's code, and if people would try to come over to us at the exact time we started to make our way across.

Second Street was already filling with people, and Deborah parked her car at the very end of the street and at the very front of what would be a long line of cold, terrified souls. Naples has a little over two thousand residents and—considering others who had been on the island because of the July 4th holiday—I would have sworn I saw at least twice that amount of people pour into the street like ants. They came with their flashlights and camping lanterns, and they were of all sizes and shapes: young, old, and everything in between. Many came prepared. They had gone into their closets and their garages and pulled out their raingear and umbrellas. By 7:45, the street looked like a parade waiting to begin.

Deborah's team had done a good job organizing, especially considering the limited time and resources that were available. She had authorized her team to break into a clothing store on Second Street and "borrow" some obnoxiously bright orange

T-shirts that were on the discount rack. It made them easier to recognize. Her orange-clad crew lined both sides of the street, and they did their best to keep order, keep everyone in the street, and when the window of opportunity opened, they would usher everyone across the water.

"Stay in the middle of the street and away from the side-walks," Deborah said through her vehicle's P-A. "The men and women in orange along the perimeter of the street are here to assist you with anything you need. Please be patient and organized."

They had also thought ahead. Her crew had rounded up some rafts and surfboards and piled them close to where Deborah stopped her car. These were for the elderly and the wounded or those who couldn't swim. I was amazed to see how many flotation devices Deborah's team had rounded up in so short a time. Her team had also advised as many people as possible to line up along the periphery, to gather along the docks, so that when the signal was given as many people as possible could get in the water and begin their trek without getting bottlenecked in the street.

But although I hated to admit it to myself, the sheer number of people I saw filling Second Street made me realize the virtual impossibility of what we were attempting. Only a ten-minute window? Was it even possible to get so many people across the water in so short a time? Would we even be able to get half of these people across?

Another thing troubled me as well. I've never been one for triathlons, but an old friend in college used to do them all the time. I remember how he talked about the swimming portion and how it was important to keep your space, because if you didn't, you'd get virtually beaten by the swimmers next to you. I was willing to bet this would be far worse than that.

Deborah was also worried about something. She got out of the car, despite the onslaught of rain, to assess the situation.

She was thinking the same thing that I was. When she looked upon the sea of terrified, shivering, citizens waiting like the Israelites to cross the Red Sea, I recognized the doubt in her eyes.

"There are lots of kids out there!" she yelled because of the volume of thunder. "They should come up front!"

"I thought the same thing," I cried. "Lots of women and children! They should all be up front!"

Just then, the clouds threw down a volley of lightning. Several lightning bolts struck light poles along the street, spraying sparks and glass over the crowd. It was difficult to hear their screams over the sounds of the storm, but I could see many of their frightened faces beneath their umbrellas and the hoods of their raincoats. I wondered if anyone should even be holding umbrellas; would they attract the lightning?

Other bolts of lightning struck buildings along the street, and even though bits of debris and sparks flew into the sky overhead, I didn't see one person in the crowd turn around and flee. They were holding their ground.

Strangely enough, when I looked up at the dark, swirling clouds overhead, I thought I could see a small break in them; there was a tiny hole, and I thought I could see a very small, clear patch of sky beyond it. I had barely time to consider what this meant before I saw those weird lightning balls return.

Little orbs of sizzling electricity descended from the clouds overhead. Each of them looked to be the size of grapefruit, but they grew larger as they fell closer to the earth. They spread out over the entire street, and I noticed Hot-rodder scream when he saw them. He threw down his bike and crawled under the police car.

Suddenly, one of the lightning balls shot toward us like a wasp. I was momentarily blinded and heard a loud humming sound that drowned out the sounds of thunder.

When my vision cleared, I saw that Toby had been

enveloped in an electrical cocoon, and even though he was kicking and screaming and clawing at the inside of the sizzling orb, he couldn't break free.

He wasn't alone. All of the other balls of lightning had done the same. Nearly fifty or so people screamed and clawed in their spherical cages just above everyone's heads. They began to slowly ascend back toward the swirling mass of destruction overhead.

The storm was taking them.

I hardly had time to think. Not knowing if it would electrocute me or kill me, I grabbed onto Toby. Amazingly, I was able to take hold of his hand. My hand passed through the outer shell of electricity easily, but I had a feeling it wouldn't be the same in the other direction. A strange, tingling sensation ran up my arm, and I was sure my hand was now stuck inside the orb. Where it went, I went.

"Dad!" Toby screamed.

"I won't let go, Toby!" I cried back. "I'll never let go!"

I'm in this place again, I thought. *Why? Why am I here again? Why with my own son?*

I pulled back with all of my weight, and I slowed him down for a moment, but I could tell that I was going to lose this fight. I couldn't stop it. I just wasn't strong enough.

Then Owen grabbed one of Toby's legs. Jesse took hold of his other arm. Deborah Blazer and Madison grabbed his pant legs. Marsha and a couple strangers in the front of the crowd raced toward my son and reached through the lightning to take hold of him. It was a miraculous sight to see—more miraculous, perhaps, than the supernatural ball of electricity that enveloped Toby.

And we weren't alone. All throughout the crowd, people grabbed onto and held back those who had been caught up by the lightning balls. Not one of them was allowed to ascend back to the clouds overhead—not one!

With so many hands on Toby and so much strength pulling him down, I felt him slowly slip out of the sizzling cocoon. There was a weird popping noise as he slipped out of the bubble and onto the wet asphalt by our feet, and the lightning ball, which now scintillated weakly, drifted away.

As I looked around the crowd, I saw the other empty lightning balls doing the same, and like the one Toby had been trapped in, they levitated toward the clouds like dying Chinese lanterns in the darkness. The rain poured down upon my face, and in an instant, Toby was in my arms and crying into my shoulder.

There was barely time to rejoice. The crowd began to part, and I saw why; Klutch rode down the length of Second Street on his Harley directly toward us.

This wasn't over yet, not by a long shot.

But I remembered what Dominic had said about the change in the static crashes, and when I looked back up at the dark clouds, I thought I could see just a little more of that hole in the storm. All the pieces came together.

I looked up defiantly as the rain poured down on my face.

The storm had been trying to destroy us. It had been trying to rip us apart. It was devouring our fear, our anger, our paranoia, and feeding from the lesser angels of our nature. That's why it had grown strong, but that was also why I saw it weakening. It was fractured.

Dominic was right.

I looked around and wondered. If we could show this cloud—this demon—that we are more than what it thought us to be, it would go away.

That's what we needed. To cut off of its food supply. To starve it.

"I know what you're doing, you monster," I said. "I know what you're doing."

Chapter Thirty-Two

As the crowd parted, Klutch drove his Harley through the rain. He was alone, which was a good sign at least.

I reached down to pick up the shotgun I had dropped when I pulled Toby from the lightning ball. I think everyone else was equally concerned. Klutch rode through the crowd, water spraying from under his tires in a V. He drove right past us and closer to the water's edge. I was surprised, considering how the lightning had been taking out people close to the water. It was closer than I would have felt comfortable going.

He stopped his Harley and slowly got off his bike, and I thought I saw him stagger drunkenly in the rain. I remembered that Owen had told me Klutch had been drinking, and I wondered if he'd tanked up again before this. He stood beside his bike and looked up at the clouds as the rain poured down on him and incessant streams of lightning filled the sky overhead in a freakish display of power. I think he was most fascinated, however, by the lightning balls still levitating in the sky.

I looked down at my watch: *7:58*. This wasn't good. Klutch was standing in our way, and the window was going to open in a mere five minutes. He pulled a handgun out of his jacket. He didn't point it at us, just held it at his side so we could get a long, hard look at it. Officer Blazer immediately ushered our group behind the vehicle for protection, but Jesse and I remained standing with our hands on our weapons.

Owen didn't take cover either but remained standing beside me, and I'm pretty sure his hand was on his gun as well. I thought about ordering him down behind the car with his mom and brother, but I knew not to. The storm had changed things. It had changed all of us.

He looked at me for some gesture of approval, and I nodded. He knew what that meant.

"You all need to keep your sticky hands to yourselves!" Klutch yelled. Now that he was closer, I was convinced he'd been drinking. The lightning flashed across his angry, drunken face, and he staggered forward a couple steps. "You went and took my arsenal because you wanted to stop me, didn't you?"

"We didn't take anything of yours!" Jesse yelled.

Klutch, who recognized Jesse, only grew angrier. He focused on him alone and seemed unaware of anything else around him. To my amazement, Jesse walked around the police car to approach Klutch. He wanted to calm him down and talk him out of what he was doing. In a weird way, they looked like two gunslingers about to have a duel on the storm-filled street of a Western town.

Jesse's position made it difficult for me. I would never be able to use my shotgun with Jesse in the path, and Owen wouldn't risk a shot either. Even Officer Blazer, who was crouched behind the vehicle with her gun drawn, would probably find it too risky to fire her weapon.

Jesse had slowly taken his firearm out of his pocket and held it at his side. He stood right in front of Klutch, mere feet away.

I looked at my watch: *8:00.*

The lightning was lessening. It was shutting down. This had to end quickly. Very, very quickly.

"I'm afraid I'm not gonna be able to allow your friends to pass," Klutch said. "First you steal my knife, then you steal my weapons, and now you wanna put this whole island in danger. This is weaponized weather, my friend. Even if you make it to the other side, you're gonna let 'em know that we're all alive here. There's a reason I never lost a man in my convoy. And you're gonna have to kill me if you wanna pass."

"We don't want to hurt you, Klutch," Jesse said with a surprising amount of calm. "I'm going to nicely ask you to step aside."

"You must not be listening. I already told you I'm not moving."

"Where are all your followers now, Klutch?"

"They're not warriors," he said. "They're civilians. It takes a warrior to do what I'm doing. But you need me! All of you need me! You're making a huge mistake!"

"You're the only one making a mistake here, Klutch," Jesse said, "and if you don't step aside right now, I'm going to have to—"

What happened next was a blur.

Impatient and angry, Klutch raised his weapon and shot twice. Jesse took two bullets to the chest, but not before unloading a shot at Klutch himself.

Jesse hit the ground first, and Klutch staggered back and looked down at the bleeding wound in his gut. With Jesse on the ground, Officer Blazer took full opportunity and unloaded four more bullets into the berserk biker. Three ripped into his chest, and the fourth got him right between the eyes. He stood there for a moment, bewildered, his eyes rolling upward in their sockets.

He collapsed on the ground, and I found myself running toward my fallen friend.

Chapter Thirty-Three

"It's stopped!" Samantha said. "I think it stopped!"

She was referring to the storm and how the lightning had completely ceased. While everyone else was rushing to make sure Jesse was alright, Samantha couldn't stop thinking about getting across the water. She was ecstatic in her impatience and self-interest.

"We need to go now! We need to go now!" she kept saying, and in hindsight, it is even clearer how concerned she was with herself rather than Jesse. Yet even amongst the chaos of the moment, I remember how it angered me.

"Wait until Dominic confirms!" Officer Blazer said. "It might not be open yet, we need to—"

"But it stopped! It stopped!" Samantha screamed and then, without any warning, she bolted toward the water's edge.

"No!" I screamed, but she never looked back.

For a brief moment, I wondered if she would make it, but that question was answered soon enough.

Just as she approached the water and the crumbled parts of the bridge along the edge, three lightning bolts tore down through the sky, joined paths, and struck her down in one bright and blinding flash of white light. I saw her body, still in running motion, lift from the ground and convulse as her body filled with who-knows-how-many volts of electricity. When the lightning stopped, her body dropped to the ground, and smoke rose from it.

Nobody said a word, because we all knew she was dead, and we also knew that the portal hadn't opened yet—*if* it was going to open to all.

When I approached Jesse, he lay on the ground, coughing blood. He had two holes in his chest. Mickey jumped out of the police car and began to tend to Jesse's wounds.

"You okay there, big guy?" I said.

"I'm alright." He didn't look good, but at least he was conscious and able to talk. "Nothing I can't handle."

"Good," I said. "You hang in there. We'll figure something out. We'll get you a ride over on one of those surfboards or something, okay?"

"It just went dead," Dominic said, getting out of the car with the radio in his hand.

Now the storm was completely thunderless and black, and if the window had just opened, that meant Samantha had been only a moment too early.

The crowd of residents waited anxiously behind us. Some had fled to the sidelines because of the shooting, but many waited, knowing that to run away would certainly forfeit any hope of escape.

Blazer opened the back door of the vehicle and pulled out Drake. He was still handcuffed behind his back. Her plan was pretty simple, I think. She was going to send him ahead into the water and threaten to shoot him if he didn't comply. If he made it in waist-deep without getting struck down, she'd consider the gate open and get on her P-A to order everyone to move ahead.

Just as she moved him to the front of the vehicle, raised her weapon at him, and ordered him to get to the water immediately, Darrel, who had been hunkered down behind the vehicle and taking shelter with the others, raced toward Drake, grabbed him around the neck, and put a gun to his head. It was the same gun he'd taken out of the duffel bag in the garage from the previous night, and my heart sank as I watched all of this unfold.

"You've gotta be kidding me," I said.

We didn't have time for this. This would jeopardize everything. The clock was ticking, and this would make the possibility of getting everyone across the water even more unlikely, and if something wasn't done quickly, none of us would get across.

I was still kneeling beside Jesse, but I saw the enraged look on Darrel's face. I hardly recognized him as my friend and neighbor. He had been planning this and waiting for this moment. In a bizarre reversal of roles, Darrel now looked like the madman, and Drake, his neck caught in the other's grip, was the terrified hostage. It was quite ironic, really. One of the guns he'd stashed in order to terrorize our neighborhood was now pointed at his own head. It may have been sweet justice had it not been for the current circumstances.

"Darrel, what are you doing?" I cried, standing up.

"You killed my wife," Darrel said. He held the barrel of the gun to Drake's temple. "You took Jenna from me! You took her from me! You took her!"

"Darrel, you're killing us!" I cried. "We don't have time for this!"

"Didn't you see what just happened to Samantha? Don't you realize your plan isn't going to work?" Darrel told me.

"It hadn't stopped yet!" I cried again.

"I want all of you to see this guy get what he deserves, you understand?" Darrel said. "I want all of you to witness it!"

He turned Drake around so that Drake was facing us and

Darrel stood right behind him. I wondered if Deborah was going to take the shot. Drake's life was hardly worth saving, and it would be far better to shoot both of them and save those who were waiting to cross over.

"Shoot them both," Jesse said, below me. He yelled at Blazer, Owen, and me. "Shoot him!"

But none of us had to.

I started to scream something again, and Darrel fired his weapon. I saw half of Drake's brains blow out of his skull like confetti. I closed my eyes and looked away momentarily, but I felt blood and chunks of something spray over me.

When I looked back, I saw Darrel standing there, shaking. In one quick movement, he placed his gun in his mouth and fired.

Blood flew out of the back of his head, his knees gave way, and he crumpled to the ground beside the man he had just killed.

Chapter Thirty-Four

I raced toward Deborah. My watch read 8:06. We'd lost three minutes, and that meant many lives. And now, to make matters worse, we didn't have a guinea pig to send across the water. Maybe Darrel was right; perhaps everything had been in vain, and the first line of people crossing the water would meet the same fate as Samantha.

"What do we do now?" I asked, petrified.

Deborah had as little a clue as I did.

"I'll go," Jesse said, barely making it to his feet. He was bleeding everywhere, and I was pretty sure he was functioning on pure willpower alone. "I'm good enough to get across. I can do it."

"You sure?" Deborah asked.

"Yeah," he said very unconvincingly, grunting in pain. He turned to look at me. "Give me a little start, okay. If I'm gonna die, I'd rather go down from lightning than bullet wounds. Makes a better story, don't you think?"

"Be careful," I said.

He slapped me on the shoulder. "See you on the other side, my friend," he said, and turned away.

He ran as fast as his injured body could toward the water, and as he ran, I thought about the way he had said those words. *See you on the other side.* I didn't like the sound of them. What side did he mean?

Deborah reached inside her car for her microphone but hesitated a moment, and I knew her concern. Not everyone would make it across. Now it was certain. She would have to order them to send the children to the front of the line, which probably should have happened anyway. Finally, she began to speak.

"We think we are clear to cross," she said into the microphone, "but we have less time now."

I didn't pay any more attention. I ran to my wife and Toby and told them they had to leave. Jesse had reached the water, and there was no lightning. I felt an obligation to remain in the back, to make sure others went before me, and to assist those who would need help. There were too many in need.

My wife didn't want to leave without me, and Toby didn't either; they cried and held onto me. I even told Owen he couldn't stay anymore. I wouldn't argue with him about this one. He had to cross with his family. Marsha, Hot-rodder, and Candice had already started to follow Jesse, and I felt the crowd begin to move toward us.

"I can't leave without you!" my wife cried.

"You have to!" I said. "Take the kids and go! Go now before it's too late! Go now! I'll be behind you!"

"Daddy!" Toby cried, clinging to my shirt.

But I let them go.

This time I didn't try to hold onto them the way I had tried to hold onto my brother's hand before it slipped into the cold waters of the Kern. I knew they had to leave, and it had to be now.

Madison and the boys were caught up in the stampede of people as they all headed toward the water, and I prayed that my family, being near the very front of the line, would be the first to get across. Deborah climbed on top of her vehicle, and I followed her. The people moved around us like ants, and Deborah and I stood on top of that police car and saw the most amazing sight.

Even though Deborah had never ordered all of these frightened citizens to send the children to the front, that was exactly what happened. Women and children swept past us, and I saw a sight that I will never forget: people giving up their places in line to send forward the elderly and the young—lots and lots of people who, realizing that the window was short, sacrificed their own lives.

I saw a flash of lightening and heard the low rumble of thunder. It was coming back.

I looked at my watch: 8:11.

No way were they going to get across. Not even close. A lot of people were about to die. Maybe my own family. Those who lived would be trapped on this island until the storm annihilated us.

I looked at the clouds. Officer Blazer and I exchanged the same mournful look, and knowing that we were about to witness a terrible tragedy, our hands slipped into each other's. I looked toward those in the water and then, as I saw another flash of lightening, I closed my eyes. I didn't want to watch them die. I didn't want to see their pain and suffering.

To this day, I can't remember what was real, what was imagined, and what I pieced together from witness accounts. But I can see it with my mind's eye.

Ted Lightener, fully clothed like most of the people out here, was struggling to swim across the water. His two-year old daughter was clinging onto his back, and when the first bits of lightening began to flash and he knew that he wouldn't make it across, he turned around and told her how much he loved her. He wanted those to be the last words he told his daughter, because when his dad died of cancer five years earlier, he wasn't given that luxury.

Thom and Wendy Butler were in their seventies and realized they wouldn't make it when they were about halfway across. Married since college, they stopped, treaded water, and faced each other. Thom kissed his wife, and he imagined the flashes of lightening in the sky weren't lightening—he imagined they were ballroom lights from his senior prom, where he first worked up the guts to kiss the pretty freshman he'd invited.

Ben and Archie Mermilliod, brothers, never went across the water. Both, having dreamt of being on search and rescue teams during their youth, had endured twenty-years of desk work—and often wanted the opportunity to prove their mettle. This was it! Instead of swimming across to safety, they stood at the water's edge, crying out for the children and the elderly to go first.

And a funny thing happened.

It worked.

People stood out of the way. Gave up their position. Cleared a path for the weak, the young, and the elderly. I was far away at that point and standing on the back of the police car, but I saw the crowd part. It was as much a miracle as when the Red Sea parted for the Israelites.

I looked at my watch: 8:13.

Game Over.

There were still people in the water, splashing, and frantically moving toward the other side.

That's when I noticed the lightening had changed. A single bolt ripped through the sky, but it looked more like the filament of an incandescent light bulb flickering out, and the sound that followed it—what should have been a peal of thunder—reminded me of a cold engine struggling to turn over.

That's when I understood.

"I think it's working," I said.

"What's working?" Officer Blazer asked.

"We're doing what we should be doing. We're starving it."

But maybe I was wrong.

Now I heard a low grumbling in the clouds. It sounded like some fiendish monster was growing, awakening from its slumber, and it grew so loud, I let go of Officer Blazer's hand and covered my ears. The air felt saturated in fuzzy static, and all the hairs on my arms and hands began to stand on end.

I knew what this was. Like a dragon, the storm was breathing in, sucking up one more gulp of atmosphere, before it spat down a torrent of electricity. This was its Hail Mary attempt to finish what it started. I saw others in the crowd cover their ears, stagger, and lose equilibrium.

"You won't win!" I cried defiantly, but I couldn't hear my own voice.

There was a great burst of light. Hundreds of blue-electric bolts shot from the clouds. I thought it was over, and shielded my eyes, but something was different. When I had the courage to open them, I saw that the bolts didn't hit the water and annihilate those crossing it. Instead, each stream sputtered out, lost trajectory, and fell in slow arcs toward the water like the glittering ends of a great plume of fire that had exploded over our heads.

The clouds broke apart almost instantly, as if a sudden heavenly wind was pushing them into some netherworld.

I fell to my knees in awe.

Not because of the storm's power to generate fear.

I was in awe of how we stood up to it. How we fought it.

Maybe it really began when my son, Owen, ran through a swarm of bullets to save Mia's life, or maybe it began when most of the citizens of Naples actually banded together to make it through the storm instead of turning on each other. But I'm pretty sure it ended with what I witnessed from atop that police car: strangers giving their lives for one another while Jesse, dying and bleeding, paved the way for everyone else.

I don't think those things computed with the storm. It misunderstood the full scope of our humanity. It must have been like pouring coolant into the storm's gas tank.

Those who had thought they wouldn't make it realized what was taking place, cheered, and celebrated as they ran, and every one of us made it across. Every one!

Even though many could have stayed on the island, since the storm was suddenly gone, nobody wanted to take a chance. Maybe it would come back. Who knew?

I followed the crowd and swam across to the other side, no longer in fear that I wouldn't make it.

It was complete pandemonium on the mainland shore. Emergency crews and sirens were everywhere, but I quickly found my family and our entire group. I saw Mia and Candice first, both dripping wet. I learned later than Candice had grabbed a boogie board from the stack of floatation devices Deborah's crew had rounded up and pulled Mia across the water on it. Bessie, a pretty good swimmer in her own right, dogpaddled behind them.

Overwhelmed with joy, I clung onto everybody. I didn't want to let go. Never again.

But before long, I realized that one person was missing.

Where was Jesse?

I went searching for him, and I eventually found him. A circle of paramedics surrounded him as he lay on the sand, working on him. I didn't know what exactly they were doing, but it didn't look good. It didn't look good at all.

"No!" I cried and ran toward my friend.

One of the paramedics turned around and stopped me.

"Is he okay? Is he okay?" I asked.

"Sir, I'm gonna need you to stay back right now."

"I need to talk to him, I need to—"

"Sir, please stay back."

I fell to my knees in the sand. I knew what was going to happen. The storm had given me back my family, but it wouldn't give me back my friend. That was its nature. I began to cry. All around me, as everyone broke into celebration and joy because the storm was gone, I alone wailed in agony.

"Do you know this man, sir?" another paramedic asked. It may have been the same one who stopped me. I wasn't sure. I was lost in the madness.

"Yes," I said, weeping. "I owe him a beer. I owe him a beer . . ."

Chapter Thirty-Five

I never did find out what the storm was. But I suppose that's the way with all of the storms that confront us in life. Does the person who has just been diagnosed with terminal cancer find any more reasons for why it happened? Or what about the parent who gets that call in the middle of the night? Can those people find any more sense as to why those storms passed through their lives? Are those questions any easier to answer?

I'm afraid the answer is no.

And it certainly did what those other storms in life do to us. It taught me who I really am, and it certainly showed me a glimpse of who my son, Owen, was on the verge of becoming. I sometimes think the flashes of lightning illuminated the people we really were. I don't know why some became brave, like Owen, and why others, like Darrel, let the storm defeat them without one lightning bolt ever touching them. But I suppose that's how life works.

Maybe, in the end, it's not the storms that are important—it's the way we perceive them. Maybe there's nothing more noble than standing beneath the storm-filled sky, looking up at a power you cannot possibly overcome on your own, and putting up a fight anyway. Maybe that's what separates the truly brave from the cowardly.

Whether it was some kind of monster, alien life form, or a living creature from a dimension alongside ours, I still believe it was feeding on our fear. It wanted to destroy us in the same way that it wanted and even expected us to turn on each other. But it backfired because it didn't know us; it didn't know what we really were.

And that gives me hope.

The change in the static crashes wasn't an alarm that indicated the storm was nearing the end of its demolition. It was another thing entirely. I like to think that the change Dominic heard was the storm's own alarm because it had begun breaking down and falling apart. Code Red. We weren't pumping enough fuel into its tank, and it was preparing for shutdown.

The media made up their own stories, of course. The most mainstream of the media stations declared it the storm of the century and said scientists would be studying and discussing it for years to come. There was lots of speculation and too many theories to recount. Some, like Klutch, thought it was a weather weaponization system that had gone awry; some thought it was God's judgment and explained everything by quoting different passages of Revelations; I even heard some claim it was an alien attack, and seeing that our planet was not habitable for their life form, they left for another planet.

But I didn't care about the theories and the speculation, because when you live through something like that, you realize the answers won't make anyone feel better. And it won't bring back those who were lost.

We returned to Naples Island. If what they say is true— that lightning doesn't strike the same place twice—then I must live in the safest house in America, because no way is something like that storm going to go down twice in the same place. I'd place my bets on that.

Marsha is still my neighbor, and just yesterday, she brought over her first published story in *Urban Suspense Magazine*. My wife broke open a bottle of champagne, and we had a lovely evening together on the front patio, watching the sunset. I've come to admire Marsha more than I ever would have imagined.

Not long after the storm left, Mia was placed in the custody of a local aunt and uncle. I haven't heard from her since, but I trust she's well. I think about her sometimes, and I wonder if she will even remember the storm when she's older.

Hot-rodder is back at his parents' house down the street. They lived through the storm, hiding out in a neighbor's house. I don't think a single week passes without him coming by the house for a free soda or snack, and of course, we've resumed our word of the day tradition. I think "absolved" was the last one. I'm pretty convinced that I couldn't get rid of the rug rat if I tried, and I enjoy having him around my home. My wife does too, and ever since Owen went away to college, I feel like I have another son.

And I like it that way. I really do.

Owen drove off to the University of Arizona just a few months ago. Candice even came to say goodbye to him, even though they'd broken up long ago and are just friends now. I forget their reasons, but I was happy they broke up. He's too young, and I was scared he'd get too attached to her and not see the world. I wanted him to see things and go places and do a better job at what his old man has such a hard time doing: letting go. When he told me they'd broken up, he was pretty distraught about the whole thing, so I listened, tried to give him some fatherly advice, and reminded him that he could talk to me as much as he needed if he was having a hard time.

Then I went into my room, told my wife, and we did the

Happy Dance.

On the day Owen left for college, my wife, Toby, and Bessie said our goodbyes in the driveway, and I watched as he drove down the street and out of sight. I'd always imagined that I would go back into the house and collapse in grief, but I didn't. I looked at my wife, held her, and reminded her that Owen was never ours to begin with. Neither was my little brother.

We have so little time here with those we love, and sometimes—for reasons we don't know—they're taken from us. Sometimes it's to another city, to another state, and sometimes to the other side, as Jesse said. I suppose the best we can do is love the time that we have with them and let them go when the time is right.

That's what the storm taught me, and I don't ever want to learn that lesson again.

I miss Jesse the most, and I think of him often. He died that night, with me standing in the sand behind the team of paramedics. I wept for hours, and while I was overjoyed that my own family was alive and well, his loss hit me harder than any lightning bolt could have.

We attended his funeral the week after the storm left, and I sat in the front pew between my sons and fought back tears. I'm sure Jesse would have called me a pansy and told me to suck it up, but I did my best.

I remember the song they played: *You give and take away, you give and take away, my heart will choose to say, Lord, blessed be your name.*

I closed my eyes, and for the first time in my adult life, I struggled to formulate some kind of prayer on my lips. It wasn't pretty, and in my anger and my loss, it was filled with more expletives and cursing than was probably proper for any church. But it was real, and it came from the broken part of me that wanted to desperately understand why everything had happened.

After the preacher said some words, I walked up to the closed casket and stood beside it while my family waited outside. I just wanted a few minutes alone with Jesse. Just some time for the two of us.

Only a moment later, a young lady, probably around thirty or so, walked up to the casket beside me. She was a complete mess and could hardly keep herself upright. It didn't take me long to figure out who she was. She looked aged and worn, and the lines on her face and the grey in her hair proclaimed a difficult life.

This was Virginia, Jesse's daughter, and when I told her that I was friends with her dad and was there with him at the very end, she nearly fell into my arms. She sobbed hysterically, and I held her—even though she was a stranger—because she was still a part of Jesse.

"I wanted him to know that I loved him," she sobbed, and I held onto her.

The tears came back to my eyes again, and this time, I didn't resist them.

"I haven't talked to him in years," she said. "I just wanted him to know how much I loved him. I'm so sorry. S-so sorry . . ."

"He knows you loved him," I told her, and when I had wiped the tears from my own eyes, I looked at her very firmly. Just like with Owen, I really wanted to get this right. "And he loved you, too. He loved you with everything he had in him. And he forgives you. He wants you to know that."

In that moment, I was able to stand in the place of Jesse in the same way that he stood before me, my family, and everyone else on that island when he staggered toward the water with two bullets in his chest. It was the least I could do for him. I owe him much more.

After we drove home, I needed some time to be alone. My wife understood, and after I tucked Toby into bed and said goodnight to Owen, I went for a long drive through the city. I didn't know where I was going, but eventually I pulled into a biker bar several cities away called Chad's Corner. There was a long row of bikes out front, loud music within, and it was just the kind of place I thought Jesse would like.

I walked inside, and I was the only guy there wearing slacks, a button shirt, and a tie. A couple guys with sleeveless shirts and tats laughed at me as I walked past them, and a large woman in leather biker pants and jacket pointed at me and whispered something to one of the sleeveless guys.

It didn't bother me. I strode past them and walked across the sawdust floor to a little table in the corner. The music was loud and obnoxious, and drunken, leather-clad bikers were everywhere, drinking beer and engaging in revelry. A perturbed-looking woman with a lazy eye sauntered over, and I ordered two beers: a Crescent Moon and a Pabst Blue Ribbon.

She came back a moment later. I paid her and sipped my Crescent Moon.

I must have stayed there for at least an hour or two. I sat at that table, sipped my beer, and contemplated everything that had taken place. Jesse would have liked it here, I thought. He would have liked it a lot.

Finally, I looked at my watch and realized how late it really was. Where had the time gone? Feeling fatigued, I threw down a five dollar bill for a tip and headed to the front door.

A scrawny busboy caught me by the arm as I was about to leave, and pointing to the full glass of Blue Ribbon that sat untouched on the table, asked, "Are you done with your beer?"

"Don't rush him," I said. "Leave it there for a while."

The busboy looked at me strangely and went off to another table.

"Goodbye, my friend," I said and walked out the door toward my car.

About the Author

William Michael Davidson lives in Long Beach, California, with his wife and two daughters. A believer that "good living produces good writing," Davidson writes early in the morning so he can get outside, exercise, spend time with people, and experience as much as possible. A writer of speculative fiction, he enjoys stories that deal with humanity's inherent need for redemption.

GREAT STORIES. NO GUILT.

www.cleanreads.com

CPSIA information can be obtained
at www.ICGtesting.com
Printed in the USA
FSHW01n0735101018
52900FS